Magnate
Acquisition Series Book 2

Celia Aaron

Magnate
Acquisition Series, Book 2

Celia Aaron

Copyright © 2015 Celia Aaron

All rights reserved. No part of this book may be reproduced, scanned, or distributed in any printed or electronic form without prior written permission from Celia Aaron. Please do not participate in piracy of books or other creative works.

This book is a work of fiction. While reference may be made to actual historical events or existing locations, the names, characters, places and incidents are products of the author's imagination, and any resemblance to actual persons, living or dead, business establishments, events, or locales is entirely coincidental.

WARNING: This book contains sexually explicit scenes and adult language and may be considered offensive to some readers. Please store your books wisely, away from under-aged readers. This book is a dark romance. If dark romance bothers you, this book isn't for you. If dark, twisty, suspenseful, and sexy—or any combination of those words—interest you, then get the popcorn and enjoy.

Cover art by L.J. at mayhemcovercreations.com

Editing by J. Brooks

ISBN: 1523455500
ISBN-13: 978-1523455508

OTHER BOOKS BY CELIA AARON

Forced by the Kingpin
Forced Series, Book 1

Forced by the Professor
Forced Series, Book 2

Forced by the Hitmen
Forced Series, Book 3

Forced by the Stepbrother
Forced Series, Book 4

Forced by the Quarterback
Forced Series, Book 5

***

A Stepbrother for Christmas
The Hard and Dirty Holidays, Book 1

Bad Boy Valentine
The Hard and Dirty Holidays, Book 2

F*ck of the Irish
The Hard and Dirty Holidays, Book 3

***

Zeus
Taken by Olympus, Book 1

Sign up for my newsletter at AaronErotica.com and be the first to learn about new releases (no spam, just send free stuff and book news.)

Twitter: @aaronerotica

CONTENTS

Chapter One STELLA	Page 1
Chapter Two STELLA	Page 3
Chapter Three SINCLAIR	Page 15
Chapter Four STELLA	Page 23
Chapter Five STELLA	Page 35
Chapter Six STELLA	Page 37
Chapter Seven STELLA	Page 49
Chapter Eight SINCLAIR	Page 59
Chapter Nine STELLA	Page 63
Chapter Ten STELLA	Page 83
Chapter Eleven SINCLAIR	Page 89

Chapter Twelve STELLA	Page 103
Chapter Thirteen STELLA	Page 111
Chapter Fourteen STELLA	Page 121
Chapter Fifteen SINCLAIR	Page 141
Chapter Sixteen STELLA	Page 149
Chapter Seventeen SINCLAIR	Page 157
Chapter Eighteen STELLA	Page 165
Chapter Nineteen STELLA	Page 177
Chapter Twenty STELLA	Page 185

CHAPTER ONE
Stella

The sun's rays floated through the clear water, shining on me in dappled waves. My lungs burned. They'd been burning for a while, ever since I'd dived down to the bottom and forced myself to stay. I could almost see the edge of oblivion hovering in the distance, the darkness submerged here with me. The tile beneath my feet was a pattern of tangled vines, all emanating from the dark green 'V' in the center. The same one that graced the back of my neck.

I winced when I remembered how I got the mark. Not because of the pain it took to get it, but because of the man who had given it to me. The man with a matching one over his heart. Sinclair Vinemont. Another bubble of air escaped. My last. It wobbled this way and that before it floated to freedom.

The burning grew until my vision blurred. I propelled myself upward and broke the surface in a burst of speed. I sputtered and took in huge gulps of life. Grasping the side of pool, I coughed until my breathing calmed, my heart settled, and the water quieted. It was only moments before the surface became a smooth mirror again, reflecting the blue sky above. Nothing had changed. Would anything have changed if I'd stayed beneath the water?

I shook the thought from my head and swam to the stairs. Once out of the pool, I dropped onto my chaise and lay back. The sun was high, beating down, yet somehow failing to dissolve the humidity that hung in the air. Winter in Cuba was a lot like Louisiana in summertime, hot and bright. But there were differences.

An acre or so of verdant grass surrounded the pool patio. Palm trees dotted the lawn here and there, offering a small bit of shade from the unforgiving sun. Beyond the grass was nothing but an impenetrable wall of green—sugar cane.

I scanned the horizon. The fields stretched out around the Vinemont plantation for as far as the eye could see, a wave of emerald disappearing into the horizon. The tall, slim leaves danced on the breeze. Whenever the wind hit just right, the smell from the nearby sugar plant would sweep over the estate, encompassing me with a lingering sweetness that I didn't feel. Just like the sun bathed my skin, drenching it in warmth that never penetrated any deeper.

I turned my head to the side, away from the open sky and toward the classic Spanish style mansion. The stucco was a muted pink and the roof consisted of neat rows of brown clay shingles. It was three stories of rooms upon rooms that were a mix of modern and antique. I leaned back on the chaise, water sliding from my skin and dripping to the fabric. Even with my shades, the sun was unbearable. I closed my eyes and willed the warm light to infuse something into my heart—some flicker, some sign of life.

But when I closed my eyes, I glimpsed Vinemont's blue ones. He was always there, hidden inside, waiting for me to close my eyes or fall asleep. In my dreams or waking, I saw him. I clamped my eyes shut tighter, trying to erase him. It never worked. I hadn't had a good night's sleep in the two weeks since I'd left Louisiana.

Lucius had followed me that night—the one when my world shattered and Vinemont was the cause—back to my room. He'd promised me escape, a chance to leave the world of Acquisitions and pain. But he didn't promise me for how long. I sighed and shifted, the raised scars along my back sliding against the damp fabric.

I kept my eyes closed, even though Vinemont was there, his dark blue eyes always piercing through to my heart, the one he'd destroyed. The warm sun and light breeze lulled me to sleep under Vinemont's watchful gaze. He followed me down into the abyss. A whip in his hand, but a loving touch along my cheek. His whispers were in my ear, promising me pain, pleasure, and so much more. He ran a hand down my back, his fingertips caressing the lines of suffering he'd embedded there. I let out a soft moan when he brushed his lips against my neck.

I wanted to put my palm to his face, to look into his eyes and feel that surge of heat, but my hands were bound. I struggled against the manacles. He smiled without warmth. Cruelty lived in his eyes, his mouth. I shivered. But not from pure fear. And that was the worst part—I always wanted him. Even when he visited me with a whip, with vicious words, with pain, I wanted it all. I wanted *him*.

Vinemont's gaze darkened, what little light was in his eyes snuffed out.

"Stella?"

He reared back with the whip. My breath caught in my throat.

"Stella?"

I strained to free my wrists. It was no use. He started his swing, the whip lashing through the air. A strangled scream erupted from me.

"Stella!" Not Vinemont's voice. Someone else.

I opened my eyes, my heart racing and the scream only then dying on my lips. Lucius leaned over me, kneeling at my side and blocking the sun. He brushed a hand across my cheek.

"Are you all right?" His other hand rested on my bare waist, above the line of my bathing suit bottoms. For a moment, I caught a flash of Vinemont, but it was replaced with his brother Lucius, his chocolate hair and lighter eyes. Handsome, made even more so by the concern written in his features. I wasn't falling for it. He was just another viper.

"Fine. Just fell asleep." I tried to shrink away from him, but his hand on my waist kept me where I was.

He leaned in closer, his clean, sandalwood scent filling my nose. "It doesn't have to be like this. You don't have to be afraid, not of me."

He slid my sunglasses up my head and peered into my eyes before wiping a tear that had escaped during the dream.

"I'm not afraid of you, Lucius." I returned his stare.

"Then why are you trembling?" His voice was silky, seductive as he leaned closer.

I had to escape his gaze, his touch. "Because you remind me of your brother."

He shook his head slightly. "I'm not Sin, Stella. I thought you knew that when you chose me."

My barb about his brother hadn't worked. Lucius was still too close, his hands too warm, his words too easy. If anything, he was emboldened by my sharp tone, his gaze darting to my lips.

This is the closest he'd come since our flight to the island and subsequent Jeep ride to the estate. We had been in Cuba for two weeks. Most of the time I had remained in my room, trying to figure out what I was going to do. I couldn't go back home. I didn't have one. Not anymore. My father sold me like a piece of cattle. The memory of his signature beneath Vinemont's elegant script made my stomach churn. Bought and paid for by one Vinemont, and now another was trying to take even more of me.

"No, Lucius." The steel in my words strengthened my

resolve. I gripped his wrist and pulled his hand away from my face. "I've been played enough. By my father. By Vinemont. Now you're trying to play me. Not anymore. I'm not the same naive girl from two months ago."

He allowed me to move away from his touch, but he gripped my hand. "Stella, I won't deny I've wanted you since the first time I saw you." He smirked. "It didn't hurt that you were naked at the time."

I sat up but he didn't release me. Instead, his hold tightened. He was kneeling so it was as if we were sitting face to face. Too close.

"But you need to know you're mine now. You chose me. You are my Acquisition and you'll stay that way. Your contract is just as binding as it ever was. Your father? He still has the same sword over his head as he's always had. I can have him in prison with a phone call."

"You think I care what happens to him?" I tried to yank my wrist from his grip. It was like trying to pry it from steel.

"I know you do. I know deep down you don't want him to suffer and die in prison. Even though he sold you like a worthless trinket. I know you, Stella. I could be your ally instead of your captor. If you'd only let me." His gaze flicked to my lips again.

The worst part was that he was right. I still cared for my father. I hated myself for it, hated the stupid little girl who lived in my breast and held out hope that this was all a trick or a mistake. It wasn't. Anger rose inside me like the waves of heat from the cobblestone patio around the pool. "You don't know anything about me, Lucius. All you know is I'm an Acquisition, sold to your godforsaken family and enslaved first by your brother and now you. You own me for a year. I have nowhere to go. So stop with the mindfuck."

"That's not what this is Stella."
"Then why don't you just let me go?"
"I can't do that." His face hardened.

"Why not? If you don't want to be my *captor*, then that's the quickest way to alleviate your concern."

"The Acquisition. It's too late for that now, Stella. You're mine." The velvet faded. He was made of stone.

"Am I? I remember Vinemont telling me the same thing. Wasn't true then, either."

His eyes bored into me. "I would never let you go, not like that. Sin didn't know what he had. I do. I'm good at three things, Stella. Three. One is running the family business. The second is valuing assets. Whereas Sin undervalued you, I see your true worth."

Lucius let the words hang in the humid air. The ghost of the man who'd taken my heart and left a black, twisted hulk in its place haunted us even in the bright daylight.

Don't fall for it. Lucius was just manipulating me, the same as his brother. I let out a hitched breath as he drew even closer, his minty breath mingling with mine.

Three things? "What's the third thing?"

He smiled, wickedness in every crease. "You'll find out about that one soon enough."

A shiver shot through me at his words.

He released my hand and I got to my feet, feeling exposed in my bathing suit while he was fully clothed in jeans and a white button down. Even so, he held my gaze, never darting his eyes down my body like I would have expected from him.

"*Jefe?*" A voice carried down to us from the upper terrace.

Javier, the man who'd driven us from the airfield, and who I'd learned was the head of the operation in Cuba when Lucius was gone, appeared over the railing. I suspected he had connections with the dictator, the only explanation for how the Vinemonts maintained their foothold in Cuba. He and Lucius spent most of their days away from the plantation, leaving early and coming back well after sundown. I was glad Lucius was preoccupied with the sugar business. I didn't want to deal with anything—not the Acquisition, not Lucius, not Vinemont, not my father. For the first time in my life, I was steeped in uncertainty, but I didn't care. I just wanted to be left alone.

"I'm coming." Lucius ran a hand through his hair, ruffling it in the same way his brother did when he was frustrated.

My stomach fluttered at the familiar movement. I clamped my shades down over my eyes like some sort of shield from the onslaught of memories. I didn't want to feel anything.

"Look, Stella, just give me a chance here, okay? I'm trying to get you through this, all of it. I don't want to have to threaten you or keep you under lock and key. I will." He smirked. "Don't doubt that for a second. But it doesn't have to be so black and white. I just want…"

"What?" I flicked my damp hair over one shoulder and put my hands on my hips. My heart was hammering, a mix of anger and indignation pumping through my veins. "What do you want from me?"

"Jefe!" Javier called again.

Lucius let out a string of invective in Spanish at the foreman before turning back to me and lowering his voice. "Everything." His familiar, wolfish grin surfaced, eating me up bit by bit.

I knew it. "You'll get nothing."

"We'll see, Stella." He turned on his heel and ascended the curving staircase to the terrace, his broad back straining against his shirt. With one final look at me, he disappeared into the house with Javier.

I sank back down onto the chaise, my heart thundering in my chest, the beat in my ears, my temples. The first Acquisition trial was over, but we were still playing the game. I was still a pawn, a piece to be sacrificed so a Vinemont could rule the depraved cabal of moneyed southern families.

I eyed the pool again, the water still reflecting the

perfect blue sky. Playing the fingertips of my left hand along the scar at my right wrist, the ridges reminded me of why I could never sink to the bottom of the water and stay there. I would survive. I would make it out of this nightmare, and I would never be the same weak fool again.

Gathering up my towel, I wrapped it around my body and climbed the stairs to the upper terrace. I peered in the back windows and, once assured Lucius was out of sight, I hurried across the palazzo floor and to the right.

My room was at the end of the hall. With its own private balcony and massive en suite, the luxury it entailed was far beyond the wildest dreams of the people who lived in the surrounding countryside. The Vinemonts turned the sugar cane into gold and kept the resulting wealth to themselves. It was as if they had a particular talent for injustice, no matter where they went or what they did.

I trudged to my bathroom, turned on the shower, and took off my top before shimmying my bottoms off.

A calloused hand clapped hard over my mouth and a wide, rusty blade grazed my neck. I was yanked back and an arm wrapped around my ribs, crushing the air out of me. My scream made it no further than the palm against my lips.

CHAPTER TWO
STELLA

"NOT A WORD." The voice in my ear was low and heavily accented. "Where is jefe? What room is his? This one?"

I shook my head. I hung lifeless in his arms lest I give him any reason to cut me.

"Where?" He loosened his grip on my mouth, but kept the blade poised at my throat.

"D-down the hall. I can show you."

"I bet you can show me a lot of things, eh *mi puta*?" He slid a hand up to my breast and squeezed.

I forced my scream to stay put in my throat.

Another man spoke from behind us, near the balcony. He was clearly irritated and giving instructions in Spanish to the one who held me.

"Later, mi puta." He crushed my breast in his palm, pain roaring through me until he let up.

He shoved me forward and the other man grabbed my upper arm hard.

These were rough men. Their calloused hands and rugged faces telling a story of years of toil. And they hadn't come to talk, judging by their machetes.

"Now show us where he is. If you make a sound, I'll give you to Franco." He jerked his chin at the man who'd first grabbed me. "*Comprende?*"

"Yes." I'd heard bits of gossip here and there about how the local workers weren't happy with their cut of the sugar cane profits. It was as if the Vinemonts had started squeezing more over the past few months, increasing their own income while ignoring the burden it put on the already-strained farmers.

The tension seemed to have reached the point of no return. Would they kill Lucius? The thought thrilled me, but what would happen to me if there was no more jefe? I glanced over my shoulder at Franco, his low brow and toothy leer. I didn't think it possible until that moment, but I would fare worse if Lucius were gone.

"Go." The man shoved me forward and I began to walk, hyperaware of the attackers, their weapons, and my own nudity.

I turned toward the left, the direction of the main house, hoping someone would see us and sound the alarm. It was broad daylight, after all, and the house had a few servants. We passed some bedrooms, and I saw a glimmer of hope as Raul, one of the butlers, turned the corner ahead of us. He froze, his mouth falling open as he saw me. Then he stared at the man who held my elbow. I willed him to run, to yell, to do something.

Instead, he dropped his gaze and retreated into the nearest bedroom, closing the door behind him. *Fuck.*

Franco laughed low at my back. "*Coño.*"

I kept walking, leading them toward Lucius' study. We didn't pass any more servants, and the house seemed eerily quiet. The adrenaline in my system amped up another notch, my heart beating loudly in my ears as my steps began to falter.

"Keep up." The man lifted me by my arm, forcing my gait to stay steady.

I took a few more steps toward the closed French

doors leading to Lucius' study.

"Here?"

I nodded.

Franco seized my shoulder. "Run, *puta*. I will find you soon enough."

The men shoved me to the side and took the last step to the doors. Franco brought his knee up and kicked through them. The other man followed close behind as they rushed forward, blades drawn.

I darted away. My ruse had worked. Lucius and Javier worked the evening hours away in the library, not the study. I ran down the corridor, my feet slapping against the tile floor. Footsteps echoed behind me, Franco and the other man hot on my heels.

"Lucius!" I screamed and flew into the library. He and Javier rose as I threw the doors shut and turned the lock.

"What the fuck, Stella?" Lucius eyed my body.

"Men," I gasped, "here to kill you." I pointed to the door and scrambled back.

Javier yanked his pistol from his belt holster, and Lucius pulled out a handgun from his desk. The door handles began to rattle.

"Stella, hide!" Lucius barked and pointed to the space beneath his desk.

I was naked and weaponless. There was no other choice but to do what he said. I ran to him as the door began to give way. He shoved me under the desk.

"Don't come out until I say." His sky blue eyes were full of turmoil before he rose and disappeared.

There was an even harder thud and then the whine of wood against wood as the door splintered. Gunshots rang out so loud that I covered my ears. Shouts and curses, English and Spanish – all of it mixed as the booming noises died out and nothing was left but silence.

Lucius and Javier exchanged some words in Spanish that I couldn't follow.

"Stella, how many?" Lucius called.

"Two."

"You sure?"

"I don't know. I only saw two." Raul's frightened face flashed through my mind. "And Raul saw them with me, but he just… He did nothing."

"I'll check the grounds." Javier's voice.

"Be careful. I don't trust anyone. The staff, no one. Not now."

"Understood, Jefe."

Footsteps, then Lucius knelt down and held his hand out to me. "Come on. They won't be bothering us anymore."

There wasn't a scratch on him, but he'd just killed two men. He was calm, as if he'd only swatted a fly.

I reached out to him, only then noticing how badly my body shook. He pulled me out from beneath the desk and tilted my chin up with his thumb and index finger. Inspecting my neck, he said, "You're bleeding."

"I am?" A haze had settled over me, and my ears were ringing. The smell of burnt gunpowder hung in the air. I glanced past him and fixated on the two bodies, blood pooling around them in a crimson sea that blocked the door. How would we get out without getting their blood on us? I'd lured them in here, straight to their deaths. I was already covered in their blood, I just couldn't see it.

"Stella?" Lucius pulled my gaze back to his, a crease forming in his brow. "Come on. Let's get you out of here." He scooped me up in his arms, his pistol still in the hand at my knees.

I stiffened. "I can walk."

He shook his head at me, his light brown hair falling into his eyes. "You're in shock."

"I've been through worse."

He grazed his fingers along my back, feeling the ridges of my scars. "I know. Close your eyes. I'm going to step over them and take you back to your room."

"No." My voice shook and I looked down again, the

bodies drawing my gaze like a magnet. "That's where they found me."

"Close your eyes. Do it now." Lucius' tone was harsh.

I turned back to him and buried my face in his shoulder, but I could still feel their lifeless stares. He moved through the library, taking a final, big step across the pool of blood, and then we were out in the hallway. I opened my eyes as he turned to the right, away from my room and toward his. He moved quietly and swiveled this way and that each time he came to a door, searching for any more unwanted guests.

Easing his bedroom door open, he peered around before walking in and setting me down on the bed. I drew his blanket to my chin and watched as he checked the bathroom, the closet, and then closed and locked his balcony doors.

"You'll be safe here. I'm going to go find Javier and make sure there were only two." He clicked something on the gun and the magazine slid out. He checked the bullets and nodded to himself before looking back to me. "Don't move from this room."

I stared at the crimson stain along the side of his boot. Blood. So much of it had flowed around me. My mother's, mine, the men on the floor. How much of it was my fault? All of it?

He stalked to me, his light eyes flashing even in the now-darkened room. "Stella. Tell me you'll stay here. I need you safe."

That got through to me, his one half-truth. He needed me. He needed his Acquisition untouched until he said otherwise. Until three weeks from now at Christmas when the second trial was set to begin. Would he keep me safe then? Renee's story of torture and violation replayed through my mind, forming a lattice work of pain over the pool of blood that had already seared into my vision.

I looked up and met his focused stare. "I'll stay here."

"Good. I'll be back in a short while. Don't open this

door for anyone else. Not even Javier. Got it?" He pulled back the gun's action and checked the round in the chamber. His hands were steady, as if killing was what they were made for.

He released the metal, a smooth *shick* sound that spoke of death. Reaching out toward my face, he pushed a lock of hair behind my ear. I leaned away from his touch.

His eyes narrowed. "Stay here. No one but me gets through that door. Tell me you understand, Stella."

"Yes." I wanted him gone. I wanted all of it gone.

He raised his gun and went to the door. "Lock it behind me."

He opened it silently, peeking out, and then slid through before pulling it shut behind him. I rose, pulling the blanket with me, and clicked the bolt over. It was just a deterrent. If others wanted to get in, they would.

I scanned the room for a weapon. There wasn't much to choose from, unless I could somehow fashion a dagger from some local art or decorative tobacco baskets. I went to Lucius' bedside table. Nothing there of use. I whirled and caught his fireplace in my peripheral vision. I grabbed an iron poker, gripping it hard and getting a feel for its weight. It wouldn't do much if the intruder had a gun, but it was better than nothing.

Tossing the blanket back onto the bed, I hurried into his walk-in closet. I closed the door behind me and yanked down a white button up. I slipped it on and rolled up the sleeves, ignoring the fact that I wasn't wearing panties. The wooden racks and drawers gave me nowhere to hide.

I scratched the idea of sheltering in the closet and returned to the bed to sit and wait. It didn't matter anyway. If someone came here to kill me, hiding wouldn't stop them. They would find me.

Tension roiled along my body, every commonplace sound in the house like a bomb going off, shocking my system. The ticking of a clock, the sound of a bird on the roof nearby, the slow drip of Lucius' faucet in his bathroom. I edged back until I was sitting against the headboard, the fireplace poker next to me, the unyielding metal a strange comfort.

Would I die here instead of in the Acquisition? Maybe this end was better. Maybe this farmer uprising—if that's what it truly was—was a blessing in disguise. I absentmindedly trailed my fingertips along the scars on my left wrist. I'd wished for death back then. I still toyed with it, flirting with it from across the room with glances and coy smiles. Death watched me as if I were its next dance partner, its next sumptuous feast of flesh. How long would our flirtation last before he dragged me into the swirling mass of dancers, swallowed up by flowing skirts and dark smiles?

The air remained still, the whole house turned into a sepulcher by the two bodies, maybe more, that filled its walls. I focused intently on every noise, every creak of the house. After an hour or so, a sharp crack shattered the stillness. A single gunshot that was soon joined by others. Booming shots mixed with the sporadic cracks of pistols as I huddled under the blanket, my gaze fixed unwaveringly on the door.

The sun slowly faded through the window as I waited. The room became steeped in gloom, hours passing without word from anyone and no more shots. I didn't dare turn on a light. The adrenaline was long-since drained from my body. I scooted down in the bed, propping my head on pillows so I could keep an eye on the door. Lucius' scent surrounded me, sandalwood and sophistication sinking into my pores.

My eyes grew heavy. I should have sat up, should have moved around. Instead, I let the darkness lull me. It wasn't the first time.

The door burst open, and I scrambled from the bed. Sleep was gone and a surge of murder took its place. The poker was in my hand as I rushed forward toward the dark figure advancing into the room. Drawing my arm back, I waited for the gunshots to sound, for my blood to spill. Nothing.

I swung with all my strength but the figure caught my wrist and squeezed hard. The pressure increased until my bones ached and I dropped the metal with a cry. He clapped his hand over my mouth and snaked an arm around my waist, pulling me to him. Fear engulfed me like quicksand, dragging me down until I knew I would suffocate.

I peered up to get a better look at the person who would snuff me out. I breathed in through my nose and got a taste of his scent—woodsy, masculine. My heart drummed in my chest. I recognized him, the hard body against my breasts, the feel of his arms caging me against him.

"Stella." The deep rumble of his voice made my knees weak but also poured kerosene on the ember of hate that burned in my heart. The flame leapt, catching the rest of me on fire, setting every nerve ablaze.

I renewed my fight, kicking and opening my mouth wide so I could dig my teeth into his palm. The bastard dared touch me after everything he'd put me through—my contract, the Acquisition ball, and my father selling me. He needed to bleed, to suffer. I bit harder. He grunted but didn't release me. Even as I tasted copper and he constricted me so tightly to him that my vision dimmed, he wouldn't let go.

"Stop," Vinemont ordered, impatience dripping from his tone.

Getting nowhere, I relaxed my jaw and he withdrew his hand, but he kept the arm around me, walking me backward so he could close the door behind him.

"Where's Lucius?"

He was already drawn tighter than a piano wire, but my question made him vibrate with intensity.

"He's here tending to his foreman."

"Is Javier hurt?"

"Took a slug in the shoulder. Through and through, but still hurt like a son of a bitch based on his whining." He pushed me back until my knees hit the bed and I sat.

He took a step back and peered around, slivers of moon peeking through the windows the only light in the room. He strode back to the door and flipped the light switch. I was momentarily blinded but it didn't matter. He blotted out everything else. Vinemont, standing before me, his dark hair wild and blood running from cuts along his cheek, his neck, his arms. His right pant leg was stained a vivid crimson and still wet.

But more striking than any of that were his eyes. Deep blue, turbulent, and filled with a mix of possession and pain that rent my already tattered soul into even smaller pieces before scattering them away into the four winds.

"What—"

"We're safe." His gaze took me in, every inch from head to toe. "For now."

"What's happened?"

He ignored my question and strode to the bathroom. Though he hid it well, I saw a slight wince each time he put weight on his right leg.

He ripped open the linen closet and dug around until he found a first aid kit. I followed, lingering in the doorway as he sank onto the edge of the tub and yanked the case apart. Supplies spilled into the floor, and he grabbed the small bottle of alcohol before tearing the lid off and dousing the cuts on his arms and neck. Some were deep, the alcohol making the blood flow more freely. He'd lain a gun to his right, within easy reach.

He needed help. His arms and neck would heal, but the crimson stain spreading along his leg looked much, much worse. Should I help my enemy? The man who'd whipped me, tortured me, and told me he'd do it all again without hesitation? I chewed my lip as he dabbed at the wounds with gauze and glanced up at me every few moments, as if making sure I hadn't bolted.

When I noticed the slight tremor in his hand, I acted.

"Here." I grabbed some towels and wash cloths from the closet and sank down in front of him.

He raised his eyebrows and froze, surprise in the clear windows of his eyes. Then he looked away, closing my one glimpse into his depths. I took his hand and inspected the arm that was the worst for wear. The slashes were straight, clearly caused by a knife, and one was particularly deep. It cut through one of the thick, snaking vines of ink at the upper end of his forearm. The wound needed stitches to stanch the blood that dripped down to the white tile floor. I searched the first aid contents and found a small staple gun. It would have to do.

"I want to see your leg before I do anything else."

"It's fine. I'll heal." He reached for the half full alcohol bottle, but his tremor had increased and he knocked it into the tub. I bent over his legs and grabbed it before the entire contents rushed down the drain.

"Just let me see." I sat back on my knees. "Take your pants off."

He smirked. "Missed me?"

I was a moth trying to aid the spider. *What was I thinking?* I started to get up. "Go fuck yourself."

"Stop." His voice shook the slightest bit. "Please." He reached to his dark leather belt and unbuckled it before unfastening his pants.

I swallowed hard, giving him an angry stare before I gripped his jeans at the sides of his hips and pulled as he lifted up a bit. He settled back down heavily, the hand I'd bloodied with my teeth slipping as he sank and painting a bright red smear along the white porcelain. His boxer briefs were the only article of clothing not soaked with crimson. I drew the pants the rest of the way down and gasped when I found the stab wound through his calf. It was longer and deeper than the gash on his arm. The edges were ragged, oozing blood.

"How?" I looked up into his sapphire eyes.

"He came at me." He lifted his arms and I could tell the wounds were defensive. "I fought back." He rotated his wrist so I could see his bloodied knuckles. "And when he fell, he got one last good stab in before I…" He turned his hands over and stared at his palms, his brow wrinkling. He looked back at me, his eyes haunted.

What little compassion I had left was his, though he had no right to it. "You did what you had to. It's going to be okay."

He snorted a tiny laugh, but there was no smile, no spark to him. "I seem to keep doing that."

"What?"

"What I have to do, no matter what. No matter who gets hurt. No matter who I destroy." His voice thickened, mournfulness in every note, before he straightened his back and looked away.

Remorse? I would have laughed. I wanted to, the crazy impulse bubbling up and almost spilling from my lips. Instead, I pulled the belt from his jeans and looped it around his thigh, yanking it tight to momentarily slow the blood flow. When he winced, I felt somehow vindicated. Then I removed his boots and stripped his socks and pants the rest of the way off.

I soaked a washcloth with the alcohol and dabbed at his wound. He hissed but kept still. It had to hurt like hell. *Good.* I cleaned the wound more as his breathing grew ragged. The white washcloth soaked up his blood, his life with each swipe. Once I was satisfied the gash was as clean as I could get it, I gripped the stapler with one hand and used my other to squeeze his damaged skin together.

"Ready?"

He turned to me, his face back to its angular stonewall,

and nodded. I squeezed the trigger and the machine made a loud *tick* as the staple clamped. He fisted his hands but gave no other sign that it hurt. I did another, then another, continuing until the wound was sealed. Blood still flowed around the edges, but most of the damage was contained so I could release the makeshift tourniquet. After stripping off his shirt, the now-familiar Vinemont emblem blazing from his chest, I moved to his arm and did the same. Once the largest gash was sealed, I used gauze and medical tape on the rest.

When I was done, the shirt I was wearing was a mottled crimson and white. I wiped the sweat from my brow with the back of my arm and sat next to him on the edge of the tub.

"Thank you." He stared straight ahead, his neck tight, his jaw tighter.

I'd healed the spider, gotten him into tip-top shape so that he could destroy me even more thoroughly the next chance he got. I had no doubt he would. My flesh would be ripped, my blood spilled, and he would be the one to do it, just like before. I was a fool.

My gaze dropped to the gun only inches away, and I itched to take it. Could I kill him? End him and run? As much as my head wanted to say yes, my heart remained treacherous and refused.

As if reading my thoughts, he palmed the gun and stood, but swayed on his feet. He'd lost too much blood—the towels were soaked right along with his clothes. I pushed up and put my arm around his waist, helping him to Lucius' bed. He eased down, set the gun on the pillow beside him, and looked around, a haze over his eyes.

"Just rest for a minute. You need to recover. I'll go to the kitchen and get you some juice and whatever else I can find." Distance. I needed it to clear my head, to cope with the shock of him bursting into my life again. I got one step away before he grabbed my wrist.

"Stay."

"No. You need liquids. To replenish your blood." I pulled my wrist, but it was useless.

His palm rested over my scars, the very reason I knew how to help him build his blood back up. I'd been hooked to an IV for days even after a transfusion.

I sighed. "I'll come right back."

"No." He yanked and I fell into the bed next to him. "It's not safe." He wrapped his bandaged arms around me and pulled me to him, his hard chest pressing into my back.

"Vinemont!" I tried to push away from him, but I was caught.

"You aren't going anywhere. Too dangerous." His fingers played along the edge of my shirt, no doubt feeling the dampness of blood. "Take this off."

I stiffened. There was no way I was going to lie in bed with him naked. "No."

"Off." He growled and gripped one side, yanking the shirt apart, buttons bouncing off the hardwood floors as he pulled the shirt roughly down my arms and tossed it.

"What the fuck do you think you're doing?" His body was hot, alive, and hard at my back. I couldn't stay here. Not with him. Not in this bed like we were lovers, like we were two people who could seek solace from each other. We weren't. We never could be those people. "Stop!"

He caged me, my struggles nothing to him even in his weakened state. "You aren't leaving this bed. Get used to it. Don't fucking try anything."

I stopped fighting. There was no point. I would just have to wait until he fell asleep.

"You're mine, Stella." He tightened his grip with each word. "I don't care where you run, who you choose, what you say, or what you fucking do. You, all of you, belongs to me."

"I'm not a thing you can own," I hissed.

He laughed, the sound low and full of heat. "You can hop countries like a skipping stone for all I care. I'll find you, and you'll wind up right where you are now."

I tried another tack, one designed to knock him back to reality. "Besides, if I belong to anyone, it's Lucius."

He stopped laughing and drew his free hand up to my hair, stroking through the strands before gripping so tight it hurt. I yelped.

"Has he touched you?" His voice was in my ear, danger and seduction cutting through me like the knife had his skin.

"Fuck off."

He yanked. "Has he?"

I barked out a harsh laugh. "Yes. Every night. Every night he fucks me until I scream his name. He gives it to me so good he's all I can think about. I want it from him. I dream about him. When he puts his cock in my mouth I've never been happier. I beg him to fuck me in the ass. When he does, I come so hard I black out."

He relaxed his grip and nuzzled into my hair. "You done?" His laugh was low, seductive. "Or do you have some more lies for me?"

My body warmed under his touch, his breath, his voice. I willed the memory of him whipping me into my mind, the memory of him showing me the contract where he'd bought me from my father. I wouldn't fall for his tricks. Not again. I was done being his plaything.

He released me for a moment and gripped the white duvet, throwing it over us and marring it with blood. I edged away from him, separating our bodies, but it didn't matter, he reached across me and turned off the light with the remote before crushing me against him. This time I felt his half mast dick pressing into my ass.

"Stop." My voice quavered, the turmoil inside me spilling out in uncertain notes.

He spread his fingers along my bare stomach, his index finger brushing against the bottom curve of my breast. "Tell me to stop again. Please, Stella. Tell me again and see what happens."

His words were a dark promise that sent a thread of electricity straight between my thighs. I was in his web again, caught and cocooned as he slowly sank his fangs into every bit of me.

I remained silent. I had no other choice.

"No?" He teased his lips down my neck. "You don't want to find out? You don't want me to put you on your stomach, slap your ass, fist your hair, and fuck your tight pussy until I make you come on a scream? Tie you up, make you come again and again while I'm deep in your ass until you beg me to stop? You don't want all the things you just lied to me about? I can make them true, Stella. Every last one." His fingertip moved back and forth against the sensitive skin of my breast, every nerve in my body focusing on that one small movement. "I could break you and you'd love every minute of it."

"You will never break me. Never." The venom in my voice surprised me. I realized then how much I meant it. How much I intended to fight. There would be no more sinking to the bottom of the pool. No more toying with death over drinks and dancing. I intended to walk across the room, wrap my arms around death's neck and pull him down to me. Kiss him like there was no tomorrow and dare him to do a thing about it. Fuck him. Fuck Vinemont, too.

"We'll see." Though his voice spoke of exhaustion, his grip on me didn't falter.

He fell asleep soon after, his breaths becoming deep and even, tickling my neck.

I tried to slip away twice after he lost consciousness, but I only managed to put a few inches between us before he wrapped his arm around me like a vise and yanked me back, a growl in his throat.

Eventually, I drifted off to sleep, awash in Vinemont, regret, and the faint scent of Lucius.

CHAPTER THREE
SINCLAIR

STELLA SLUMBERED PEACEFULLY on my chest, her red locks fanned out along my upper arm as if entwining with the vines that covered me. The sun had risen without any more bloodshed, though there had been plenty the night before. I'd killed men. My fair share, maybe more, to keep the Vinemont stronghold alive and well.

I didn't blame the farmers, or the instigators, or even the paid mercenaries our competitors hired to keep the unrest churning. No, I blamed the Sovereign. If Cal wasn't squeezing us for an even bigger cut of profits, then none of this would have happened. The farmers were just collateral damage, pawns in a much larger war that was going on hundreds of miles north of here in the bayous of Louisiana.

I smoothed my hand down Stella's back. The tiny ridges marred her skin like braille beneath my fingertips. I'd written our story on her fair flesh in blood and violence. Regret tolled in me, but what I'd done was necessary. Just like all the trials.

Her eyelashes fluttered against my chest and she let out an angelic sigh. Her breasts were pressed into me and her smooth thigh was slung over mine. She was soft and warm, a wet dream come to life in my arms. I breathed her in, her hair smelling of lavender and vanilla.

I moved my hand back up and dug my fingers into her hair. I didn't want her sighing. I wanted her screaming, my name on her lips, my ecstasy pulsing through her veins. But it wasn't so simple. It never had been. I needed so much more from her than simple surrender. And the past two weeks without her under my control had been nothing short of torture.

She had run away. My fist tightened.

Away from *me*. Her eyes opened.

She chose Lucius. I gripped her hard right at her scalp.

"Vinem—"

Before she could even say my curse of a name, I settled on top her, pushing my knee between her legs as she struggled. Her attempts to buck me only made my cock harder. She was my Acquisition. Mine. She needed to know it. I was foolish to indulge her for as long as I did. Foolish to let her hope, to let her think that she could hold any sway over my heart. Maybe if I could do this, if I could commit this transgression, I'd finally stop seeing her as something more than a possession.

"Don't." Her eyes went wide, all traces of sleep gone and fear in its place.

This was what I needed. Her fear. Her loathing. I slapped my hand over her mouth and stared into her eyes. She dug her nails into my back with her free hand while I pinned the other above her head. My cock was against her hot core, only the fabric of my boxer briefs separating us. I could take her. Take everything.

"I should have done this the first day you showed up at my house, Stella." I crushed my palm into her lips, surely bruising them. "I was weak. You made me weak. From the first moment I saw you, you were a fucking poison."

But then something sparked in her emerald depths. Not fear. Defiance.

Her eyebrows lowered the tiniest bit, as if daring me onward. She let out a roaring sound against my palm, deep and guttural. The heat between her thighs had me pushing my hips against her. She was wet and wanting even as her eyes were full of vengeance. I wanted her, wanted every last morsel of her rage, her hate.

Even so, I knew if I did this, she would never forgive me. And then I would have truly lost her. Could I bear it? It didn't matter. I had to do it. Breaking her was the only way to win. And I would win no matter what.

A searing pain exploded through my calf at the same time she bucked hard. She'd dug her heal into the wound. I rolled to my side and reached for my injured leg as she slid out from under me and off the bed. She scrambled away, the skin of her knees squealing against the polished hardwoods. I recovered and lunged after her, jumping on my good leg before sinking to my knees and gripping her by the hair. I landed on her back as she cried out, pinned beneath me.

"Do it. Just fucking do it, you psycho!" Despite her words, she still fought me, pulling against the hold I had on her hair.

She was helpless. I pushed my hips against her, the friction of my hard cock on her soft ass almost unbearable. I pulled her head to the side and licked her ear before capturing it between my teeth and biting down.

She whimpered, her nails scratching at the floor as I kissed down her neck, tasting her skin the same way I'd thought about every second she'd been away. I'd waited for her to come back, to realize she'd made a mistake. She didn't. She hadn't. I bit the flesh over her jugular, wanting to punish her for running, for taking what was left of my heart with her when she did.

She surged beneath me, one last effort to escape. Not a chance. I rose and flipped her onto her back, pinning her wrists to the floor and studying her face. Her chest heaved and her pussy was on fire, making my cock leak. The morning light made her eyes sparkle even through the hate I found in them.

"You are pathetic. All of you. Just get it over with." She fisted her hands, but couldn't do a thing with them. Her gaze was nothing short of scorching.

As she goaded me on, I knew I couldn't. And that knowledge sealed my fate. If I couldn't break her, I would have to pay the price. The Acquisition demanded it.

A sudden flash of light at my temple turned into a gloomy dark and then a pair of hands were on me, lifting me up and throwing me down onto my back. My vision cleared. Stella shrieked and turned over to her side, rolling into a ball. Lucius stood over me, his brow wrinkled in fury.

"Don't you fucking touch her, Sin!" He went to her and scooped her up in his arms. She clung to him and buried her face in his neck.

I tried to get up, but my injured leg gave way and I landed back on my ass. Lucius backed out of the room, Stella clutching him.

She gave me one last look, her eyes awash in tears and pain. Then she was gone, all hope right along with her.

CHAPTER FOUR
Stella

LUCIUS SAT ME on the edge of my bed and pulled my duvet up around me. He eased down next to me and rested his palm on my cheek. I flinched away, but he wrapped his other arm around my waist, holding me still.

"Did he hurt you?" His sky blue gaze searched my face.

"No." I shook my head, ignoring the tremor in my voice.

"He'll never hurt you again." His jaw tightened, but his touch remained soft.

"I'm fine." I shuddered at what Vinemont had done. His threat had grown in the two weeks since we'd been apart, not lessened.

"You're not fine. Don't lie to me."

I pushed him away. I refused to be manhandled or bullied by any of them. Not anymore.

He sighed and released me. "I'm not him."

I let my gaze travel the ink peeking from the edges of his sleeves. Even if the brothers didn't see eye to eye, they would always be bound together, on the same side.

His face softened a bit. "Stella, listen—"

"What happened yesterday? Is it safe?" I didn't want

any more mind games. I only wanted to know if I'd survive the day.

He glowered, fine wrinkles turning the corners of his mouth. "Local unrest spurred on by outside interests. It's taken care of for now. I had to fix up Javier and then meet with useless government officials until late."

Blood stained his shirt in several places, most of it already brown in the morning light. He seemed none the worse for wear, save a few scratches, making me wonder whose blood he carried in the threads.

He continued, "That was the only reason I didn't come back to you. I sent Sin to protect you because I couldn't. I run the business here, so I'm the one who had to calm things down. I didn't realize he would…"

"Looks like you don't know your brother as well as you thought." I pulled the blanket up higher, covering every inch of skin below my neck. "Don't worry. Your little investment is protected and plenty *useable* for the next Acquisition trial. No harm done."

He slumped the slightest bit. Whether it was fatigue from the long night or my sharp words, I didn't know. "There are traditions. Things have to be done a certain way. You wouldn't understand."

I arched an eyebrow. "Do *you* understand? Vinemont says you don't even know the rules yet you jumped right in and started playing."

"I don't need to know any rules to win, Stella." He met my eyes.

I didn't lean away. I wouldn't cower for him or anyone. I could play the game, too. "You're full of shit. Playing second fiddle to your brother has made you rash."

He pulled at the duvet slowly until my shoulders were uncovered, though his eyes never left mine. A heat kindled in them, intense and immediate. "I've always been rash. This is nothing new."

He stroked his fingertips along my collarbone, the gentle sensation so at odds with the ravenous look in his eyes. "I've given you two weeks. Two weeks to adjust to being mine. I would never try to force you. I'm not my brother, Stella. Two weeks—has it been enough time?" He slid his fingers lower, pushing the duvet down my bare skin and to the swell of my breast.

My breath hitched in my throat as I glared at him. "I'm not yours. It doesn't matter what some contract says or what some bullshit Acquisition rules say. I will never be yours."

He smirked and shoved the duvet the rest of the way down before pulling me into him. His mouth was hot on mine, his tongue desirous and seeking. I shoved against his chest, but his grip on me was unshakeable. His lips were firm, insistent.

He sank his tongue inside, exploring and groaning as he tasted me. Heat pulsed through me but it was all wrong— his scent, his voice, his lips. Even as my body warmed to his advance, my thoughts strayed to his brother. The way he'd handled me before, the feel of him between my legs, the pain and determination in his eyes as he told me I was his poison.

Vinemont was right. I intended to poison them both. So I opened my mouth further, letting Lucius hold sway over me. Letting him think I chose him. He pushed me back on the bed and moved one hand to my breast, kneading it as his hard length rested against my thigh.

I faked a moan. His touch was pleasurable, but didn't send the shock of adrenaline through me like Vinemont. It didn't matter. I would use Lucius. I would do what I had to do to truly turn him against his brother. I tangled my hands in his hair and he moved his knee between my thighs. I lifted my hips to him, my pussy tingling at the friction.

"Jefe?" Javier's tentative voice came through the door.

Lucius broke the kiss and sat up, pulling me with him. I yanked the cover back in place.

"What?" he barked.

"The jet is ready. I found Mr. Sinclair in your room. One of the hands is helping him."

"We're coming." Lucius smoothed a hand through my hair and rested it on my cheek. "This isn't over," he whispered.

No, it isn't.

He stood and squared his shoulders, all business again.

"We're leaving?" I asked.

"Now that we've tamped down the uprising, Javier will run the plantation until after the Christmas trial." He glanced away at the last words, unable to look me in the eye. *Coward.*

Reaching out, I brushed my fingers along his. "Tell me what the trial is."

He lifted his fingers, seeking more contact. I let my hand stay there, our skin heating wherever we touched.

"I'm not sure. I haven't spoken to Sin since we left, not until yesterday when I got word of trouble. And then we didn't have time to discuss the trial. I know generally what it is." He glanced away again. "But that rat bastard Cal will be sure to make it more interesting since it's his year."

I dropped my hand, a deadness spreading in my chest. "Renee told me about her year. I know what's going to happen to me."

"It can't be helped." He knelt in front of me, his eyes pleading. "All I can tell you is that once I'm Sovereign, I'll make it all up to you."

"Just let me go." I ran my fingertips down his chiseled jaw, the stubble sharp and thick. "You could let me leave. Or we could leave together."

"No, Stella. You don't know what you're asking me. When I'm Sovereign, I can give you anything you want. Anything you've ever dreamed about. These trials will just be some hazy memory when we're flying on our private jet or vacationing in the Maldives or having tea with the fucking royal family. Don't you see? If I lose, then all of that's gone. The Vinemonts will spend another ten years under someone else's thumb. Someone who may be even worse than Cal. Stella, look at me. We can do this." His face appeared almost boyish in its earnestness.

I laughed, the sound cold even to my ears. "Now it's a team sport? 'We'? Are you going to watch as your friends rape me? Hold me down? Cheer them on? Keep count? Gag me to cover my screams? Will all of that be a hazy dream to you once you're Sovereign?"

He rose, towering over me. "I will do what I have to do to become Sovereign. It's the right play, Stella. You'll see."

Turning his back, he strode away with renewed purpose, as if our chat about my defilement put his head back in the game. "Be ready to leave in half an hour."

My chin dropped to my chest as he closed the door. Lucius had made up his mind, just like Vinemont, to win at all costs. To them, the value of being Sovereign outweighed my well-being, my freedom, my everything. I stood and dropped the duvet before going to the shutters and throwing them open.

The fields of sugar cane waved in the light breeze as the sun blazed down. The rays were painful, sharp, and unrelenting, but the sugar cane soaked up the punishment and grew stronger, sweeter—more valuable. Every moment under the oppressive heat was a gift, a dose of life when there would otherwise be none. Surviving and thriving.

Was strength always born of fire, of torment? I nodded at the silent question. I would have to suffer to survive. But I would come out the other side. And when I did, I would burn the entire Acquisition to the ground.

CHAPTER FIVE
Stella

THE JET RIDE lasted a few hours, the sun already fading from the sky as we neared land. The dark waters of the Gulf retreated and a twinkle of lights sprouted along the horizon. New Orleans was ablaze, the city vibrant even from the air.

Neither Vinemont nor Lucius spoke to me or each other as they piloted the plane from the open cockpit. Despite the lack of words, the animosity between the brothers had grown into something almost palpable. It swirled around the cabin, making every moment strained. I smiled and relaxed back into my seat, enjoying the tension in both of their backs as they sat at the controls in front of me. Maybe tearing them apart wouldn't be as difficult as I'd first imagined.

We landed at a private airfield outside the city and taxied over to a hangar. A driver waited out front next to a black limo. Once we came to a stop, Lucius stood and opened the hatch, letting the stairs down so we could exit. He held his hand out for me.

"Don't touch her," Vinemont growled.

"Fuck off." Lucius didn't waver.

I took his hand and stepped down, glad to be out of the tight cabin. The weather was chilly for Louisiana; winter was in full swing despite the high, bright sun.

The driver greeted me with a smile and opened the back door. I slid in as he went to help gather the bags and other items from the plane's storage hatch. The car was running, and Christmas music was playing low on the radio. I almost laughed. *Merry Christmas to me.* Gallows humor had taken on a particular relevance for me in the past few months.

Even though I was here for the Acquisition trial, I was still glad to be back in the States. I allowed my thoughts to flit to my father for a split second before forcing them down. The last I'd heard he was in ICU. I hadn't inquired any further. I couldn't. Not after seeing his name on Vinemont's contract. Had the hospital stay truly been a ruse as Vinemont suggested, or was my father ill? I shouldn't have cared, but I did.

My eyes stung, the wound still fresh. He'd committed an unforgivable sin against me. Even so, I couldn't wish for his destruction, no matter how much I wanted to. Too much of me was caught up in him, too many memories, too many years of relying on each other and surviving despite the weight of Mom's death slowly crushing us. I blinked the unshed tears away and tilted my head up until they receded. I may not have wanted my father dead, but I'd be damned if I cried for him.

The car shook as the driver loaded up some belongings in the trunk. Vinemont slid in next to me and locked both of the back doors. Lucius stood outside and glared at his brother before climbing into the front passenger seat.

"Back to the house?" the driver asked.

"Yes, Luke." Lucius kept me in his peripheral vision.

I edged away from Vinemont. He was still banged up, fresh bandages down his arms and angry red wounds along his neck. He was healing, but it would take time. He studied me, his eyes fixing on mine as he tapped his fingers on his knee. What could he be thinking after what he'd tried to do earlier that morning?

The memory of his hard body on top of mine sent a rush of heat spiraling through me. I'd been afraid at first, but then I'd become something more. Livid. I dared him to do it. I wanted him to take that last step, to seal his doom even further.

My body may have been fooled by him, desperate for his touch. My mind was anything but. I knew he couldn't follow through. I knew he wanted me as more than just his Acquisition. His twisted heart had a glimmer of love left and I'd touched it, felt it. Now I would use it to break him.

Luke sped down the interstate, farther into the Louisiana countryside toward the Vinemont estate. Lucius kept glancing back like a chaperone insistent there would be no funny business on his watch. Vinemont said nothing, just continued studying me, as if he were dissecting me piece by piece to discover what particular magic made me tick.

The Christmas music persisted for the entire drive, telling us all to be joyful as we pulled up to the vine-covered gates and I entered enemy territory once again. It felt like a homecoming of sorts—the winding road, the secret bayous, and the familiar oaks. My eyes strayed above the tops of the trees to the dormer windows on the third floor. A light glowed into the night from one of them. Was Vinemont's mother watching our approach?

We arrived at the house, the stately white façade and wide porch greeting us like always. The front door opened, and Farns and Renee appeared, both smiling as I got out and clambered up the steps.

Renee folded me in her arms and squeezed hard. "I missed you."

"I missed you, too." I buried my face in her familiar jet black hair.

"Ms. Rousseau, so nice to see you again." Farns gave a slight bow.

I smiled up into his weathered face. "Ever the gentleman."

"Why, thank you. The house wasn't the same without you." His smile faltered, as if remembering I wasn't exactly a willing guest. He covered by telling Luke he'd help with the bags, though he eased down the stairs with ginger steps.

Renee pulled her shawl tighter around her narrow shoulders. "Come in, come in. Too cold out here to be standing around."

A biting wind blew past, as if to illustrate her point, and I followed her into the foyer. Everything was the same—honey oak floors, glittering chandeliers, and impeccable southern architecture. Still, a shift had occurred in my bones, maybe even at my most basic level. The last time I'd arrive here and entered those doors, I hadn't known what to expect. This time I did. This time I could face my future and, hopefully, have a chance of weathering the storm.

"When I got word you were on your way, I went ahead and drew you a nice hot bath. How's that sound?" Renee led me up the stairs and into my room. Lavender and vanilla permeated the air and drew me into the bathroom.

She didn't need to tell me twice. I stripped out of my jeans and t-shirt and slipped into the fragrant water. I moaned in sheer pleasure as Renee bustled around making sure I had towels and anything else I needed.

I finally waved her toward the small hamper. "Sit down and tell me what happened while I was gone."

She laughed and took her seat. "I think you need to tell me why you're back so soon first. I heard there was trouble brewing, but from the looks of Mr. Sinclair, it seems to have boiled over and scorched."

I nodded and lay back, letting the heat relax my muscles. I recounted my two weeks of wandering around the Cuban estate, swimming in the pool, and doing everything in my power to avoid thinking about Vinemont.

When I told her about the uprising she clucked her tongue.

"That sort of trouble has happened before, but it was a long time ago."

"When was that?"

Her dark eyes scrutinized me and she furrowed her brow as if she were trying to make a choice.

I willed her to tell me something, anything. Information was like to gold to me. It always had been in this house.

She sighed. "Well, I guess it doesn't matter. I'll tell. Maybe it'll help."

I leaned forward and propped my chin on my knees. Renee must have missed me to be so ready to spill information.

Her fingers were already in a twisting war with each other. "When Rebecca was Sovereign, she had a problem with a neighboring sugar cane plantation in Brazil. It was owned by another family, the Roses. The Roses had been steadily eating up the open farmland around the Vinemont fields and gained a stranglehold on the crop in that particular area with the help of paramilitaries. It was a lawless place that far inland. Still is. Anyway, once Rebecca won Sovereign, the Roses had already been doing everything they could to get the Vinemonts out of Brazil." More hand wringing.

"Go on."

"Well, the Sovereign has a certain set of powers." She halted, clearly wondering how much information she should give.

"What powers?" I had to keep her talking.

"Well, the Sovereign can bring families in."

"Like the Vinemonts?"

"Yes." She avoided my gaze. "Like them."

She scratched at her neck before forcing her hand back to her lap. "And the Sovereign can cast families out."

"What happens when a family gets cast out?" I asked.

"It means that, should the Sovereign will it, the family's assets and lives are forfeit."

I cocked my head sideways at the idea of such a one-sided remedy. "Why doesn't the Sovereign just do that to everyone and take everything and call it a goddamn day. To hell with the Acquisition?"

"Because the Sovereign may only do it to one family during their entire reign. He can bring one in and he can kick one out. It helps keep everyone in line, you see?"

It made sense. Casting a family out fortified the Sovereign's wealth and position. And just the threat of it was likely enough to keep the families under the Sovereign's thumb. Being able to add an ally? Priceless. It was like stacking up pieces around the king on a chess board. "What happens to the family that gets the boot?"

"It depends. Some are allowed to go, move away, try and rebuild. Some aren't so lucky. The Sovereign controls fortunes, controls life or death..." She dropped her gaze to the floor, a pall falling over her.

"What happened with Rebecca and the Roses?" The water couldn't have cooled in such a short time, but I felt a chill rush down my spine all the same.

"The Vinemonts weren't always one of the main families. Some of the older families looked down on them, tried to take advantage—"

"Families like the Roses?"

She nodded but still didn't meet my gaze. "By the time Rebecca became Sovereign, she was a different person. Before, she would work with the local farmers and try and sort out the issues the Roses were creating at the plantation. But after the trials, she decided to make an example of them. She waited until they instigated another supply problem—Rose trucks blocking the roads and keeping the workers from getting the sugar cane to the processing plant. She went down to the farm, flew herself as she used to do, and took Mr. Sinclair with her. I told her he was too young. She didn't listen. That poor boy..." She finally returned my stare, her dark eyes swimming with unshed tears.

"What happened?"

Renee took a deep shuddering breath. "I really shouldn't be telling you this."

"Tell me." I needed to know the rest of the story like I needed my next breath.

Her eyes flickered to the ceiling and then back to me, and she dropped her voice to barely above a whisper. "She rounded up every farmer on the Vinemont property, armed them, and set them on the Rose plantation. It was burned to the ground within hours. The fields charred. The workers killed. Mr. Rose was down there at the time. He never returned. A month after that, the Rose plantations were Vinemont plantations, and the Rose clan was no more. The little boy that left with his mother never came back, either."

"Why would you tell me this now?" I couldn't keep the anger from my voice. She had so much more information that she wasn't sharing. She doled it out in tiny spoonfuls and I was hungry within seconds after each bite.

"Because I've seen the way Mr. Sinclair looks at you. I saw how he was for the two weeks you were gone. He needs you, Stella. More than he's ever needed anyone. I think…I hope." She chose her words haltingly. "I hope that you may be the one thing between him and a lifetime of regret. I wasn't strong enough to save Rebecca. But you're different." A tear rolled down her cheek, hesitating in the small crease next to her mouth before falling to the floor.

"You want *me* to save *him*?" I couldn't begin to wrap my head around the mix of Stockholm Syndrome and pure fucked up insanity she'd just said. "I'm his prisoner, his plaything, the ant he likes to use a magnifying glass on. I have no power to save myself, much less him. Whatever feelings he may have for me are nothing compared to the darkness inside him. You've seen it."

"I've seen it." She held my gaze. "But he's not the only one with darkness inside him, Stella. We all have it."

I closed my eyes and sank beneath the water, for once sated with information. I didn't want to think or hear any more about the child Sinclair, how scared he must have been, how horrified at the violence he no doubt witnessed. I had to think of myself. It didn't matter what sort of rules he adhered to now. The fact was he could still let me go if he chose. He could leave my father alone. He could still turn his back on the whole Acquisition. He only stayed in it to reap the rewards and benefits of a system that was built on darkness, on the vilest impulses of human nature. He was a part of it, participating willingly.

No, I wouldn't save him. I refused. But I would save myself.

When I emerged from beneath the surface, Renee had disappeared.

After I'd soaked as long as I could in the hot water, I rose and dressed in some new pajamas I found in my dresser. Renee had been busy during my absence, the closet full of new clothes and the dresser bursting with even more. I ate in my room that night, not willing to sit through a meal with the Vinemont clan. I picked through the roast chicken and vegetables Renee had brought until there was a knock at my door.

Adjusting my tank top, I pulled the blanket up over my shorts. "Come in."

A blond head of hair peeked through. "Hi."

"Hi, yourself." I smiled, happy to see Teddy. Of all the Vinemont brothers, he was the most genuine. Teddy telegraphed his motives clear as a bell and his boyish manners endeared him to me, though he was only a handful of years younger than I was.

He came in and shut the door behind him before easing onto the foot of my bed.

"I heard some things about Cuba. You okay?"

I set my plate on the nightstand and drew my knees up. "Things were hairy there for a minute, but I'm safe."

"Yeah, Sin doesn't look so good. Dr. Yarbrough is

patching him up right now. But Sin said you took care of him, doing staples and all that?"

I nodded, remembering the way Vinemont had watched me as I knelt before him, cleaning his wounds. "I did."

"Why?" He angled his head so I could look down the line of his strong jaw.

It wasn't an easy question, and I had no easy answer. "He needed help."

"But why would you help him after he…" He glanced up to my shoulder, as if he could see the lash marks there.

I shrugged. "I don't know."

He traced the stitching on the quilt at the foot of my bed with his fingertip. "I think I know why."

"Enlighten me."

He met my gaze, his hazel eyes shy but also seeking. "I think it's the same thing I feel with Laura. Like, you would do anything for that person, even if you're mad at them or even if they've done something terrible."

I tilted my head to the side. "Are you talking about love?"

He shrugged, his lanky arms rising and falling with the movement. "I guess, yeah. I don't know. I've never been in love. I just know that if someone hurt her, I'd make that someone pay, and then I'd do everything I could to help her. Does that make sense?"

"It does. For you and Laura it does."

"But not for you and Sin?"

I sighed and leaned back against the pillows. "I think whatever is between me and your brother is much more complicated than what you've described. And I think you know why."

"Because of the Acquisition?" He kept tracing the same pattern of seams over and over, his index finger moving to its own silent beat.

"Yes." In some other life, there may have been love. Maybe if Vinemont hadn't been born into his role and I hadn't been born into mine, then maybe. But as it was, we had no future and our past was murky at best.

"I just wish…"

"What?"

He shook his head and rose. "I'll let you get back to your dinner. I just heard you were back and wanted to come say hi and that I missed you. And thank you for taking care of Sin when he needed it."

I held my arms out and he came and gave me a hug, squeezing me almost as tightly as Renee did, but not quite.

"You're welcome," I whispered.

"Okay." He stood and retreated to the door. "I'll see you in the morning at breakfast then?"

I couldn't refuse his honest smile. "Yes, I guess so."

"Good."

Once he left, I snuggled down into my bed. Why did the other two have to be so vile when Teddy had turned out so normal?

I tried to fall asleep but couldn't. Not until I dropped to my knees and reached up into my nightstand. Once I felt the familiar blade still securely taped to the underside of the drawer, I crawled back into bed. I'd brought the knife here as a weapon, but the simple act of touching it strengthened my resolve. It was more of a talisman than anything else at this point.

I didn't need it to keep me safe. I could do that on my own. And I would.

CHAPTER SIX
Stella

Breakfast the next morning was oddly calm. Vinemont was already at the table, sipping his coffee and watching my every move as I walked in and took a seat next to Teddy.

"Happy to be back?" Vinemont set his cup down and leaned forward, his perfectly pressed business shirt doing nothing to hide the muscles underneath.

"I wouldn't say that." My sharp tone made the corners of his mouth turn up, a smile trying to break free. The half-smile died as Lucius entered the room.

He was on a call, fluent Spanish rolling off his tongue as he gave orders to someone, most likely Javier. He wore a navy polo and jeans that fit his narrow waist and lean hips perfectly. When he was done, he tossed his phone down on the table.

"Well?" Vinemont asked.

"Javier says it's all over. But now we have to pay the local militia for their *assistance*."

Vinemont glanced to Teddy and shook his head at Lucius. "We'll finish this discussion later."

"I'm not a kid anymore, Sin. You two can tell me

what's going on." Teddy swept his hair off his forehead, perhaps aiming for a more serious look.

"It's nothing." Vinemont waved his hand as if a militia fighting a farmer uprising was nothing more than a simple labor disagreement.

"Sure." Teddy wasn't convinced.

"All under control, lil bro. Don't worry, we're keeping your trust fund stocked." Lucius grinned.

"Douche." Teddy crossed his arms over his chest as Lucius' grin broadened.

I elbowed him. "Ignore him. Tell me what life is like out there. What's going on at school?"

He smiled. "I aced my classes this semester—"

"And every semester, dork." Lucius cut in.

Teddy raised an eyebrow at his brother. "So I'm almost done with my pre-med coursework."

"So you're well on your way to being Dr. Teddy, then?" I asked.

"Yep. I've already been accepted. I should graduate undergrad in the spring and roll right on into med school."

A surge of misplaced pride welled inside me. After all, Teddy wasn't my blood. Still, I smiled at him and patted him on the back. "Well done."

"Thanks."

Laura came in and set out plates full of biscuits, gravy, country ham, and eggs. She and Teddy avoided each other's eyes. It was glaringly obvious they were in love and trying desperately to hide it.

Vinemont scowled and speared a chunk of ham. Lucius smirked and gave me a wink.

I decided to help Teddy out and erase some of the awkward. "What sort of doctor do you want to be?"

"Gynecologist, right?" Lucius didn't miss a beat.

Teddy choked on his orange juice. I clapped him on the back a few times and glared at Lucius.

Teddy tried twice to speak before he could do it without sounding strangled. "No, I was thinking cardiology."

"What do you know about hearts?" Lucius grinned at Laura as she came around and refilled our coffees.

"Nothing yet. That's what the medical degree is for."

"Touché." Lucius laughed.

Vinemont remained silent. I thought he'd at least encourage Teddy to do something other than hang around this house and its godforsaken occupants. But he didn't say a word.

"And how many years will you have to be in school?" I tried again.

"Four years of school, three years of residency, and maybe another three years of fellowship after that."

I elbowed him. "You'll be an old man by the time you finish all that. I'm glad you started young."

Vinemont's fork and knife clattered to his plate. He fixed Teddy with an inscrutable stare before turning his burning gaze on me.

"Sin, what gives?" Lucius said. "Shouldn't you applaud the little bro's fine, upstanding life plans? Better than running a sugar business and playing lawyer like we do. Let's toast." He raised his mimosa.

Teddy and I reached across the table and clinked glasses with Lucius. Vinemont rose, threw his napkin down, and stormed out.

Teddy's cheeks bloomed red and his shoulders fell.

"Sin!" Lucius stood and strode after his brother.

What the hell just happened? I put my hand on Teddy's arm and squeezed. I was just as in the dark as he was.

A door slammed down the hall—Vinemont's study.

Knocking and banging echoed through the corridor. "Open this fucking door, douchebag, and apologize to Teddy!"

Nothing.

Before long, Lucius returned and sat down. "He's just being a dick as usual, Ted. Don't worry about him. He's told me before that he's all for you getting a medical degree."

"He's told me that, too. So, I'm just..." Teddy shrugged and placed his napkin next to his plate. "I'm going to go upstairs for a while." He pushed his chair back and walked out, head down.

"What the hell?" I asked.

Lucius shook his head. "Not a fucking clue."

Laura came in to check on us, but her pleasant smile faded when she noticed Teddy was gone.

"He's upstairs." I said. "Some company might be welcome right now."

She blushed and retreated back to the kitchen.

"You shouldn't encourage that." Lucius leaned back and linked his hands behind his head, the broad expanse of his chest appearing even wider.

"I don't live by your snobby rules." I wiped my mouth and set my napkin on the table.

He raised an eyebrow. "No?"

"No."

"I'm pretty sure you're bound by quite a few more rules than I am." He smiled, wolfishness taking the place of his anger at Vinemont.

"I'm not in the mood, Lucius."

He let his gaze run down the scoop neck of my sweater and lower. I stood and moved toward the door. He darted faster down his side of the table and blocked me in.

"I think you are." He shoved me into the corner, caging me in with his hands at either side of my head. "Want to know what I've been thinking about? What I thought about last night while I stroked my cock?"

I met his light eyes and fisted my hands at my sides. "No, but I'm sure you'll tell me."

He moved closer. I tilted my head back so I could hold his gaze. He was dangerous. Taking my eyes off him wasn't an option.

"I thought of you." Pressing his fingertip into my jugular, he traced down my bare skin to the edge of my sweater. "The way you looked in Cuba, naked underneath me. The way these were hard." He pinched my nipple and I pressed back into the corner. "Just like they are now. How much I wanted them in my mouth. How deep I wanted to be in your pussy. You know what got me off, what pushed me over the edge?"

I forced myself to stay put, to see this part of the game through. "What?"

"This." When he pressed his lips to mine, I closed my eyes. He tasted like champagne and oranges, heady and sweet.

I clung to the front of his shirt. He sank his hand down in my pants, gripping my ass hard and pulling my hips forward.

I tried to shove him away, but he growled into my mouth and ground his thigh against my pussy. I dug my nails into his chest, but he only kissed me harder, his tongue plundering my mouth. Heat raced through my body, pooling between my thighs. He grabbed my hair and pulled my head back before kissing down my neck, biting my throat and then fastening his lips to my collarbone.

"Lucius." I was panting, caught up in a man who was no better than the devil I'd given my heart to. "Please."

"Beg me. That's right, Stella. It's time to finish what we started." He kissed lower, his mouth hot and luscious on my skin. "Beg me to give you what you want, what you need."

He rubbed against my clit, the friction making my head spin. I gasped.

"Beg me to sink myself so deep in you that you can't tell where I end and you begin."

"Don't." I breathed as he released my hair and pulled my sweater and the cup of my bra down.

I moaned—not a fake—when cool air hit my nipple, his mouth following close behind.

This was wrong. All wrong. I dug my fingers into his hair and pulled, but he sucked me in harder, his teeth grazing along the hard peak of my breast. He groaned into my skin and palmed my ass viciously, rubbing me against him in a slow, teasing rhythm.

"We can't." I sounded unsure even to myself.

He swirled his tongue once more around my nipple before coming back up and resting his forehead against mine, his hand on my cheek. "You're already mine. I'm going to taste every bit of you. Every inch of skin. You're going to take all of me, Stella, and beg for more. And I'll give it. I'll give it every time you ask and even when you don't."

His words buzzed around my mind like a swarm of bees, stinging me but with the promise of something sweet.

He leaned in to kiss me again but I pushed harder. I couldn't do this. Not here. Not now. I wanted to snare him, but not with Vinemont a few doors down.

He gripped my wrists and pinned them above my head. "I know you want it, Stella. I know you want everything I have. If you say you don't, you're lying to yourself." He brushed his lips against mine again, making me believe his lies. *Were they lies?*

"I could take you right now. I could yank your jeans down and feast on your sweet cunt." He shoved his hips into me, his hard cock substantial in his pants. "I want to, Stella. Oh, how I want to."

"Please, don't. I-I can't." I was stumbling, falling, begging the wolf in front of me to catch me.

He stole another kiss, this one lingering. My heartbeat was like a drum in my ears as his tongue swirled against mine, teasing and tasting. He pulled my wrists down from the wall and wrapped them around my back at my waist, making my breasts jut out against him.

He kissed to my ear. "I'm going to take it all, Stella."

"Never." I tried to shake myself out of the haze he'd put me in.

His deep laugh was in my head as he nipped at my

neck. "We'll see."

He pulled away and stared down at me, his eyes calculating. "I'll give you a pass this one time, Stella. Just once. But the next time I get you alone and you try to tease me—" He grabbed my palm and ran it down his hard length "—you're going to get all of this. And then you're going to thank me when I'm done."

He dropped my wrists and backed up another step. "Go," he commanded, "before I change my mind."

Stunned, I brushed past him and into the hallway. All the oxygen had been out here, not in the dining room where Lucius had made it impossible to think. I stumbled over the runner before gaining my feet and taking the next few steps. I pulled my top back into place as I fled. The doorbell stopped me. I turned and glimpsed a figure through the transom windows.

Lucius was already in the hallway, adjusting himself in his pants before striding to the door and swinging it open.

The visitor wore an old-fashioned servant's livery—even stuffier than Farns'—who ambled up and shook his head at Lucius. The man handed Lucius a card, gave a perfunctory bow, and whirled on his heel.

"You shouldn't get the door. That's my job, Mr. Lucius," Farns chided gently.

"I've gotten my hands dirty plenty over the last few days, Farns. Trust me. This is nothing."

Vinemont appeared, his dark hair a tousled mess as if he'd been running his hands through it. He glanced up at me and quickly looked away. I felt a surge of guilt that I batted away. We weren't together. We never would be. Seducing Lucius was part of the plan. Or was Lucius seducing me?

"What is it?" Vinemont's voice was gruff.

"Invitation." Lucius swiped his finger under the wax seal and broke it open before unfolding the parchment.

The brothers read it together as I walked to them, curiosity overcoming my shaken cocktail of emotions.

"Fuck!" Vinemont whirled and punched a hole in the foyer wall, plaster falling in a heap at his feet. I flinched and went to stand at Lucius' elbow to get a better look.

Farns shook his head and scurried down the hallway, most likely for a dustpan and broom.

"What is it?" I asked.

"Cal wants us to come to his New Orleans house tomorrow night. Welcome party for some new family or something." Lucius flipped the page over, as if searching for more writing on the empty back.

"All of us have to go?" I thought I was done with the bastards until Christmas.

"Invite says Sin, you, and me."

"He knows." Vinemont shook his head, his brows pinched.

"Knows what?" I scanned the invitation, the stark lines of a New Orleans address and a time with an oak tree watermark.

"He knows my Acquisition has changed hands. He knows or he never would have invited Lucius." Vinemont's violence had reopened the wounds in his knuckles. Blood dripped to the floor, but he didn't notice. A vein thrummed in his neck as he stared murder at Lucius.

"Hey, I didn't tell him. But what does it matter?" Lucius put his hand around my waist. "It's true."

Bad move. Vinemont was already on a hair trigger. He lunged for Lucius, grabbing him by the neck as they fell in a heap on the floor. I stumbled backward and sat down hard.

With a guttural roar, Vinemont flexed his bloodied knuckles as he choked his brother.

Lucius gripped Vinemont's hands and ripped one free before leaning up and head-butting him. Vinemont groaned at the impact and slammed Lucius back down, pressing harder with the one hand still at his brother's throat. Lucius reared back with his right hand and aimed a fist at Vinemont's jaw, the blow sending him crashing to the floor. Lucius jumped on top of his brother, both men slugging away.

I should have been happy. My plan was working. This was what I'd wanted—them tearing each other apart so that I could stand over their shredded remains. But as they fought, I wanted nothing more than for it to stop. The sickening thuds of fists on flesh, the blood, the grunts and anger.

I covered my ears. "Stop!" I didn't realize I was capable of the scream that tore from my lungs.

Lucius held his fist ready to strike before pushing himself off Vinemont, landing with a heavy clunk that made the chandelier overhead rattle. Both men stayed put, breathing heavily and eyeing each other as if waiting for it to start again.

I heard footsteps on the staircase behind me, and then Teddy's voice. "What the fuck is going on?"

"Don't worry about it." Lucius grinned and put his hand in the air, giving Teddy a thumbs up, though he didn't take his eyes from Vinemont. "Everything's fine, Teddy."

"Fine." Vinemont agreed and sat up.

"Sure. Right." Teddy offered me his hand. "Nothing in this house is fine. Come on, Stella."

I took it and he pulled me to my feet. I could feel two sets of eyes on my back the whole way up the staircase until I turned the corner toward my room.

"Are you okay? What was that about?" Teddy asked.

We hurried down the hallway and into my bedroom. I dropped down on my bed before digging the heels of my palms into my eyes. Teddy sat next to me and put his hand on my back, rubbing it gently.

"I'm okay. Thanks, Teddy. And that was about me. Well, actually, I think it was about me and Cal Oakman."

Teddy blanched. "I hate that guy. Always have."

"You and me both."

He wrapped his arm around me and pulled me over so my head rested on his shoulder.

"Are we going to make it through all this, Stella?" He sounded tired, far beyond his years.

"Honestly? I don't know. But I think your chances are a smidge better than mine." I smiled weakly. "So there's that."

He rested his chin on top of my head. "I would have taken that whipping for you. If I'd known about it. Which I didn't."

His unexpected kindness was like a balm, though tears stung my eyes and I swallowed hard. "I wish you didn't know about that. And I don't think that's how it works, anyway. But I appreciate the sentiment."

He took a deep breath. "I wish a lot of things. I wish there was no Acquisition. I wish we weren't here. I wish Laura and I could be together. I wish…"

"I know. I have my fair share of wishes, too." A flash of images sparked through my mind—Mom, Dad, and the spider who haunted my waking moments along with my dreams. Wishes for each of them. Some good. Some bad.

We sat silently for long enough to hear Vinemont and Lucius go to their respective corners, and to hear Farns start cleaning up downstairs.

When Teddy left, I realized all three Vinemont men had made inroads into my heart.

And I cursed them for it.

CHAPTER SEVEN
Stella

Renee flitted about, bobby pins hanging from her mouth and test smudges of eye shadow along the back of her hand. She had been working on me for over an hour, but it was obvious that getting ready for a fancy party was a bit out of her skill set. Still, she gave it her best—rolling my hair, curling my lashes, doing my makeup. I'd argued at first, told her I could do it myself. With a raised eyebrow and a shake of her head, she'd whisked me off to my room.

Now, I was as close to ready as I was going to get. She'd pinned the sides of my hair up, and the rest flowed down my back in red waves. My skin appeared luminous under the vanity lights.

She'd gone heavy on the dark brown eye shadow, but otherwise I was fine with everything. It didn't matter to me. Not really. I didn't want to impress anyone. Maybe I should have gone the dowdy route, made myself less appealing for the upcoming Christmas trial. Though I knew what they had planned for me wasn't about sex. Not really. It was about violence. About taking something from me.

I took a deep breath and did my best to smile at Renee in the mirror. She tossed the last bobby pins on the counter and returned my smile. "I think I've done it. You look amazing. Maybe not as fabulous as you did for the ball, but you had professionals helping you…"

She let her words trail off when I dropped my gaze to my hands.

She placed a hand on my shoulder. "I'm sorry. I shouldn't have brought that up."

I placed my hand over hers and met her dark eyes in the mirror once again. "It's fine. It's my life now, after all. And we're sort of in this together, right? Just twenty years apart."

"That's exactly how I feel." She sighed. "I know it's you. I know you're the one going through it, but I still feel it, you know? It's like a wound that never fully healed. When you went to the ball, I knew I couldn't save you, but I felt it as if I were there again, reliving it. Instead of a fresh pain, it was a dull ache. The emotions—they were the same. I-I felt it. I understand."

If she still felt this pain, would I twenty years from now? Would I still be here, helping the next sacrificial lamb prepare to have its throat slit? I shuddered at the thought. *Never.*

"And there's one more thing." She pulled open the small drawer on the far left of the vanity and plucked out a syringe.

A ribbon of worry streaked through me. "What's that for?"

"For you. It's your usual prescription." She wrinkled her brow. "To be effective, you need it now. Just in case… at the trial, you see…"

I studied the syringe and my eyes widened with recognition. Birth control. My last shot had been three months prior, so Renee was right on time. Vinemont had left no stone unturned, getting my medical information and keeping me in tip top shape for the Christmas trial. My eyes burned with angry tears.

"This is so twisted, Renee." I balled my hands into fists, my fingernails digging into my palms. "So fucking twisted."

"I'm sorry. I just—"

"No. It's fine." I fought the tears, not letting a single one drop. "Just do it."

I offered my arm and she ripped open an alcohol wipe, cleaned a spot, and injected me. A slight sting and then nothing. *Now I'm protected.* I didn't know if I wanted to laugh or cry at the ridiculousness of the thought. I would never be protected, never be safe until I was free of the Acquisition.

She tossed the syringe into the waste basket. "I'm sorry."

"It's not your fault." I shuddered at the thought of carrying a child as a result of the Christmas trial. "And thank you … For doing it for me, I mean."

Renee kissed the crown of my head before laying her cheek against my hair for a few moments. I was surprised such a small gesture could impart so much solace. But by the time she straightened, I felt her warmth flowing through me like a mild transfusion.

She smiled big enough to almost convince me it was genuine. "Wait 'til you see the gown I picked for you."

"If it's got feathers—" I grimaced. "—I'll pass."

She laughed and shook her head, her dark hair shining. "No feathers. Not this time. Come on."

I followed her into my bedroom and stopped when I spied the dress she'd laid out on my bed. It was black with a plunging neckline. The hem would fall to my ankle, but the high slit would leave little to the imagination.

I frowned and crossed my arms over my chest. "I don't think I can pull that off, Renee."

Renee threw her hands on her hips. "Modesty is confidence's ugly sister."

I laughed. For a woman who'd I never seen in anything

other than prim black and white, Renee surprised me.

She pushed me forward. "Put it on. I know it'll be perfect."

"Fine. For you. I'll try it for you." I shrugged out of my robe and trudged to my dresser for some underwear.

Renee cleared her throat. I turned to look at her over my shoulder. "What?"

She pointed to a thin piece of black material that I hadn't noticed next to the dress.

"Is that a g-string?"

She smoothed her skirt. "Well, that dress clings, and you can't have panty lines. Or you can go no panties if you like that better."

I definitely did not like that better. I gave up my quest for comfortable cotton panties and pulled on the barely-there thong. My ass was totally exposed, but at least my pussy had some semblance of fabric over it.

"I'm guessing no bra, either?"

She shook her head and eyed her feet. "The back is open, so no."

"Fine." I lifted the dress and dropped it over my head. Renee was right, it clung as it slid down my body and settled. The front dipped low between my breasts in a draping cowl that thinned into spaghetti straps and tied at the top of my shoulders. The straps multiplied into three thin strips that flowed down my back and joined the sides at elbow level, leaving the rest of the back open almost down to my ass. The slit was so high that I was glad I chose to wear the panties.

"You are perfect."

"I take it this isn't a jeans and t-shirt event?" I snorted and walked to the full length mirror to get a better look. Renee had created a fashion plate in record time.

"Never. You need to impress the Sovereign. Play to your strengths."

"To help Vinemont?" I narrowed my eyes at her in the mirror. "I have to dress like a street walker to help my captor?"

"Yes." Renee pushed my hair over my shoulder and perused my tattoo. "Though I never had a dress this nice when I was a working girl."

That raised my eyebrows.

Renee shrugged and blushed. "I told you about my past, and I'm not proud of it. But I'm just saying that yes, you are being taken somewhere to be shown off as an Acquisition, but enjoy the little pleasures. That's all. One day you won't even have those. So—"

"Did you just tell me to *carpe diem*?" I turned and smiled at her, willing away her embarrassment.

"I did." She smiled back, the clouds of memory giving way to the present. "Now let's see about your shoes and, the best part, your jewels."

She went into the closet and brought out a pair of velvet stilettos with red soles.

"I don't know if I can manage those. Got anything with a shorter heel?"

"Nope. These are the ones." She set them down in front of me and I stepped into them. They were almost impossible, but not quite. As long as I was on an even surface and not doing any running, I might survive.

"And these." She practically pranced to a box on my dresser and flipped the lid before pulling out a dazzling necklace. An array of emeralds in an art deco layout. The jewels dangled from silver chains, with the center emerald hanging lower than the rest.

"Do the Vinemonts own all the choicest emeralds in the world or what?" I walked over to her and lifted my hair so she could fasten the priceless strand around my neck.

The earrings were similar threads of silver with an emerald dangling at the end. I put them in and smoothed my hair back down.

Renee clasped her hands in front of her. "This is going to help us. It has to."

"Us?" I turned to her, searching her dark eyes for some

clue as to what she meant. Obviously, I wasn't in this to help the Vinemonts. I couldn't care less who became Sovereign.

"Winning will help everyone, Stella. You included."

I peered down at her. "Did winning help you? You're still here, aren't you? Are you living out your wildest dreams? Did things perk up after your lover was ruined by becoming Sovereign?"

She waved my comment away with an impatient flick of her wrist. "Rebecca was strong, but Mr. Sinclair is stronger. Even Lucius is stronger. When either one of them is Sovereign, there will be so much they can do for you, for their mother, for the family, for all of us." She closed the jewel case, her fingers shaking slightly. "Now that we're in the running, winning would be the best outcome. There's no way around the trials. But if you win," she turned, an iron glint in her eye that I'd never seen before, "and you've played your cards right, you have a great deal of power at your fingertips. Power to destroy the ones who hurt you."

"Like the Roses?"

She nodded. "Like them and others."

I'd meant it as a barb, but she wore the Roses' destruction like a badge of honor.

"Have you destroyed people, Renee? The ones who tortured you most during the trials?"

She took my elbow. "We should get you downstairs. Mr. Sinclair will be antsy to leave."

"Renee, you can't just cut me off. I need to know." I hadn't actually considered the proposal Lucius made in Cuba—the power he would have after winning Sovereign. But Renee was echoing his sentiments: win, and then everything else will fall into place. Was Renee right? Was helping the Vinemonts win the surest route to destroy the entire game? Take it all down from the inside? Maybe, but it hadn't worked for Renee.

"You need to go. You can't be late for Cal's party. That

would be a bad start to your night." Renee swept past me and opened the door before ushering me through it.

I'd been around her long enough to know that the discussion was tabled. She was practiced at evading my questions. I just wished I could break down her walls, see everything inside and leave with the spoils of information. It would never happen. Not with Renee. Whether she'd always been evasive or was forced to be so because of the Acquisition trials, I'd never know.

I maneuvered slowly down the stairs in my heels with Renee at my side. Once downstairs, I heard voices on the front porch. Lucius and Sinclair.

"Tell me all about it when you get back." She pulled a long, dark fur from the foyer closet.

"Is that for me?" I didn't do fur, but the coat glowed with an amazing luster and begged to be touched.

"I had it brought from the climate controlled storage this morning. It's the sable." She held it out.

"I'm not sure." I ran my fingers down the front, each strand of fur silkier than the last.

"I am. Come on. It's cold out there."

I turned and slipped one arm and then the next into the coat. It was heavy and warm, the softest thing I'd ever felt. I studied my appearance in the foyer mirror. Even in the few months I'd been involved in this cruel game, my eyes seem to have hardened. Or maybe it was what was inside that had changed, grown stronger. I tilted my chin up the slightest bit, as if steeling myself for what was to come.

Renee swept my hair from the coat and draped it over my shoulder. "Everything will be fine. They won't harm you between trials."

"Do you know that for certain?" I opened the front door.

"Nothing is ever certain." Renee gave me a wry smile.

With that cryptic bit of wisdom, I walked into the cold night. Vinemont and Lucius quieted as I approached, but a heavy tension roiled in the air.

"Stella—" Lucius began.

Vinemont turned and stepped in front of his brother before offering me his arm.

Both men wore clean black tuxes, expertly fitted. Lucius's hair was tamed down in smooth waves while Vinemont's was his usual dark and tousled perfection. Clean shaven lady killers. They were beautiful, each in their own way. Lucius sleek and refined. Vinemont rough, almost gritty, even though everything about him was polished.

Luke waited in the drive, the limousine competing with the inky black of night. I ignored Vinemont and gripped the stair rail, holding on for dear life while I clicked down each step in my stilettos. I let out a silent sigh of relief once I was on level ground again.

"Ms. Rousseau." Luke tipped his hat and opened the back passenger door for me. I slid in, the fur moving across the leather like butter in a warm pan.

"Don't fucking try it." Vinemont's voice wafted past the engine noise and he sank down next to me.

Lucius took the front passenger seat once again, turning and giving me a winning smile. "You are fucking gorgeous."

Even though I knew it was a trick, just words, I couldn't stop the heat in my cheeks. "Thank you."

"Drive," Vinemont barked at Luke.

The limo eased down the driveway, and soon we were whistling along the interstate, heading into the heart of New Orleans.

Vinemont's eyes bored into me until I turned and matched his glare. His gaze slid to my mouth, then lower to the open top of my coat. Warmth raced through me, and I was thankful the fur covered my hardened nipples. His tongue wetted his bottom lip and I found I couldn't look away.

His mouth, the sharp line of his jaw, the elegant silhouette of his neck in the darkness of the car—all of it was somehow a lure. And like every other lure, there was a sharp hook in it, ready to catch and draw blood. I dropped my gaze, though I could still feel his burning into me, making me hotter than I should be to the point where I wanted to shrug out of the rich coat.

"Take a fucking picture, Sin. Jesus. You're making her uncomfortable." Lucius caught my eye and winked at me, his white teeth momentarily glinting in a passing street lamp.

"You don't know a thing about her comfort."

"Oh, I think I may have a few ideas. Don't I, Stella?"

I shifted in my seat, away from both of them.

"What is he talking about?" Vinemont smoothed a hand down my sleeve before gripping me lightly through the coat. "Stella?"

I ripped my arm away and sank even further back. "You two play your twisted game. I'm going to sit this one out."

Lucius laughed and faced forward again before cranking up the music to an almost painful level. Some angry rock song with a thumping beat. At least it cut off the conversation. I stared out the window at the passing cars, wishing I was in one of them. Any would do, just so long as it was going away from these people, from the Acquisition.

The rest of the drive was filled with Lucius' brash musical stylings. The city loomed ahead of us, the lights beaming out into the night like a million lighthouses luring us toward safe harbor. Luke took us into the city's beating heart, live music on the street corners and the smells of fried food seeping through the vents. The houses grew statelier the farther we drove, until we were in the midst of the Garden District. Mansions rose on every side, elegant and stylish, with high wrought iron fences separating their inhabitants from the rest of the tumultuous city.

We eventually pulled up in front of a three-story Victorian that seemed to take up half a block. It was almost garish in its ornate grandeur; turrets and a widow's walk ran along the roof. Two hulking magnolia trees stood guard over the walkway, and a sweeping porch wrapped around the entire house. Every light in the windows burned, and people congregated on the porch and spilled out the front doors.

Luke stopped out front and opened my door. I rose and made it to the sidewalk without tripping. It was a win. But my next step landed on a rock or something else I couldn't see in the dark. My ankle turned and I made a strangled noise as I started to fall.

A strong hand grabbed my elbow and righted me easily. I looked up, but somehow I already knew it was Vinemont. Suspicion confirmed as Lucius came to my other elbow. Vinemont offered his arm again, this time a slight smirk on his face.

I accepted it for no other reason than to avoid breaking an ankle. We climbed the three steps to the yard, strode down the wide walk, and then ascended a few more steps to the front porch. The impulse to run grew stronger with each moment. Vinemont must have sensed it because he pulled my arm into him, steadying me more as we walked past some guests and into the brightly lit entryway.

A servant came for my coat. Vinemont helped me take it off and froze when he saw my dress. His gaze tore down my figure, as if memorizing every line, every curve before he met my eyes again.

Lucius strolled up next to me and pulled on his cuffed shirt sleeves. "This should be fun."

The house was beautiful with exquisite woodwork on every corner, above the wide doorways, and along the sweeping stair. Partygoers milled around, all dressed in black tie or dresses that screamed Hollywood glamor. Music played upstairs, a deep beat drifting down and completely at odds with the antique, elegant nature of the home.

"The Vinemonts made it!" Cal was halfway down the

stairs, his gaze fastened on me and a huge grin plastered on his face. He pulled a petite blonde along with him. I recognized her—Brianne, Red's Acquisition. She stumbled trying to keep up, but Cal just pulled her into him and dragged her the rest of the way down before setting her back on her feet. He was just as much a showman as he had been at the ball—his tux flashy, his salt and pepper hair perfectly coifed, and every word spoken two tones too loud.

Brianne clung to him, her red dress revealing the tattoo along her chest and a fair amount of skin. I could only assume Red had chosen her attire for the evening. Her eyes were glassy and she looked through me, no recognition sparking to life in her face.

"Glad you could come to my little soiree." Cal shook Vinemont's hand, then Lucius'. I didn't offer my hand, so he grabbed both of them and pulled my arms out, staring down my body as he licked his lips. "You look good enough to eat, Stella."

Vinemont twitched at my side, but did nothing. Cal released me and cocked his head up the stairs. "Come on. The real fun is on the second floor. And Stella, if you're lucky, I'll invite you up to the third and give you a surprise."

A cold tremor ran down my spine. I wanted to stay as far away from the third floor as possible. Even so, Vinemont took my elbow and led me forward as we followed Cal and Brianne upward toward the pounding music. *Is the second floor a rave?*

Brianne swayed, but Cal gripped her ass firmly, sinking his index finger deeply between her cheeks as he lifted her up stair after stair. He glanced at me over his shoulder and winked. Anger gurgled in my throat, threatening to come out of my mouth in a scream. I wouldn't let it. Renee and Lucius had made me think more about seeing the entire game board before making any decisions on moving pieces. If playing along got me in a better position to destroy these people, then I would do it.

We reached the landing and the beat was even deeper, vibrating in my chest and shaking the chandelier that hung above the foyer. Cal continued forward toward an open set of double doors, exchanging pleasantries with the partygoers that crowded around. People gawked and stared, but I kept my eyes straight ahead. They could look and leer, but I held on to what Renee had told me. They couldn't hurt me. Not tonight.

A man pushed through some guests and came up to us. Auburn hair and beady eyes—Red.

"Oh, there you are." He glowered at Brianne.

"She's just helping me greet my guests, Red."

"You're welcome to her, Cal. Anytime." Red flicked his eyes to me before letting his gaze fall to my breasts. "Nice to see you again, Stella."

"I can't say likewise." I still wanted to scratch his eyes out for how he'd treated Brianne. Then again, I was standing here holding onto a man who'd whipped my back until I bled. The scars were on display even now in this backless dress. Is that why Renee had chosen it?

Red flipped his too-long hair out of his eyes. "Still a cunt, I see."

"Shut the fuck up, Red." Vinemont tensed next to me, a warning.

"Don't like it when I insult your whore?" He laughed, his teeth slightly purpled from wine.

Vinemont took a step forward and Red drew up his fists.

"Boys, boys. Save it for Christmas!" Cal laughed and patted them both on the back. "I've come up with a pretty clever way for you to release your aggressions, trust me."

Fight or flight kicked alive inside me again. My stomach churned and bile rose in my throat. Renee's tale of her Christmas trial was bad enough, but I knew Cal would make mine as horrible as possible. I had a momentary flash of trying to kill him. Maybe slipping down to the kitchen and grabbing a knife and slitting his throat right in front of all these ghouls. Would that end it? Would that stop the entire corrupted machinery from turning? Or would I just put a new Sovereign in charge sooner than expected?

"You and I are going to have a very Merry Christmas, Stella. Count on it." Red backed away and grabbed the nearest woman before sinking his tongue into her mouth. She moaned and went limp, letting him reach up her short skirt and finger her.

Vinemont took my elbow, roughly this time.

Cal clapped his hands and gripped Brianne. "That's more like it. Now, come on. I want to show you the fun."

We followed him toward the large double doors where the sound emanated from. The room beyond was dark, but we plunged ahead. The music grew louder, a techno beat. It was a ballroom on a much smaller scale than the one at the Oakman estate. Still, it was large and took up almost the whole second floor.

Nude men and women writhed to the music on four platforms that dotted the room. Stuffy paintings and ornate sconces lined the walls, totally discordant with the scene. Couches sat against the periphery, some occupied by people doing drugs or having sex, sometimes a mix of both. I couldn't tell if they were more frightening now that they were unmasked.

I should have realized at the ball that these people had no limits. But now I knew the ball wasn't an anomaly. It was them. *This*—the woman snorting coke off a man's hard cock, the two men fucking while a semi-circle formed to watch, the needles and the glassy eyed women—this was what these people were.

"Isn't it something?" Cal yelled over the din.

"Impressive." Lucius nodded, his gaze glued to the nearest platform where one woman knelt and licked between another's legs.

"I like to throw these parties every so often. Keep things fun as Sovereign. This one is a welcome party, of course. But I certainly hope the next Sovereign keeps the tradition of impromptu get-togethers alive." He yanked Brianne into his side and looked from Vinemont to Lucius. "But which one of you is in the running?"

"I am." Vinemont and Lucius spoke in unison, though their voices barely carried over the music.

Cal shook his head and glanced to Brianne. He grabbed her chin roughly and pulled her face to his. "Only *one*, isn't that right little Acquisition?"

"Y-yes. One." She nodded, seemingly even more out of it than she had been downstairs.

Cal turned back to us, his face stone cold sober, all hint of a smile gone. "Sinclair, you know the rules. Did she choose him or not?"

Vinemont snaked his arm around my middle. "She did, but—"

"But nothing, Sin." Cal's face broke in a wide smile, the façade back in place. "Lucius, my favorite sugar magnate, looks like you're in the running."

"I am. She's mine." Lucius stepped closer to me.

"Excellent, excellent. Now, has Sinclair given you all the rules or do I need to give a little lesson?"

Vinemont's fingers pressed into my waist hard enough to leave bruises. I didn't protest, hoping Cal would enlighten me on the rules.

"I'll handle it," Vinemont said.

Lucius cut his gaze toward his brother and then back to Cal. "I'm sure Sin will give me all the details."

Cal nodded and grabbed a cocktail from a passing waiter with a tray. "He better." He toasted to nothing and no one before downing his drink. "Now let's have some fun."

CHAPTER EIGHT
SINCLAIR

IT WAS DONE. Even though I pulled her close to me, even though I wanted nothing but her, she was no longer mine. Her scent, her skin, everything about her had sunk even more deeply into my bones since she'd returned. And now, I'd lost her.

Cal leered and pulled Brianne away to a nearby sofa. No doubt he would drug her again. I toyed with drugging Stella to make this night seem more transitory, less sharp edges, but I couldn't. She deserved to see it, to feel it all. I couldn't save her from it any more than I could save myself. We would all have to play our parts, damned as they were.

"Vinemont." Stella's sharp tone cut through my thoughts. "You're hurting me." Her green eyes were luminous with each flare of light from an adjacent strobe. I eased my hold on her waist, though I didn't want to. I wanted to pick her up and run with her. I couldn't. I was just as shackled to the Acquisition as she was, and now Lucius had unwittingly wandered into the same trap.

"Let's get a drink." Lucius took her hand and led her away, farther into the room.

I followed. I didn't intend to let her out of my sights no matter what my fool brother had done. Her leg showed through the slit with each of her steps, giving me a chance glimpse of the dark fabric covering her tender flesh at the juncture of her thighs. I didn't care if Lucius claimed her, I still owned her, especially there where I'd already tasted. My cock grew hard at the memory of her spread before me, her soft moans and the frantic movement of her hips. I wanted it again. I hadn't been able to think about anything but her for quite some time.

We wound through the crowd, halted by several people who wanted to shake hands. At least the music was too loud for chit chat. A wide bar was set up along the back wall, and servants poured, rolled, or razored into a line any substance imaginable. Lucius shouted out a drink order and leaned down to take a line. Stella's eyes widened as he snorted it and then pinched his nose. He smiled and handed her the straw.

"Try it."

She eyed the lines of coke.

I knocked the straw from her hand. "Lucius, I'm warning you."

She glared up at me. "I'm a grown woman, Vinemont. I don't need your permission."

"You already have mine, Stella. Go ahead." Lucius handed her another straw.

"I don't need your permission either. Jesus!" She turned and peered over my shoulder before the ghost of a smile graced her face. "You two do me a favor and go have a pissing contest with Cal. I see someone I know."

She brushed past me, her flower and citrus scent wafting over the smell of lust and liquor. *Who could she possibly recognize?*

She maneuvered through the dancers and shook her head at a couple of eager gentlemen. Her destination reached, she stopped in front of one man in particular. He turned. Gavin from the ball.

Lucius handed me a drink as we watched her. "Who the fuck is that?"

"Eagleton's Acquisition."

"Want to fuck him up?" Lucius downed his drink and motioned for another, the coke already speeding up his movements.

"That's against the rules."

Lucius laughed. "Guess you'll have to tell me all of them now."

I took a drink, the bitter flavor hitting my tongue just right. "I will."

He studied me before following my gaze to Stella. "You know the difference between you and me, Sin?"

"I know of several."

Lucius smirked and leaned against the bar. "I can do what needs to be done to her. I can win this. I can make her cry, make her hurt, leave her in a bloody heap, and never look back. I can win this for us. The Vinemonts can rule it all again. But you..." He drained another glass. "You can't. That hot pussy of hers has got you on your knees. That's why it needs to be this way. That's why it's a good thing she chose me. I'll break her and become Sovereign. You'll see."

As if it were that simple. As if all he had to do was make her cry, make her bleed. I shook my head. I let Lucius talk despite the acid that roiled in my gut. That's all it was—talk. I'd seen the way he looked at her when he thought no one was watching. I'd hated him for it, for his desirousness that edged on something more.

He may have fooled everyone else, but not me. His boldness would falter, and he would fail. And the consequences would destroy us all. I had to get her back, to somehow remedy the situation, but I was out of plays. I had to wait for other pieces to go into motion before I could make a move. I chafed at the waiting, just as I always had.

"Look at that motherfucker." Lucius shot his hand out

toward Gavin.

Gavin smiled down at Stella, genuine pleasure at seeing her written all over his handsome face. I wanted to break his nose. It was ridiculous, that aggression, that need to keep her to myself. But it was there and I couldn't ignore it. I'd done far worse than beat a man over a slight, but I'd never fought over a woman. Not until Stella. I swallowed more of the bitterness, letting it run down to my center and mix with my own.

"I still want to fuck that guy up." Lucius slammed his glass down. "Is it against the rules if no one sees us do it?"

I wanted to say we could take Gavin out back and bloody him for even speaking to Stella. That we could end him and dust off our hands like we'd just taken out the trash. But we couldn't. Too much was at stake to break the rules now.

The rules. I shook my head and finished my drink.

"You don't know what you've done." I said it too softly for my brother to hear me over the din. But the words were true.

Lucius had taken my spot in hell. He just didn't realize it yet.

CHAPTER NINE
Stella

"I GET THREE squares a day and a bed. That's more than I got when I was on the streets." Gavin shrugged, his eyes a deep amber. "I don't even see Bob. I saw him for the ball. Otherwise, I sort of have the run of the guest house on his property. Nobody bothers me. I guess I could try to run, but he's assured me he'd find me and drag me back. Nowhere to go even if I did. I'm just going to see it through. I don't really have any other option at this point." He sighed. "How about you? How'd you get talked into this?"

I sipped the drink he'd handed me. "Betrayal, deceit, lies, and a contract. Same song, different verse."

"I get it. Trust me, I do." He glanced around, the glaring strobe flashing in his face, making him ghostly one second and solid the next. "Hey, do you want to get out of this room? Go somewhere we can talk without so much noise and so many ears?"

"Yes, please." The cacophony of music and the blur of bodies was overwhelming, and I couldn't help but notice some of the guests pointing at Gavin and me. They knew who we were.

He took my hand and pulled me through the dance floor, past the frenetic dancers and the sex performers. The hall still thumped from the beat within the ballroom, but it was calmer. Delving further into the house, we turned a corner and found a small alcove backed with a stained glass window in a floral pattern. We sat on the window seat thigh to thigh, both silent as our senses became accustomed to the light and freedom from prying eyes. He was warm next to me, his body heat seeping into my bare leg that was revealed by the high slit.

"You look beautiful tonight, by the way." He leaned back and let his head rest against the panes.

"Thanks. You do, too. Handsome, I mean." I followed his lead, leaning out of sight from anyone further down the hall.

"Thanks."

I glanced up at him, his eyes even warmer now that light reflected from them. "Are we going to survive?"

"Yes." He answered so quickly that I wondered if he misheard my question.

"How do you know?"

"I've always been a survivor, and something tells me you have, too."

I wobbled my head back and forth on the glass. "No, I've given up before."

"Maybe, but I knew the moment I saw you at the ball that you had steel in your spine. The way you stared out into the crowd as if you were above all of them, the way you tried to help Brianne, the way you took the…"

"The whipping?"

He nodded and his hand found mine. "I don't remember much of that night. Maybe I blocked it out, but I do remember how strong you were, how I wished I could be strong like that, too."

"I think you have me confused with some other helpless woman caught in an antiquated trial for supremacy among rich sadists."

He snorted and squeezed my hand. "No, it's you. And nothing about you is helpless."

"Don't let the jewels fool you. I'm just as caged as you are."

"I know you are, but your strength gives me hope. Don't make me doubt it. I need it to keep going." His voice was somber, pleading.

"Okay. I'll try."

"That's all any of us can do."

We fell into a comfortable silence, listening to the music and watching as guests staggered past, high and lit. I kept my hand in his, forming some sort of bond that I hoped strengthened the both of us.

After a brief respite where we were simply able to exist, someone laughed raucously and stumbled down the hall in our direction. I recognized the voice—Red. I tensed and tried to shrink into the alcove.

"What is it?" Gavin dropped my hand and put a steadying palm on my thigh.

"Red," I whispered.

The steps came closer. I shivered.

"Oh, fuck. That guy?"

"That guy." If he noticed me, I wasn't sure if we could avoid an even worse confrontation.

Gavin looked down the hall and then back at me. "Trust me?"

I nodded. Then his lips were on mine, his body crushing into me and shielding me from the hallway. His eyes slowly closed as he slanted his mouth more, covering my face so that all Red would be able to see was Gavin's dark hair.

I'd frozen at Red's voice, but Gavin's body heat tried to thaw me. He rested one hand at my waist and planted his mouth on mine. He didn't seek entry with his tongue, just kept himself poised over my lips. Red's voice grew closer, and I closed my eyes, praying he wouldn't see me.

Red bellowed a string of profanities. He was so close it

startled me and I opened my mouth. Gavin took the small chance I gave him and lightly darted his tongue inside, teasing along the tip of mine. He tasted like vodka and some sweet mixer. I gripped the lapel of his jacket as his hand slid up my bare thigh.

"Well look at this shit." Red's voice. "We got Acquisitions fucking each other now?"

Damn. Gavin broke the kiss, his brow creased, before pulling away from me.

"You horning in on Sin's little cunt here?" Red swayed and leaned against the wall opposite us, his head almost bumping into an ornate sconce.

"Fuck you." I stood and stared him down.

He leered at me. "Wait 'til Christmas, little cunt, then I'm going to be balls deep in your ass while you scream for me to stop."

Rage lit me from the inside out and before I knew what I was doing, I'd slapped him, leaving an angry red handprint along his cheek.

"You fucking—" He lunged for me, his eyes wide with wrath. His hands were at my throat, pressing the metal of the necklace into my skin as he constricted my airway. I clawed at his wrists, drawing blood and wanting to do much, much worse.

Gavin yanked him off me, but I wasn't finished. While Gavin was pulling Red backward, I walked up and kneed him right in the crotch with every ounce of anger I had. Red yowled and bent over. Gavin released him and held his hands up as if he'd just touched something filthy.

"You fucking bitch, you fucking bitch." Red kept saying the same thing over and over with wheezing breaths as he cupped his balls and stared up at me from his hunched position.

Gavin came back to my side. "Stella, we need to go—"

I couldn't look anywhere but at Red. The desire to inflict more pain blotted out any thought about Acquisitions or trials or who was watching or consequences. "You are never going to touch me, you sick fuck! You got that?" I seethed with hate, and pulled my hand back to strike him again, but Gavin gripped my forearm.

"Don't."

"That's right, bitch. Don't." Red was trying to stand up straight, but kept clutching his crotch. "I'll get you back. Don't worry. In a few weeks, I'm going to fuck every hole you got. And there's not a fucking thing you can do about it, you stupid cunt. Merry Christmas to me." He laughed in a high-pitched cough.

I struggled against Gavin's hold, desperate to hurt Red, to make him feel even an ounce of the pain I'd already endured.

"Gavin?" A voice floated down the hall. "Gavin, where are you?"

"Shit. It's Bob." Gavin pulled me next to him and forced me to turn my back on Red and walk away.

Red was still laughing. "Oh, I'm going to have a good time with you Stella. Such a good time. Can't wait to see you at the Christmas trial. Come hungry."

Gavin kept leading me away even though I wished I could go toe to toe with Red and win. I wouldn't. He would beat me. And worse, I feared his words were true. There was nothing I could do about the Christmas trial, no way to pull myself back from the brink. Red would capitalize on it, make me hurt in ways I never had before. He would always have the last laugh, just like everyone here. Even so, I still held onto the slim hope that I could somehow stop it.

"Gavin?" Bob's voice, closer now.

"Right here." We turned the corner to find Bob, Lucius, and Vinemont.

My expression must have tipped Vinemont off that something happened because he was towering over me in an instant. "What?"

"What do you mean?" I dropped my gaze to the floor.

I didn't need his help and I certainly didn't want it.

He leaned back to get a view down the hall we'd come from. Red barreled around the corner, mirth still lighting his eyes.

Vinemont advanced on him until they were standing chest to chest. "Red, stay the fuck away from her. I'm not going to tell you again."

"You don't have to. I'm done. Don't worry, I'm a patient man. I'll get my turn at Christmas." He winked at me, though he still kept a protective hand over his crotch.

I hoped his dick was bruised and swollen. I only regretted that I hadn't tried to rip it off.

Lucius stepped up next to his brother. "Stella belongs to me now, Red. If you touch her, speak to her, do anything to her without asking me first, I will skull fuck your little sister." Lucius smirked. "She eighteen yet? Not that it matters."

"Don't you fucking talk about my sister!" Red screamed. His anger was raw, unexpected, the sound catching in his throat.

Somehow, this anger was far more real than any other emotion I'd seen from him. It was strange to think he cared for someone other than himself. But there was no mistaking it. Lucius' jab had hit home. Why?

Vinemont put a hand on Lucius' arm. "Come on. Let's get the meet and greet done and then we can bow out." Vinemont pulled Lucius back, reining in his younger brother.

Red shook his head as if to clear it, the auburn strands sticking to his sweaty forehead.

"Gavin, come." Bob tottered away, his round body swaying like humpty dumpty as he headed toward the staircase to the third floor.

Gavin gave me a small smile and turned to follow.

"We're going, too." Vinemont placed his hand on my lower back, his fingertips hot against my bare skin, and led me forward.

Lucius was close behind and Red followed. We climbed the stairs. The music faded as we rose, until it was only a slight rhythmic bump.

We turned right at the landing and entered a solarium. The glass ceiling above opened to the night sky. Exotic plants that were painstakingly curated to give the appearance of wildness filled the room.

Branching ropes of wisteria climbed central pillars and fanned out across the panes, creating a patchwork of bark and greenery. I imagined how it must look in the spring, heavy lavender blooms hanging beneath the blue heavens. I closed my eyes, etching the image into my mind so I could paint it later. It would have been beautiful, but tonight the sky was nothing but a dark blur through the glass, no stars, no moon. The air stagnated with conversation and stale cigar smoke. Whatever beauty this room might hold was covered with a fine layer of grime from its occupants.

About two dozen more guests settled here, lounging, talking, drinking. Several older ladies in one group turned toward us, whispering and eyeing me with haughty disdain. Though they were long past their prime, their faces were frozen in an impression of youth—lips too plump, brows too unlined, smiles too improbably white. Like some of the plants in the room, they were sickly sweet and entirely predatory. I shivered and edged closer to Vinemont.

He wrapped his arm around my waist and something inside me calmed. The tempest of emotions Red, and now this room, had whipped up mellowed under Vinemont's touch, and even though I knew I wasn't, I felt safe.

I glanced up and caught his eye, the dark sapphire blue stopping my breath for a second. The memory of him in the cabin that day during the storm, the way he'd worshipped my flesh with his, flitted through my mind. A distant echo of those same feelings scattered through my heart and multiplied until the only thing inside me was his name, a whispered prayer. *Sin*.

He leaned toward me until his lips were at my ear. "I should have told you before. But I have never seen anything more beautiful."

My heart stopped, and then a warmth spread from it to the rest of me. His words were unexpected, and my steps faltered as I tried to keep his pace.

He straightened and looked ahead so that all I could see was his strong profile against the backdrop of the shadowy sky. His grip never failed, I gained my feet again, and we glided through the room.

Unlike the dance floor below, the atmosphere was almost cloyingly serene, and a string quartet played in a corner. The older guests here were sedate, perhaps having swum long enough in an ocean of privilege and depravity that they were now content to sit on the shore and watch the rest of the swimmers struggle and drown.

Cal rose from his perch on a love seat, Brianne sitting next to him, and greeted us. "Welcome, welcome. Make yourselves comfortable. Relax. It's a party after all."

He stepped forward and took my hand. My skin crawled, and Vinemont's fingertips pressed more firmly into my waist.

"Come, let me chat you up. These boys can do without you for a few minutes, right Sin?"

Vinemont froze and focused on me. *Would he refuse?*

Cal faked a laugh. "But, wait, what was I thinking? Lucius is the proud owner now. I was confused, what with the girl on your arm, Sin, instead of your brother's." He gave Vinemont an acid smile and turned to Lucius. "So, may I speak with Stella for a moment?"

Lucius grinned and pulled Brianne up from her seat. Her eyes still bore a glassy sheen, and I wondered if she would even remember tonight. "You talk to that one. I want to *talk* to this one."

"That's my man." Cal laughed as Lucius dragged Brianne a couple of sofas over and hauled her into his lap. "Now, Sin, if you don't mind? I do believe Lucius gave permission." There was an edge in Cal's voice, and his fingers started to crush mine.

"Sin?" Red jerked his head toward the door. "Can I speak to you?"

"You're speaking to me right now." Vinemont didn't look at Red.

"I mean in private, asshole." Red's anger flared like the head of a match in the dark.

I held my breath. Maybe Vinemont would refuse Cal. Maybe something had changed. I was desperate for it to be true.

It wasn't. Vinemont dropped his hand. Cal sat and yanked me down next to him, the seat still warm from Brianne's presence.

Vinemont held my gaze, unwavering even as Cal put an arm around me and pulled me closer. Renee's words about playing along echoed in my mind, but I still had the urge to fight Cal off, to do anything other than submit. I wanted Vinemont to pull me up and take me out of here. Instead, after a second prompting from a jittery Red, Vinemont broke our connection and walked away to speak with him.

Lucius had long since gotten lost in Brianne, his hand in her dress and his mouth on her neck. I was left with Cal.

"So," he leaned in and inhaled at my ear, "tell me about you, Stella."

"What, you aren't going to drug me first like Brianne?" I tried to shift away from him but his grip tightened on my upper arm.

"You think I drugged her?" He tsked and pierced me with a withering look. "She drugged herself when she got here. She's weak. Can't handle it. You, on the other hand, handle all of it with surprising grace. The way you took that whipping..." He made a humming sound, as if the memory was particularly tasty for him. "I'll never forget the blood on your pale skin."

He released my arm and ran his fingers down my back. I struggled to stay calm.

"You're something special." He moved closer, his mouth at my ear. "Did Sin know you were special when he chose you? Or did he only figure it out once he had a taste?"

"Get off me." I leaned away from him but he clutched my waist and kept me tucked to his side.

"Do you ever behave?" He laughed and let his gaze drop to the deep neckline of my dress and then to the slit at my thigh.

"I'll scream." My heart was racing, fear oozing along my body wherever Cal touched me.

"Do you think anyone here will care? Come now. I just want a little taste is all. I have a thing for redheads." When his lips hit my neck, I had to tamp down my cry. I scanned the room for Vinemont, but he and Red must have stepped into the hall. I couldn't see Lucius, though I had no hope of help from him anyway.

Cal licked up my neck and I couldn't bottle the sound of revulsion that leapt from my lips.

"It's not so bad, is it?" He gripped my chin and wrenched my face to his while he eyed my mouth. I pushed on his chest, ready to scratch and bite if I had to. I couldn't play along, not with this.

"Cal?" A woman's warbling voice sounded from behind us.

Cal released me and I was finally able to breathe again. I scooted away from him until my back hit the arm of the love seat.

He adjusted his bow tie and stood, the fake smile already back on his face. "Ms. Devereaux, back so soon?"

Wait, *Devereaux*? She spoke again. I knew her voice. Something like déjà vu but darker swirled in my stomach. I turned. There, standing at my back were my former stepmother, Marguerite Devereaux and my stepbrother, Dylan.

CHAPTER TEN
Stella

"Dylan?"

My stepbrother rushed around the love seat and sat next to me before folding me in his arms.

"How?" My vision swam, hope trying to fire in my breast but unsure if this was some trick by Cal.

"Are you okay?" His embrace crushed me to the point I had to push away just to breathe.

"I am now. But how are you here?" I searched his eyes, willing it all to be real.

"Because, Stella," Cal interrupted, "the Devereauxs have long been a family in the upper echelons of society." He gave Dylan's mother a respectful nod. "But in just this past month, the lovely Marguerite expressed an interest in finally joining our particular party—the very pinnacle of all society. And we are more than happy to have her and her son, of course." Cal smiled like a toothy shark.

I wondered how much Marguerite had to pay to be accepted into this den of monsters. We had never been close when she was briefly married to my father. She saw me as more of an inconvenience than anything else. This must have been Dylan's doing.

Dylan smoothed a hand across my cheek. "Are you okay?"

"I'm fine. I just don't understand—"

"And you never will, Stella. Because we're different breeds." Cal looked down at me, as if I were an unruly child who needed to learn her manners. "Dylan here has an affection for you, clearly, but how much affection can a lion truly have for a lamb? He doesn't realize it, but you're beneath him, just like you're beneath everyone else in this room. It doesn't matter if we dress you up, put jewels on you, or whatever else."

"You don't have to talk to her like that." Dylan's voice was gruff, though he still palmed my cheek tenderly.

"I'm just stating the facts, Dylan. That's all. No need for unpleasantness. Marguerite, may I show you my particular favorite orchid here in the solarium? Give these two a chance to catch up?"

Marguerite stared at me and then her son before shaking her head and taking Cal's arm. She'd studied me the same way the entire time I'd known her, like I was a curious animal or insect. Interesting enough to examine, but too low to approach or engage. Without a word, she walked away as Cal began waxing poetic about plants.

Dylan hugged me again just as fiercely before holding me away from him. "It worked. I can't believe we're in and I'm here with you." He smiled, youth beaming from his tanned skin and light brown eyes.

"Can you get me out?"

His face soured, the corners of his mouth turning downward. "I don't know. Cal hasn't been very forthcoming about the whole process you're caught up in."

"The Acquisition?"

He nodded. "Right. He says there's going to be a big Christmas party next weekend where we'll get the idea of what it's all about."

"Next weekend?" I thought I had more time. I thought I had at least two more weeks. But no, Christmas was coming early. A wave of nausea washed over me, but I had to focus. I needed information.

"Yeah, he says it's a big to-do out at someone's house in a forest up north of here. Two-day party. I have no idea. I'm not much of an outdoorsman, but Cal assured me I'd enjoy the hunting." He shrugged, completely oblivious.

My heart sank and tears burned in my eyes. "So you're coming to the Christmas trial?"

"Yeah, we kind of have to. It's part of the whole joining the club thing. And maybe once I get more in with them, I can get you out. You'll be there, right?"

"Yes." I stared at the floor.

"Stella, what?" He gripped my hands. "And what do you mean by trial?"

"Christmas. It's a trial."

"Like with your dad?"

I shook my head and looked at him again, my tears barely held at bay. "I've already been through one trial."

"I'm not following." He held my hands tighter, as if the pressure would somehow make him understand. But there was only one way he would comprehend what I was talking about. I had to show him.

I twisted my body so I faced away from him. The gasp when he saw my back and the touch of his fingers along my skin made two tears fall—perfect, transitory drops that were lost in the black fabric of my dress.

"Who did this to you?" Dylan's voice was a strangled whisper.

"They all did."

"Cal?" His fingertips stroked across each mark.

"No, but it doesn't matter who did it. It's them. All of them. They all do it." Why didn't I want to tell him Vinemont had inflicted the wounds? I could have said, could have named him, but I didn't.

I looked up and caught Lucius staring at me, his eyes burning even as Brianne was pliant under his touch. She was straddling him now, her skirt hiked up and her hands in his hair. He palmed one of her tits, his other hand on her ass, as she kissed his neck. Even so, his direct gaze was on me, pinning me to the spot. My mind spun out of the conversation with Dylan even as his fingers still traced the memory of the tortures written on my skin.

Lucius gripped Brianne's breast harder, her head lolling back as he twisted her nipple. I swallowed hard, a tingling erupting along my same breast. He pulled down Brianne's dress and latched his mouth on her nipple, his eyes never leaving mine. Her moan cut through the string ensemble and my heart sped up. When he gripped her hair and yanked her head back so that she arched into him, I let out a pent up breath.

"—Stella?"

I forced myself to look away from him, to engage with the one man in this cursed place who I knew cared about me.

"Are they going to do that to your back again at Christmas?" Dylan's face was pale, the color drained like water from a sink.

"No."

He let out a sigh of relief. "Thank God. I don't think I could handle something like that."

"Have you seen my dad?" I blurted it out. I shouldn't have cared what happened to him, but seeing Dylan brought my mangled feelings for my father back to the forefront. Had Dylan's message that my father was ill been true?

"He's fine. Not sick or anything. Don't worry. Just concerned about you. He's the one that thought of this. There was no way to get you out, he said. But maybe if the Devereauxs could get in, we could help you. You're all he talks about. Trust me, he wants you away from here. He wants you safe and back with him."

Dylan's words were meant to comfort me, but they were a rusty blade in my stomach. My father had not only betrayed me, but now he'd betrayed Marguerite and Dylan.

Entering this realm was not something done lightly, and though I didn't know for certain, I was sure there was no easy way out. My father had doomed Dylan to become one of the monsters that was seated around us now, the villains in beautiful clothes with perfect manners and a taste for blood.

"Don't change the subject, Stella. What happens at Christmas?" He furrowed his brow.

How can I tell him?

"What happened before...to my back." I shook my head. "Christmas will be worse."

"What could be worse?" He pulled me into his arms and ran his palms down my shoulders. "What could be worse than this?"

A shadow fell across us. "Get your hands off her." Vinemont glowered at Dylan, his hands fisted at his sides, the still-bruised knuckles turning white.

"You bastard. You did this to her, didn't you?" Dylan stood, rage already turning his cheeks a bright shade of crimson.

Vinemont sneered and affected a bored air. "You don't know what you're talking—"

Dylan shoved him, and Vinemont took a few steps back before smirking. "I've been wanting a good fight since I got back from Cuba." He appraised Dylan. "Too bad I still won't get one."

Vinemont was fast, his fist crushing into Dylan's jaw in a scant moment. But Dylan didn't fall. He was strong, well-muscled from rowing and lacrosse. He took the impact and rushed forward, seizing Vinemont around the chest and slamming him into the marble floor. The other guests, smelling blood, stopped their small chatter and watched the show.

"Dylan, stop." I stood and stepped toward them, but they both ignored me.

Vinemont laughed as Dylan caged him with his knees and started raining blows on his face. Vinemont wasn't blocking them, just taking the vicious hits until he saw his moment. Then he aimed a powerful fist to Dylan's ribs. Dylan wailed and fell sideways, clutching his side. Vinemont pushed Dylan onto his back and put a knee on his chest before raising his fist.

"No. Please, don't." I grabbed Vinemont's arm. I knew what he could do, what he was capable of. "Don't."

He turned to me, his eyes wild and wrathful. I let go of his arm and ran my hand down his face, brushing my thumb over his split lip. His flesh burned beneath my touch, but his eyes cooled and he leaned into my palm the slightest bit. I felt it then, the one thing I wished had completely died that night when he'd shown me how truly alone I was. The string that bound us together, the inexorable link that ran from his heart to mine, came back to life. The connection tightened, and he rose as Dylan sputtered. Vinemont took my hand in his and leaned over me. He was so close. Everything stopped. My eyes closed of their own accord and I wanted his kiss, his blood, him. I just wanted him.

"Fuck, Sin. If you aren't going to finish it, I will."

I opened my eyes to see Lucius aiming a kick at Dylan's side. "Stop!"

Too late. Dylan howled with pain as Lucius' foot connected. I dropped to my knees and draped my arm across Dylan as he curled into a ball. I held my free hand up, trying to ward off Lucius.

Lucius straightened his coat and smiled. "Lesson of the day, *Dylan*. Don't fuck with us or our property."

"She's not property." Dylan coughed and rolled to his back.

The chatter started again, the momentary blood sport at an end.

"She's mine, you little shit. That's all you need to know."

"Ignore him. Come on." I helped Dylan into a sitting position. "Are you okay?" I felt along his ribs and he winced. They could have been broken for all I knew. "Can you walk?"

"I-I think so."

Lucius stepped over Dylan's legs to stand at my side and peered down at me. "Come on, Stella."

I glared at him, acid in my gaze. "No! Back off, Lucius."

I hitched my hand under Dylan's arm to try and help him to his feet, but a searing pain along my scalp had me crying out. Lucius wrenched me from the floor by my hair and brought my face to his.

"You will do as I say, Stella. Every—fucking—time." His eyes flashed and his voice was thick with malice.

I spat in his face, anger flowing up through me like lava. "Fuck you."

"Enough," Vinemont growled, and wrapped his arm around my waist, pulling me away from Lucius. I dug my fingers into him and tried to pry his hand loose. His mouth was at my ear. "Stop making a scene. Stop making us have to hurt you."

I stilled against his chest, but scowled at Lucius. He drew out his kerchief and popped it before wiping his face. He smiled as he did it, as if enjoying some private joke.

Everything had turned into a fight. More blood, more pain—I was awash in the cruelest of emotions, and in a few days, things would only get worse.

Dylan struggled to his feet, his breath coming in quick pants. I wanted to go to him, but I didn't. Vinemont's strong arms had me rooted to the spot.

Cal and Marguerite emerged from amongst the fronds and fountains, laughing politely. Dylan smoothed his jacket and shot Lucius a dark look before turning to his mother.

"How was it?" he asked.

"The orchid? Glorious," Marguerite simpered. "Makes me think of having the greenhouse at the Acres rebuilt."

Cal gave a slight bow and handed Marguerite off to Dylan, who smiled despite what must have been an aching pain in his ribs on both sides.

"What did I miss?" Cal asked.

Given his narrowed gaze and even haughtier demeanor, I surmised Cal never missed much of anything.

"Just some rough and tumble antics. You know how it is when boys get together." Vinemont's smooth words covered the jagged scrapes and bruises of only moments before.

"I do. But we want to treat our new guests with utmost respect at all times. We are so pleased to have them here in our midst." Cal's chiding tone was buried in an over-friendly smile as he patted Dylan on the back.

"Of course. Glad to be here." Dylan fell into his easy manners, learned through a life of the best schools, fancy dinners, debutante balls, and the like. He wasn't rocking the boat in front of Cal. Maybe he was smarter than I'd given him credit for in the past.

When he shook Cal's hand, I realized that some of what Cal had said was true. Dylan was one of them. He was born and bred to fall right in step with these people. Doubt crept into my mind. Marguerite must have made a sizeable investment to get into this party. Dylan would be risking his family fortune and his future if he tried to take my side in anything having to do with the Acquisition.

"Well, it's been fun, but Stella here will turn into a peasant—I mean pumpkin—if we don't get her back home soon." Lucius patted Dylan on the back far too hard, and Dylan gritted his teeth at the second assault.

Vinemont stayed at my back the entire time, his clean scent enveloping me, and his heart beating against me. His arm was still at my waist, a sturdy band of bone and muscle that kept me locked tight to his body. I got the feeling that if Cal asked for me to sit with him now, Vinemont would tell him to go to hell.

Once Lucius was done with Dylan, he stalked over to me. I kicked my chin up and met his stare. I was trapped between the two Vinemont men, the one at my back an enigma, the one in front an open book of deceit.

"Take my arm and walk out of here, Stella." Lucius' voice was a low, dangerous purr.

"Do it." Vinemont's voice in my ear. He shifted and pulled his arm away, his fingers trailing along my stomach and making my skin tingle as he went. I wanted to stay with him. I wanted to believe that maybe something was different, that maybe he felt the same connection I couldn't escape. But he'd turned me over to Lucius.

Dylan gave me the slightest smile, a hidden "chin up" that tried to warm my heart, but fell short. He didn't know what Christmas would bring. I did.

The string quartet began playing "Silent Night" as I took Lucius' arm and turned my back on the one small bit of sanctuary I'd found since all this began.

The car ride back was silent. I chose the front passenger seat before another idiotic fight could break out. Luke smiled as he got the door for me, perhaps aware of what I was doing.

As soon as we stopped at the house, I darted out of the car and up the front steps, my shoes left behind in the car. Farns opened the front door and I blew past him, seeking the shelter of my room. I had to think about what happened, to sort out what Dylan's presence might mean for me. And, most of all, I needed to talk to the one person who might be able to shed more light—Renee.

Though I didn't hear following steps, I closed my door and leaned against it. It felt as if the filth of the party coated me, Cal's fingerprints meshing with my skin and tainting me just like everything else he touched. I stripped the dress off, not caring that I left it in a heap in the floor along with the panties and jewels.

I ran a hot shower and stood beneath the steaming rain, my makeup running down my face and my hair wilting. I just wanted to be clean, to have not a single trace of Cal or Red or anyone else left on my skin. I picked the bobby pins from my hair and shampooed all of it. Then I lathered myself up, scrubbing until my skin was raw. I rinsed off and stepped out.

I reached for my towel, but it wasn't on the bar. Movement behind me had me whirling. It was Vinemont, the towel in his hands. He wrapped it around my shoulders and clutched it closed in front of me. He still wore his tuxedo pants, but his jacket was gone and his shirt halfway unbuttoned, as if he'd been in the middle of disrobing when he'd changed course and come to see me. His eyes were half hooded, lust and heat wafting from him like a fire.

My body tingled, anticipation and fear playing along my skin. "Were you watching me?"

"Yes." His voice was a low rasp. He was so still, but his jaw was tight and the sinews in his neck even tighter.

I moved the towel down under my arms and tucked one end into the other over my chest. "If you're done with your peep show, I'd like to get dressed and get some sleep."

I edged past him even though he took up so much space. The room, my head, and my heart were all filled with him.

"Dylan can't save you." His words were cold, far colder than the heat of his eyes.

"I don't expect anyone to save me. I expect to save myself." I forced myself to walk slowly to my dresser, not even looking as Vinemont approached. I grabbed a pair of panties and shimmied them up my legs beneath the towel. Then I chose a tank top and pulled it over my head, dropping the towel once it was in place. I turned back to him, my hands on my hips. He was so close, having crept up behind me while I dressed.

"What do you want?"

"Do you think this will stop me?" He plucked the hem of my tank top and ran his fingers over the edge.

"One minute I'm beautiful, the next you're in here threatening me?"

"This isn't a threat. I'm simply telling you." His eyes bored into me as he fisted the material of my top and pulled me to him. "Dylan can't save you. You can't get out of this. I will never let you out of it. Understand?"

"Understand what? That you want me, that you have feelings for me, but you'll also gladly let me be raped by all your friends so you can win some game? I got it. Now get the fuck out." His fist had tightened as I spoke, drawing me closer.

Without heels, I had to crane my head up to see him, to look into the dark pools of his eyes. "I will do anything to win, to make sure Lucius wins, to beat the others. Anything, Stella. Even if that means that every fucking man in Louisiana rapes you a hundred times over. No matter how much that sickens me. Yes."

I should have seen it coming, should have known that nothing I thought about him was real. No one who had feelings for me could say such a thing. My eyes watered. I should have been used to pain. I'd endured so much of it over the past weeks, but his words struck at my very center, like a shard of ice skewering my soul.

"Get out." I stared at the floor, not wanting him to see my tears when they fell.

"If Dylan contacts you, I'll know." He gripped my hair and wrenched my eyes back to his. Tears ran down my temples as he spoke in a harsh whisper. "Don't try anything. If I find out you've been speaking or even trying to speak to him, you can say goodbye to this room, these nice things." He yanked my shirt hard, the seams splitting under my arms. "These clothes. Everything. I'll have you kept naked and bound in the stables with a horse blanket for warmth. See, Stella? That was a threat. And I intend to make good on it if you even so much as think about trying to fuck us in this Acquisition. Do I make myself clear?"

I swallowed hard, tears thickening in my throat as terror pounded in my heart. Vinemont shook me, my arms flailing before I latched onto his shirt. My already scattered mind exploded in waves of desperation. I had to get away from him.

"I asked if you understood, Stella." His intense gaze crushed me more than his hands ever could. "Do you?"

"Yes."

He shoved me back into the dresser.

"I'm glad we had this little chat." He turned and walked out, slamming my door behind him.

I sank to my knees, the sobs uncontrollable. I thought I had something figured out. I thought I was getting Vinemont to turn, to put me ahead of being Sovereign. I was wrong. So wrong. I sobbed until I couldn't breathe, until I thought I would vomit. I cried for what felt like hours. So much of me poured out and into the rug beneath me.

Where was Renee? She should have come. She had to know I was here. I lay on my side and clutched my arms to me until the last tear fell and I was silent. Everything inside me was fractured and broken. Vinemont had taken what I was and smashed it into the ground.

But I was the one who'd given him the ability, who'd let him in. I'd allowed him to hurt me by foolishly hoping I could change him. I was the one who'd changed, who'd let myself be taken in by a man whose sole desire was to use me in every way possible before tossing me aside. When would I learn?

I picked myself up and crawled into my bed, the soft whir of the ceiling fan the only thing competing with the sluggish beat of my heart. My thoughts flickered to the hidden knife before I shoved the thought back in its box and turned the lock.

This was a setback, and, I forced myself to believe, a

good thing. Now I could seduce Lucius and turn him on Vinemont without any second thoughts. I burrowed into my crisp linen sheets and forced my breathing to even out, forced my eyes to close, and forced myself to give up any hope of warming Vinemont's cold heart.

CHAPTER ELEVEN
Sinclair

I PACED MY study, tossing back a bourbon before pouring another. It was close to daybreak. I'd been in here for a couple of hours, steeling myself for what had to be done next. A dull ache emanated from my chest and I wondered if it would ever go away. But it was necessary. All of it.

I should have gone even further with Stella, but I couldn't. The pain in her eyes was enough. The fear—even better. I wanted her afraid. It was the only thing I could use to keep her in line now that she knew about her father. So much was riding on her, how she behaved, how I, and now Lucius, treated her. It was all a skillful dance put on for the entertainment of the Sovereign. Tonight, I could feel his favor slipping. And after my conversation with Red, I realized things were even more precarious than I'd thought.

I had to tell Lucius. It was time. After his performance at Cal's party, he needed to know the real stakes, the real penalty. And our grasp on Stella was weakening by the moment now that Dylan was a possible player. Could I trust Lucius to stay strong with the weight of the truth bearing down on him?

I poured another glass and left my study as the first rays of the sun shot out across the dead grass and peeked through the leafless trees. My legs were heavy on the stairs, each step painful in more ways than one. Stella had done well fixing up my leg, but our doctor had cleaned the wound and re-stitched it just the day before. It still burned like a son of a bitch. Fatigue clouded my vision. I only hoped it hadn't clouded my judgment.

I passed my bedroom on the way to Lucius'. I wanted nothing more than to sink into my bed and into a dreamless sleep. No, that wasn't true. The one thing I wanted more was to walk to the other wing of the house and get in Stella's bed, pull her close, and fall asleep with her head above my heart. But that would require her trust and something more—her love. I almost laughed, my chest shaking from the strained chuckle caught beneath my ribs.

I'd heard her sobs, stood outside her door and listened to the aftermath of what I'd done. She would never let me in again; not in her bed, and definitely not in her heart. It was better for her this way. I had to destroy her or watch my brother do it. Wanting her, feeling her entwined in my very soul, had nothing to do with the Acquisition. And it couldn't. I wouldn't let it interfere.

I tucked a glass under my arm and swung Lucius' door open. His room was dark, his curtains drawn so that only a slice of the growing daylight showed through.

"What?" An orange circle flamed in the dark and then faded.

"Mom would kill you if she knew you were smoking in the house." Wisps of smoke circled in the air across the room, folding back in on themselves before spreading into nothing.

"Good thing she doesn't know, then. What do you

want?"

"We need to talk." I closed the door behind me before settling at the foot of his bed and holding out the second drink.

"Your good bourbon?" He took the glass and stubbed out his cigarette. "Did shit just get real, or what?"

"It got real a while ago. As soon as I was chosen for the Acquisition this year."

"You finally going to tell me the rules?" He sat up higher against his pillow and sipped his drink.

"Yes." I sighed and drained my glass, wishing the alcohol would kill the stings that ricocheted inside and out of me.

"About fucking time. Shit. Hit me. I'm ready, drama queen."

"There are only seven." *Seven rules to see you through. Seven rules to live by. Seven rules to make it hurt. Seven rules to kill by.* Mom's voice when I'd told her we were chosen this year echoed in my mind. I'd known for quite some time that the mother from my earliest memories was gone. But I didn't know how far gone until I'd heard her scratchy song, sung with glee.

"Seven rules? I'm all ears." He leaned forward, the strip of daylight cutting across his face.

"Let's start with the first, and most important rule." I wondered if a weight would lift after I'd told him, if I'd suddenly be lighter or freer. I doubted it.

"What's that?" He polished off his drink.

I met his eyes, knowing I was about to knock the wind out of him worse than I ever could with my fists. It would kill him just as sure as it was killing me, but it couldn't be helped. Not anymore.

CHAPTER TWELVE
STELLA

THE MORNING CAME, and with it, still no Renee. Then another dawn, and another. I hadn't seen Vinemont or Lucius in the days since the party. Farns apologized profusely, but gave me no information about what had become of Renee. Laura took over Renee's duties in my room. She was tight-lipped, far more than she had ever been before.

It was as if the house had just shut down around me, shunning me and making me the outsider I was. No information, no interaction. Just me, sitting here, and waiting until the Christmas trial. Four days away and still no sign of my friend. The only person I spoke to other than Farns and Laura was Teddy.

"Want to go for a ride today?"

I glanced out the window behind him as we ate breakfast. "Is it going to rain? Or storm? Or hail? Or *lightning*?"

He grinned and checked his phone. "Nope, only sunny and cold. It'll be fun. I'll save you from any danger, promise."

"Aren't you the valiant one?" I smiled and took a bite

of French toast. Cinnamon and sugar played on my tongue to the point I wanted to moan.

"At your service, my lady," Teddy said. "I've been meaning to go out for a ride. Get some air and just cruise, especially since Sin and Lucius aren't around to tell me no."

"Where are they? Do you know?" I'd already tried to get some Renee information out of him to no avail. Might as well take my chances and see if he'd spill about his brothers.

"There was more trouble in Cuba. Lucius flew down a couple days ago." He finished his orange juice. "I don't know where Sin got off to. He was here yesterday on a conference call with Lucius and some investors, but then he was gone again. Maybe back in town? I'm not sure. He keeps tabs on *me*, not the other way around." He shrugged, his broad shoulders pulling at the buttons on his plaid flannel shirt.

"Will Lucius be back by Friday?" That was when the trial was supposed to start. If Lucius wasn't back, did that mean I wouldn't have to go? I didn't dare to hope, not for a second.

"I don't know. What happens Friday?" He leaned back and set his napkin on the table before patting his stomach like it was full. Even under the shirt I could tell he was all lean muscle, just like his brothers.

"Nothing. I'm not really sure." The Stella who lived in this house, who wore my clothes, and answered to my name was a liar. I wondered if that would be something that remained, something I would never be able to shake, just like so many other dark souvenirs from my time here.

"Stella?" He put his warm hand on mine. "What is it?"

I forced a smile. "Let's ride. I think it'll do me good and clear my head."

"All right. Don't tell me. Just like everyone else here never tells me anything." He rolled his eyes. "Come on. I need to change. You do, too. Got any leather?" He stood.

"Leather?"

He grinned. "Yeah, for riding."

"I need leather to ride a horse?"

He looked over my head and out toward the garage. "Depends on what sort of horse we're talking about."

I took his meaning and crossed my arms over my chest. "I don't ride motorcycles."

"You do today." He gripped under my arm and pulled me up. "Live a little. Come on."

Maybe he was right. It wasn't like I had a lot to lose. Not anymore. I grabbed my coffee and downed it before slapping the cup back onto the table. "All right, hell on wheels, let's do it."

We went upstairs, and I inspected my closet. Renee had, in fact, gotten me a brown leather jacket. I pulled it from the hanger and inhaled deeply, the smell delicious and strong. I yanked on some jeans, socks, and boots. Then a tank, sweater, and the jacket, along with some gloves. After pulling my hair into a low, messy ponytail, and snagging some sunglasses from the back of my closet, I felt almost badass enough to ride a motorcycle.

Teddy swung my door open and strolled in, his shitkickers making steady clumps as he walked around my room.

"Don't knock or anything." I stepped out of the closet.

"I gave you plenty of time not to be naked. And like you said before, I'm valiant. I wouldn't have looked or anything." He waggled his eyebrows. "Well, let me rephrase. I wouldn't have taken pictures, but I definitely would have looked."

"Perv." I gave him the finger and walked past him. "I'm ready to meet my maker. Let's go."

We pounded down the stairs and took the short walk to the garage. I'd glanced in here a few times, but I'd never actually been inside. Cars and bikes filled every bit of free space. I had no clue what I was actually looking at, especially given that most of the cars bore emblems I didn't even recognize.

Teddy stepped toward the back to a row of polished bikes. He chose one on the end, its black metal glinting under the shop lights.

"This one's mine. I named her Black Widow."

"That's not a very reassuring name for a motorcycle." I ran my fingers down the smooth leather seat. The chrome was rubbed to a high shine, and the bike was low and sleek. If it was half as fast as it looked, I might be screaming my head off before we even made it off the property.

"You'll love it. Here." He tinkered with a black helmet and handed it to me. I removed my sunglasses, slid the helmet on, and then snugged my sunglasses back over my eyes.

He slipped his helmet on, and his voice crackled to life in my ear. "It has Bluetooth, so we can talk as we ride. Also, music." He tapped the screen of his phone and a deep bass starting pumping, backed by someone shredding a guitar. "I've already got some tunes picked out."

"Born to be wild." I couldn't help but smile.

He walked the bike out to the front of the garage and threw his leg over. I followed and climbed on behind him.

"Hang on to me. I don't mind." The music dimmed as his voice sounded clearly.

"Yeah, I'm sure you don't." I wrapped my arms lightly around him as he fired it up. The rumble shook me in all the right places and made my thighs tense against the seat.

"Sounds like heaven, doesn't it? You ready?"

I propped my chin on his shoulder, our helmets touching. "I'm ready."

He gunned the engine and we were gone, shooting up the drive, past the house, under the trees, and out into the daylight that filtered down through feathery clouds.

The wind whipped around us as he sped up, the tires devouring the distance to the gate. It was already opening by the time we reached it. He must have had a remote key somewhere on the bike. He turned right, toward town and away from the interstate.

I clung even more tightly to him through the curves and twists in the road, pressing my chest into his back as we tore through the barren countryside. The fields were gray, crops long since harvested. His music changed from hard rock to some sort of electronic dance music. We kept going until the road widened into more lanes, the traffic increasing slightly as the area became more populated. I didn't know how long we would ride, but I didn't care. I wanted to fly with him, to just be alive for a little while and not worry about the trial.

"Ready to go a little faster?"

"Faster than this?" I asked as the countryside whizzed by.

"Way faster. Straightaway up ahead. Hold on to your tits, Stella."

I laughed, but the roar of the engine drowned out the sound as he pushed the bike harder and we hurtled forward, passing a couple of cars until we made it to the straightaway. The road rose up to meet us as he leaned forward, me glued to his back. We sped so fast that we were nothing but a whoosh of speed and sound, oncoming cars only a transitory blip. My heart pounded, pure adrenaline pumping through my veins.

"Wooo!" Teddy's voice in my ear. No, it was both of ours. Both of us let out the exhilaration and soaked up the danger, the life, and the realness of the moment.

His heart pounded against my palm, matching the chaotic beat of my own. This was the freedom I longed for, a beautiful escape, if only fleeting.

We glided for a little while longer before he let off the accelerator, the bike calming down though our hearts still raced.

He reached back and squeezed my knee. "Fuckin' A, right?"

"Couldn't have said it better myself."

We rumbled into town, the familiar streets no longer holding the same charm for me they once did. He drove through the town square. We passed the courthouse where my father's trial had been held and the jail where he'd been taken after his arrest. Dark memories tempered the excitement of only moments before.

"Can we go left here?" I asked.

"Sure. Whatever you want." He turned as I'd directed, and I gave him a few more instructions before we cruised down my old street.

"Down toward the end." Toward my father's house. There was no reason for me to do it, to torture myself like this. But I had to see.

We rolled up and I gasped. The house's roof was gone, the top of the windows blackened, and the front porch fallen in.

"What is it?" Teddy cut the music. "What's wrong?"

"That's my father's house." Worry twisted my insides.

Teddy pulled into the drive and stopped, shutting the engine off and kicking out the stand. He helped me off and I walked up to my home, or what was left of it. I pulled off my helmet and tucked it under my arm.

"What happened?" Teddy stood beside me and craned his head back to see the charred tips of what remained of the sloping eaves.

"I don't know. I had no idea..." All I could do was stare, shell-shocked that this piece of my past had been erased. All my paintings, the mementos I had to remember my mother—gone.

Teddy pulled a glove off and went to the nearest window before pressing his fingers along the wood. "Not wet and the inside looks dry, too. It must have happened a while ago."

"Why would no one tell me?"

"Because you didn't need to know." Vinemont's hand clapped down on my shoulder and I jumped.

Teddy turned. "Sin—"

Vinemont cut him off. "Imagine my surprise when I was driving home after spending all night at the office and I saw a bike speeding past me at an insane clip. Who could it be?" He squeezed my shoulder so I couldn't turn around and face him. "I wondered who was foolhardy enough to drive at such a breakneck pace, who was dumb enough to ride at his back, and further, who did I know that had such a fast bike?"

I gripped his fingers and pried two of them loose before darting forward and whirling. "Keep your fucking hands off me, Vinemont."

He wore a dark blue dress shirt, the throat open, and a pair of black slacks. The sun lit his hair, coloring the deep brown a milk chocolate. He had a shadow of light stubble across his cheeks, rough and masculine. In his eyes I saw a seething anger.

"Look, Sin. I'm sorry. It was my idea, though. Not hers." Teddy walked up beside me. "You don't need to like, punish her or anything."

"I don't need to be having this discussion while at least two neighbors are watching through their curtains, no." He kept his voice low, but each word was tinged with wrath. "But here we are anyway. One big happy fucking family."

"Sin, we'll go the speed limit on the way back, okay?" Teddy grabbed my helmet and lifted it above my head.

Before he could put it on, Vinemont said, "Leave it. She's riding with me. You are riding ahead of me the whole way and *we* are going the speed limit. Got it?"

"I'm not a kid, Sin. I don't have to do what you say." Teddy handed my helmet back to me and squared his shoulders.

"I have ways of keeping you in line. Don't make me use them."

"What, are you going to cut me off?" Teddy threw his hands out to his sides and his voice rose. "Make me pay for college? What are you going to do?"

"No. None of that. But do you remember the first day you met Stella?"

Teddy shifted from one foot to the other. "Yes."

"I can make her do a lot more than just stand naked. And I can make you watch all of it. Is that what you want? Would you like that? And another thing, in case that's not enough to get your attention. Laura. I can make sure you never see her again."

Teddy slammed his helmet on the ground. "Goddammit, Sin! Why are you like this? What happened to the you that existed before the Acquisition? The one who helped me with homework because Mom was too drugged up or spaced out to notice I was even there? The one who encouraged me to go to med school? The one who taught me how to ride a fucking bike?" He pointed to Black Widow. "Where did you go?"

Vinemont remained completely unmoved. His placid demeanor in the face of such a heartfelt plea sent a chill down my spine. How had I thought for one moment that he was anything other than a monster?

"The same place you're going. Right back to the house, in front of me, and at a reasonable speed. Now shut the fuck up, get your helmet on, and get on the bike. Stella, get in the goddamn car." He turned on his heel and stalked through the unkempt grass, back to the car.

"Just go." Teddy was defeated, crushed under Vinemont's elegant shoe. Just like me. "There's no talking to him like this. I'll see you back at the house."

"I'm sorry, Teddy."

"It's not your fault." He glared at his brother but then his expression softened. "If I told you he wasn't like this, not really, would you believe me?"

I didn't want to give him the bad news—I already knew this was the real Vinemont.

"Ride safe." I gave him a weak smile before walking to the black sedan. I tossed the helmet into the back and sank into the passenger side before slamming the door shut.

"Did you do this?" I asked as he pulled from the curb.

"Do what?" Vinemont sighed and waited for Teddy to ride out ahead of him.

"Burn down my house."

He laughed, the sound filling the car's interior and making me flinch. "Are you still laying your father's crimes at my feet?"

"What?" I glanced back at the ruined house that held so many memories for me, good and bad. "Are you saying my father did it?"

"Oh, look who finally figured something out. Well done, Stella, really. I'd clap, but as you can see, I'm driving." His sneer had me looking away, looking at anything but him. "You don't believe me?"

"I didn't say that." After what my father had done to me, I wouldn't put anything past him.

"Money, Stella. Insurance money, to be exact. He torched it all. He cashed in on that house, just like he cashed in on you."

He drove around the square and turned onto the highway that led back to my prison. My breathing turned shallow as I thought of everything that had happened to me in the burned-out husk behind me, how the last time I'd left it, I thought I was doing it for all the right reasons. The betrayals layered on betrayals began to suffocate me like dirt on my grave, and I couldn't get enough air. The metal and glass closed in on me, and I clamped my eyes shut, trying to ward off my rising panic.

"Stella?" Vinemont's voice came through like we were at opposite ends of a tin can telephone.

I gulped in more air, trying to stay alive, to breathe. I just had to make it to the next moment, to keep going to the next and the next until they all fell over like a long line of dominoes, and at the end was freedom, *my* freedom. But my thoughts began to dim and I still couldn't get enough air.

"Stella!"

The car stopped and hands were on my shoulders, pulling me out and into the cold winter wind.

"Breathe, Stella. Slowly. Slowly."

I opened my eyes and stared up into Vinemont's face. I staggered back, shrinking away from him even as something in me reacted to the worry in his eyes. I shook my head. He was only worried I wouldn't be able to win for him. He would violate me. They all would. I couldn't breathe. I couldn't see. I stumbled and fell back against the passenger door as he advanced.

"No," I croaked.

"Stella, please." His voice, so different from just a few moments ago, was soaked in the same pain that burned in my lungs, in my mind.

He took another step. I finally got my breath and used it to scream. I screamed and screamed, the sound ripped from my throat and piercing the air. Each peel of despair carried every horror, every unwanted touch, every painful lash, and every desolate thought. I couldn't breathe, I couldn't be free, but I could scream. I screamed until I crumpled. He caught me in his arms and crushed me to his chest as my lungs gave out, the last shriek dying on the wind as he held me close.

No one heard. Only the desolate fields, the withered scarecrows, and Vinemont.

CHAPTER THIRTEEN
Stella

I COULDN'T SLEEP. The last full night of rest I'd gotten was when Vinemont had brought me home after my meltdown on the roadside. That restful night had more to do with a dose of narcotics from the family doctor than anything else. I hadn't cared about being drugged. I was emptied out. Every last bit of me had been screamed into the cold air as my tormentor held me.

But the trial was here. Lucius had returned from Cuba the previous night. I knew he would. There was no escape for me. I would be abused, likely many times over, and it would start today. The sun had risen an hour ago, the rays illuminating the quilts, each one telling a story I didn't care to hear.

Renee was still missing. Her absence added to the long list of disappointments already lodged in my heart. I'd stopped by her room several times, but she was never there. Her bed was always neatly made. I'd peered at the stairs to the third floor, and even taken a few steps once before Laura hurried down the hall and shook her head, warning in her eyes. After that, I'd stopped asking about Renee.

A knock at my door made me turn my head. "Yes?" My voice was scratchy.

"It's time." Lucius didn't barge in and order me around. He stayed out of sight.

"I'm coming."

"Downstairs in an hour. Dress warm, and wear comfortable shoes."

Before I could get in a snide reply, his footsteps were already retreating down the hallway. *Dress warm.*

I rose and showered, taking my time to feel every bit of the hot water. I ignored the paleness of my face in the mirror, the shake in my hands as I brushed my hair. Dressing as instructed, I donned a dark green sweater, black puffer jacket, jeans, and boots. I couldn't shake the feeling I was dressing myself for my own funeral. I didn't bother with makeup. I knelt next to my nightstand and took out the knife. The unyielding metal gave me an odd sense of comfort and served an even more basic purpose—defense. I turned the blade over and over in my hands before I wrapped the tape around it and shoved it down into my boot.

I met Lucius and Vinemont downstairs in the breakfast room. Lucius had dressed warmly in a black sweater and jeans, and Vinemont wore his usual work attire. Neither man looked at me.

I took my seat and picked at my food. If I ate a bite, I was sure it would come right back up. Lucius didn't seem particularly hungry either, and Vinemont only drank coffee.

I stopped even attempting to look interested, laying my fork down and sitting back in my chair. "I hate the waiting. Let's go."

Lucius nodded in agreement and stood. Vinemont ignored him, staring straight ahead as if he watched a ghost known only to him. I rose and followed Lucius out of the dining room and down the hall. In the foyer, he turned, his face more solemn than I'd ever seen it. There wasn't so much as a hint of amusement or his acerbic wit. Only focus.

His seriousness scared me more than anything. I couldn't control the shudder that went through me.

He grabbed my hands and brought them to his chest. "You can do this. We can do this, okay? Remember what I said to you in Cuba? All of it still stands. You just have to get through this."

I lifted my eyes to his. "And then I have to get through the next, and the next? What are the last two, Lucius? Are you going to flay my skin from my body? Scar me beyond recognition? What?"

"One thing at a time. And, no. None of those things. This one is…"

"The worst?" I finished for him.

"I think so. But I don't know what Cal is planning for the other two." He gripped my neck and pulled me toward him before dropping a kiss on the top of my head. "Trust me. We'll get through it. We'll get through all of them."

I wanted to be heartened, to take his words as some sort of comfort. But they were hollow. Getting through this trial was my cross to bear, not his. I would be crucified right along with the other two Acquisitions while Lucius threw dice at my feet.

I closed my eyes and remembered my father. The way he was before his arrest, before his trial, before any infernal contracts. The one that had held me as I cried for my mother on nights too numerous to count. The one who'd saved me from my own attempt at self annihilation. The one who, even as I felt the sting of his deceit, still lived in my heart. I needed my loving father there, giving me courage to do what I had to do, even if he was nothing more than a specter haunting my memories.

Farns rolled a couple of suitcases through the foyer, jarring me from my thoughts. I followed him onto the porch.

"I hope your trip isn't long." He smiled down at me,

clueless about what was going to happen. If he'd known, he never would have smiled like that.

I hugged him. Just an instinct. He made a surprised noise and hugged me back.

"Thanks, Farns. I just needed..." I stepped away from him. "Just thanks."

"Anytime, miss." Pink crept into his paper thin cheeks.

"Stella?" Vinemont appeared as Lucius took the bags down to Luke, the driver. "A word?" I couldn't read him—asking or intimidating all seemed to have merged into one.

Farns shuffled past him and into the house.

"What?" I didn't move toward him. I wouldn't.

He walked out to me, the sun highlighting his tired eyes and sunken cheeks. He looked like he hadn't slept or eaten in days. When he stuffed his hands in his pockets, the muscles in his forearms flexed, making the vines writhe. "I just wanted to say, not that it matters, not that it will help..." He sighed, as if having trouble grabbing ahold of his thoughts as they flittered away before him. "I would gladly take your place if I could. But I can't. And I need you to get through this. And I need..."

"What?" I asked again. He'd already taken so much, and now he was asking for even more. That connection between us, the one I'd felt so strongly, was withered now, dead on the vine. He couldn't ask any more of me. But I had to know, all the same.

"Stella?" Lucius called, but had the good sense to stay by the car.

I held Vinemont's gaze, demanding he finish his thought. "What else do you need from me?"

"I need you to come back to me." His words were so soft and low I almost missed them.

I stared at him and tried to misinterpret his words, tried to make it seem like he wanted me to come back so the Acquisition could continue and the Vinemonts could win. But seeing his eyes, and the sadness and pain welling in them, I knew it wasn't that. He wanted me to come back to him. No, he *needed* it. He'd only given me glimpses of this man—the one who hurt, who felt, who needed. And now he'd laid himself bare.

"Stella. We have to go. Come on."

Lucius' irritated command knocked me out of my reverie. I did have to go. I had an appointment to keep, one that would leave me scarred and broken for the rest of my life. And the reason I had to go was this man, the one whose regretful eyes and words were nothing compared to the pain I was about to feel. It took everything in me, but I wasn't going to help the spider anymore. I wasn't going to hasten my own downfall by jumping into his web. Not again.

I turned without a word and hurried down the stairs. Luke helped me into the back seat and closed the door. I didn't look at Vinemont, even though I knew he hadn't moved, his gaze still seeking me out even behind the privacy glass. Lucius slid in and settled next to me as Luke drove away. I kept my eyes down, never turning back.

Lucius and I didn't speak as we drove steadily northward. He took some calls, half of them conducted in Spanish as we cruised along the smooth pavement. My hands couldn't stay still, worrying away at each other or twisting the hem of my sweater. Eventually, Lucius reached out mid-conversation and snagged my right hand in his, pulling it over onto his thigh as he kept talking about sugar cane crops and the costs of production.

I let him keep it. I could worry away on the inside just as well with or without that hand. I kept trying to clear my mind. Thinking about Vinemont's words or, alternatively, replaying Renee's story of hypothermia and unforgivable violations only made the fear roar louder than my hatred. I wanted the hatred to win out, to suffocate my fear until I was nothing but a raging flame of anger. Even as I tried to master it, the dread seeped in, coloring every thought with a dirty film.

The landscape changed during the drive, the trees getting thicker as more pines mixed in with the dormant oaks and hardwoods. We were in the middle of national forest land when Luke pulled off the interstate onto a two-lane highway. Our route took us farther into the woods, the bleak trees creeping up close to the road on either side.

Lucius tapped his phone off, finally ending a particularly heated call with Javier. He gave my hand a light squeeze but didn't look at me.

After another half hour, Luke turned into a paved lane blocked by a gate similar to that on the Vinemont property. At the top of each door was a stag, its horns magnificent and overdone. Luke rolled down his window and spoke to the attendant standing out front. Then we passed through the gate and into the encroaching woods. The drive meandered through rolling hills, the sun shining with ease through the barren trees.

Before long, we spied the glint of a car ahead of us, and we joined what seemed to be a long procession winding along the narrow drive. Eventually, the woods opened into a wide clearing, and a massive log structure rose from the side of a hill. It was enormous, the size of a small hotel, out in the middle of nowhere. The roof had several apexes, each one an A-frame with a large sheet of glass enclosing the front of the house. The oak logs were rustic, but the glass was modern, glinting in the early afternoon sun.

The cars moved in an orderly row, each pausing at a valet station before parking in a field off to the right. Luke pulled to the front of the line, and the valet greeted us and opened our doors. I stepped out into the bitter air and stuffed my hands in my pockets. I didn't want anyone to touch me.

Lucius walked around to me after telling Luke to bring up the bags.

We climbed the stairs behind an elderly couple who had a hard time managing it. Neither Lucius nor I offered to assist. If they fell down and broke their necks, it was all the better for me as far as I was concerned.

We made it to the upper deck where all the windows opened out onto the landscape. I looked back and realized the house was situated on the highest ridge of the area, giving an expansive vista of the forest beyond.

"Come in, come in." Cal's voice had me slowing my pace. I could stand the frigid air more than I could stand his presence.

"Sheriff Wood! Welcome. Glad you could make it." Cal rattled off names with his usual exuberance as the greeting line moved along.

The elderly couple finally made it into the house through a pair of rustic wood and metal front doors. Lucius put a hand on my lower back and guided me forward. Cal, wearing a ridiculous Christmas sweater, gripped my upper arms and air kissed me on each cheek.

"So nice to see you again, Stella. Lucius, welcome."

Thankfully, Cal went on greeting the people behind us so we slipped in without any more fanfare. The house was a work of art—beams in a lattice work across the high ceiling, and glass giving a full 180-degree view of the ridges and valleys in the distance.

People were everywhere, talking, drinking, and mingling. The sound system played jaunty Christmas tunes as I caught pieces of conversations about the "fun of the last Acquisition Christmas trial" and "what does Cal have up his sleeve for this year?" My stomach churned as they crowed about what a good time they intended to have over the weekend.

I spotted Gavin ahead, his tall frame giving him a boost above most of the surrounding guests. Surging forward, I pushed through to him.

"Stella." He hugged me.

"Hi."

"I can't exactly say I'm glad you made it." He pulled me away and shook his head, the dark circles under his eyes telling me he hadn't slept, either. "But, if we have to be here, at least we're together."

"You aren't together." Lucius caught up to me. "Bob, get your Acquisition on a fucking leash, would you?"

Bob began stuttering, his face turning red almost instantly. "Gavin. Stop talking to her. She's the enemy."

Gavin bent down by my ear and quickly whispered. "I got your back."

He straightened and moved away toward Bob before I could reciprocate. I didn't know if it would be true, me saying I had his back, but I would do my best.

"What did he say?" Lucius maneuvered us toward another set of stairs with an attendant at the top.

"Nothing."

"Lucius?" A blonde woman in skin-tight jeans and a thin white sweater rested her hand on Lucius' arm.

"Oh, hey…"

It was obvious he couldn't remember her name, but that didn't stop her. "I'd heard you'd somehow jumped into the running. It's been a while. What, last year sometime?" Her voice dropped to as much of a husky whisper as possible to still be heard over the multitude of other people chatting.

Lucius nodded. "Yeah, I think that's right. I had a great time."

I stared at him as the lies rolled off his tongue. He clearly had no clue who she was or when he'd fucked her.

She moved her hands to his shoulders and tiptoed to whisper in his ear, rubbing her breasts all over his chest while she did it. He only smiled when she dropped back down and stared up into his eyes.

"Sounds good. Soon then."

"Soon." She winked and turned back to her conversation as Lucius pushed me even faster through the throng. We finally made it to the stairs and climbed until we came to another attendant. He was dressed all in black which did nothing to hide his portly girth. He had an air of self-importance that rankled.

"We need our room," Lucius said. "Lucius Vinemont and Stella Rousseau."

The attendant flipped through screen after screen on his tablet. "Oh, you're one of the competitors. Your room will be up one more flight of stairs, last door on the left. It's one of the larger suites."

"Key?" Lucius held his palm out.

The attendant shook his head. "No keys, sir. Trust is implicit."

"Come on, Stella," Lucius said.

The attendant cleared his throat. "Oh, no. I'm sorry. I didn't make it clear. The suite is solely for you, Mr. Vinemont. She will be staying with the other Acquisitions."

"What?" Lucius turned back to the attendant. "No, she stays with me."

"Those are my instructions from Mr. Oakman. I'm sorry if they aren't palatable, sir." He didn't seem the least bit sorry.

"But one of the other Acquisitions has a dick." Lucius was fuming.

"No need to worry about that. She won't be sullied until it's time."

Sullied? I tried to stay calm, to keep up what little barrier I had to these people and their minions. But this was already too much. I snatched the tablet from his hands and tossed it over the rail. Someone below yelped but the sound was quickly drowned out by the clamor of voices.

The attendant's nostrils flared and he scowled at me. "You can't do that."

"I just did." I may not have been able to stand up to anyone else here, but this guy? I was more than happy to grind him under my heel and piss on the dust that was left.

The attendant's eyes narrowed. "Michael," he called over his shoulder, "please escort the Acquisition to her quarters and hand me your tablet."

One of the other attendants, a younger man, stepped

forward and handed his computer over before looking at me.

Lucius pulled me aside and spoke in my ear. "You have to go with them, but if you need me, you heard what he said. My room's up the stairs, last door on the left. Come find me if anything happens, okay?"

"This way, Acquisition." Michael grabbed my elbow.

"Back the fuck off, asshole," Lucius said. "And address her as Ms. Rousseau or I'll rip your goddamn tongue out, you fucking prick."

Michael stepped away in a hurry.

Lucius reached up as if to touch my cheek but glanced around and thought better of it. "Just tell me you'll come to me, okay?"

"I will." I wouldn't. He couldn't help me.

"All right. Go with him, but don't take any shit." Lucius took my hand and squeezed my fingers. "I'll see you soon."

His words were like a judge pronouncing a sentence. He was right that he would see me soon. I pulled my hand away from his and followed Michael down the hall.

"Where are we going?" I asked Michael's retreating back.

"As was already clearly stated to you, to the Acquisition quarters, *Ms. Rousseau*."

This kid was getting under my skin almost as badly as Mr. Tablet Overboard. "I have another question."

"What?" He let out an exasperated sigh.

"Why are you such a douche?"

He stiffened, but kept walking. *Score one for Stella.*

He led me around a few more corners before coming to a set of oaken double doors. He pushed through and we entered a room with three twin beds and an en suite bathroom. It was small, but not cramped. A tiny window in the upper rafter let in natural light, and high track lighting shined down from the wooden beams.

"These will be your quarters for the duration of your

stay with us. Don't leave until someone comes for you." He backed out of the room, smirking at me and closing the doors as he went.

Brianne stepped out of the bathroom. She was in a cutoff t-shirt and shorty shorts.

I panicked. "Why are you dressed for spring break? You need to be warm."

"Why, we're going to be inside, right?" She plopped onto the nearest bed.

"No. Well, I mean, I don't know, but—"

"Red said not to worry about it. That it wasn't a big deal." She stared at the small window. "It's just supposed to be a little fun for them."

Red was an even bigger piece of shit than I'd ever imagined. I sank down next to Brianne and took one of her hands. "We have to get you dressed warmer. Did you bring any clothes?"

She finally looked at me and her eyes had the same glassy quality as they did at the party in New Orleans.

"Did you take something?" I asked.

"No. What do you mean?" She pulled her hand away from mine.

"I mean, are you high?" I had no idea what having drugs in your system would do when faced with hypothermia or worse.

She narrowed her eyes. "Don't think I don't know what you're doing. Red told me this was a competition between you and me and that powder puff Gavin. You aren't going to beat me."

My eyes rounded in disbelief. "You think we're competing against each other?"

"We are. Now get the fuck off my bed and mind your own goddamn business," she hissed.

"Brianne, please, you have to listen—"

"I said go!" Her scream was crazed.

I stood and backed away. Red had already destroyed the girl I'd seen at the ball. Brianne had broken. Would I?

My legs hit one of the other beds and I sat as Brianne went back to staring out the window at the patch of blue sky. I dropped my head into my hands, resting my elbows on my knees. Despair leeched from the air around Brianne and into my skin.

The doors opened and Gavin strode in, the rude attendant giving the same spiel about staying in the room until someone came for us.

Once he was gone, Gavin hitched a thumb over his shoulder. "Can you believe that guy?"

I rose and ran a hand through my hair. "Yeah, I called him a douche."

"He is definitely that and then some." Gavin surveyed the room before walking over and sitting next to me. "Hey Brianne, how's it going?"

"I'm not talking to either of you, so stop trying to get up in my head." She lay down with her back to us.

Gavin raised an eyebrow at me.

I shook my head, the insane urge to laugh mixing with my desire to cry. "She thinks we're competing against each other. That somehow we're the ones who need to win the competition. I'm not sure what she thinks we'll win, but there it is." I dropped my voice even lower. "She's on something. Same thing as at Cal's party."

Gavin pressed his lips into a thin line and shook his head. "Hate to say I'm not surprised. By the time this trial is over, I may be wishing I'd brought some pharmaceuticals."

"So you know?" It was a relief that I wouldn't have to tell him.

"I do." He scrubbed a hand down his clean shaven face.

"What do you think they'll do to us? I mean other than the…" I shivered.

"I don't know. I just know we have to get through it. And we can." His amber eyes were kind, and I leaned into him.

"I wish it was over already."

"Me too."

We sat like that for a long while, Brianne silent on her bed and Gavin and I huddling for some sort of comfort. No one bothered us until night fell. Then some plates arrived with a smattering of various foods. Brianne didn't eat a thing. Gavin and I tried, if only to keep our strength up, but the food made me queasy before I'd even had a mouthful.

The room was silent except for raucous cheers every so often from some other part of the house. They must have been stoking themselves up for the next day, for our humiliation.

Footsteps sounded in the hallway and the three of us stared at the door. It opened, and Lucius, Red, and Bob walked in. Gavin put a protective arm around me, and I shrank back against him. Not that it mattered. Not that any of us could stop what was going to happen.

Lucius narrowed his eyes and came straight to me. He took my hand and pulled me up, my cheek brushing against the softness of his black cashmere sweater, and his sandalwood scent in my nose. Maybe this was how it started—a gentle touch before the betrayal, before I was feasted on until there was nothing left but bones and sorrow.

He pulled me from the room, and the others followed.

"Where are we going?" I asked.

He gripped my elbow. "To the party. Don't speak unless you're spoken to. Got it?"

I bristled but remained silent. I had nothing to say to these people. The wooden floorboards were sturdy under my feet, my boots barely making a sound as we meandered through the halls toward the sound of voices. We entered a sea of people drinking and talking. The smell of roasted meat and wood smoke floated through the air.

Cal was speaking over a microphone; his favorite. "—so let's get another look at our little morsels. Ah, and here they are. Come on up!"

Lucius led me toward the raised stage in front of one of the high windows where Cal held court.

"Yes, yes." Cal narrated. "First up, looks like the Vinemont Acquisition, Stella. And, folks, I'll tell you a secret. I may have sampled a little taste—"

The people crowed and whistled as Lucius pushed me to stand next to Cal.

"Now, now. Just a taste is all I said. Not the whole meal. Don't get jealous. But I can tell you that little Miss Stella here is sweet as sugar, and I can only imagine the rest of her will melt right in your mouth."

Laughter, wolf whistles, and a few raised glasses. More movement to the bottom right of the stage caught my eye. My heart soared when I noticed Dylan standing below, waving at me to get my attention. His familiar face gave me strength and I straightened, shouldering my burden a bit more confidently just from his presence.

"Oh, and then Gavin. Now, he isn't to my tastes." Cal put his arm around Gavin's wide shoulders. "Nothing personal, of course. But I know quite a few of you ladies and gents who are salivating for a piece of this hunk, am I right?"

Cal held the crowd in the palm of his hand, their yells and laughter feeding into his frenzy of showmanship.

He moved down the row and pulled Brianne into his side. "And, I'll admit folks, I've had more than just a sample of little Brianne here. And she was good to the very last bite, I can promise you."

Brianne was still checked out, and waved to the throng like she was a homecoming queen instead of slave whose rape was the topic of discussion.

"Now that they're all here, I have a question for all of you good people out in the audience. Which one of you is going to fuck little Brianne here?"

A roar went up, and some of the men on the front row moved in closer.

"And how about Gavin?"

Another roar with quite a few high-pitched cat calls from the women.

"And finally, Stella?"

The room shook with stomping feet and yells, one of the men below climbing the first two stairs before some others pulled him back down, all laughing.

"That's what I like to hear! Now, I'm going to let them mingle a bit, and I expect everyone to be on their best behavior." He glowered at the younger men hovering near the front of the stage. "We do this the right way. The real fun won't start until tomorrow. So, behave with the Acquisitions, but of course, you are welcome to misbehave with each other to your hearts' content."

Cal bowed, and applause coursed through the room. Lucius gripped my hand and pulled me down the stairs. He elbowed through the men hanging around the stage, and I kept my eyes down to avoid their leers. I still heard their voices, their words, their promises of violence and violation.

"Back the fuck up." Lucius shoved one of them and barreled the rest of the way through the crowd and to the bar. He pushed me ahead of him and caged my body from behind. It was protective, but also too close for me. I needed air. I'd rather be in my quarters than here.

I craned my neck around to search for Dylan, but the mass of people blocked my line of sight.

"Give me an old-fashioned. Two of them." Lucius' chest was warm against me, his hands on my hips. "You're doing fine," he whispered in my ear. "That was the big show for the evening."

The bartender poured the drinks and set them down in front of us. I took mine; the taste was bitter on my tongue, but the rush of warmth from the alcohol was welcome. I drank quickly, the liquid burning as I downed it.

"Easy, Stella." Lucius took my almost empty glass.

I leaned my head back on his shoulder and spoke into

his ear. "Please, Lucius. I don't want to feel it."

His fingertips pressed into my hip. "Getting drunk tonight will only make tomorrow worse. You have to stay strong."

"Why?"

"You know why."

"I don't." I did. I just needed to hear it, to know how much worse things could get.

"Because if you can't stay strong, I'll make sure your father suffers. I'll make sure you suffer."

I snorted and snatched the drink back from him, downing it. "Yeah. I think my suffering is a given with or without my good behavior." I avoided the topic of my father. His kind eyes flashed through my mind, though I supposed they weren't truly kind, not anymore. "Got anything else? Anything to stop me from marching right back up to that stage over there and telling all your pals to go shove their Acquisition right up their asses?" I ordered another drink.

"Plenty. Are you going to suffer tomorrow? Yes. But I can make you suffer every day after." His voice darkened and he gripped my hip painfully. When the bartender set the drink down, Lucius knocked it away. "You're mine for months and months. I can think of all sorts of nasty things, Stella. Far worse than anything you could ever dream up. Pain, torture, violations that will make tomorrow seem like a pleasant memory." He moved his hand around the front of my thigh and cupped my pussy as he pushed me into the bar, my ribs crushing painfully against the wood. "If that's what you want, then by all means, go on up to the stage."

I tried to squirm away from him, but he only pressed me harder and his fingers sank farther between my legs, massaging my core through my jeans.

"Get off me," I growled.

He ignored me, his fingers making my body come alive when I wanted to stay numb.

"But," he let off and moved his hand back to my hip, "if you do what I want you to do, then I will do everything I can to protect you. And once this is over—"

"Lunch with the queen. I got it. Now get the fuck off me." I pushed away from the bar.

"Stella!" Dylan shoved past a couple of guests and embraced me, picking me up off the floor and squeezing me to the point where I wished I hadn't had that drink.

"You're here." I was starved for an honest touch, for someone who I knew cared about me and not because of some stupid game.

He set me down. "Yes." His cheeks were red and his breath smelled of something strong.

"Are you drunk?"

"No. I mean, Cal shared some choice whiskey, but I'm not drunk." He shook his head, the movement slow.

"You're drunk." A shock of pain hit my chest. "You came here and got drunk with these people?"

"I was just trying to play along. Calm down." He put his heavy arms on my shoulders and pressed his forehead to mine. "I'm going to be the one, Stella. Tomorrow. It'll be me."

"You'll be the one to what?"

He grinned, his perfect smile unnerving more than comforting. "You'll see. But it'll be me. I'll take care of you."

"I think that's enough." Lucius menaced from behind me.

"I can talk to my sister if I want to."

"Your former stepsister, you mean?"

"Yeah, so what?"

"She's not your blood. She's no concern of yours."

"She's not your blood either, asshole." Dylan had a point.

"She doesn't have to be. I own her. Now step the fuck back before I drop you and kick you while you're down again."

"We're just talking," I said. "Can't I talk to someone? Please?" I'd never tried asking him nicely. Maybe it would work.

"Yeah, you can talk to me." Lucius put his arm across my neck, pulling me back into him. "Fuck off, Dylan."

"Stop." I elbowed him, but he didn't let go.

Dylan glowered and dropped his gaze back to me. "Remember what I said." Then he turned and moved away in the crowd.

"Get off." I rolled my shoulders and Lucius lowered his arm, but not before grazing my breast.

I turned and glared at him. "Asshole."

He smirked and took another swig. "So?"

"I'm going back to my room."

"No."

"Why not?"

"Because I need you to be seen." He set his glass on the bar and took me by the arm. "Just smile and fucking nod. That's all you have to do."

He waded through the horde of people and dragged me with him. He knew so many of them, striking up easy conversations about childhood events, fun times in college, or how the sugar business was going. But no matter who he spoke to, the conversation always worked its way back around to me.

"Stella's an artist," Lucius said for the tenth time that night.

A woman, perhaps no more than fifty, and impeccably dressed in winter white, smiled and sipped her wine. "So am I. Several pieces on display in New York and Los Angeles. What sort of galleries have you been in?"

"A gallery in my hometown has, well, had a few of my pieces," I said.

"Hometown gallery?" She raised a perfectly-drawn eyebrow and took a sip of her wine. "How quaint."

Lucius smiled. "I heard one of Stella's pieces was recently on display in New York at one of the hottest up and coming galleries. It sold for fifty thousand dollars just last week."

I cocked my head at Lucius. He certainly knew how to spin a lie.

"Oh, is that so?" She simpered at me over her glass.

Lucius didn't miss a beat. "It is. I don't know if you know the piece, but it was called *The North Star*."

Something was off. I did have a piece called *The North Star*, but it sold at the town gallery a month ago, not in New York last week. And definitely not for $50,000.

Her eyes widened. "That was you?"

"It was her." Lucius squeezed my hip and crushed me into his side, pride written into his smile.

"Congratulations. I actually saw that piece in person at La Vie Gallery and was impressed. I had no idea someone of your—" she waved her hand at me like I was some interesting animal behind glass at a zoo "— situation could create something like that."

"I would take that as a compliment, but since it wasn't, I won't." I smiled at her, wishing for her death.

Lucius forced a laugh as the woman's expression soured.

"Good luck tomorrow, dear." She gave me a tight smile, and Lucius pulled me away toward another group of people.

"Bad form, Stella," he whispered in my ear. "Try again."

We visited several more clusters of people who chatted about mundane first world problems before turning to my enslavement like it was just another topic.

The next cluster we visited included Dylan's mother, Marguerite. She didn't speak, only listened to Lucius while the other ladies laughed. Her lips were pressed into a narrow line, and her gaze never left me. I wanted to speak to her, to ask if she knew anything that could help me. And, I admitted, I wanted to ask about my father. But her face was impassable, hard.

The next group was younger; Lucius fit in easily, though I kept glancing back to Marguerite as she whispered to the ladies around her. They would glance to me from time to time. I was obviously the topic of their hushed conversation, and none of the information looked good, given their expressions of distaste.

The hour grew late and, though I knew I couldn't sleep, I was ready to be alone. At least, as alone as I could be. I didn't want to be looked at or talked about anymore. If I couldn't be numb, then I'd rather fight my fears alone instead of in front of an audience.

"Are we done?" I asked after we walked away from a particularly nasty pair of older men who leered at me and spoke of nothing other than the trial.

"We can be. Come on, I'll walk you back."

"I can find it. It's just down that hall."

"I know you can find it." His light eyes were shrewd, the liquor doing nothing to dim them. "I just want to make sure you get there."

"Fine."

He led me away, his hand at my lower back as we wove between furniture and people. The hallway was cooler, the air less full of talk and noise.

"You did well. Except for Ms. Thibodeaux. I'll never hear the end of that little art slight."

"How did you come up with that lie about my art selling in New York??"

We turned the corner toward the Acquisition quarters.

"It wasn't a lie. Your *North Star* piece did sell last week for $50,000."

"No, it didn't."

"Yes, it did."

I stopped and faced him. "How?"

"You'll have to ask Sin. I'm not sure about all the details."

I resumed my pace. "Vinemont sold my art? What for?"

"Like I said, ask him. I don't invest in art. I just know good art when I see it."

"Did you tell him my art was good?"

He shrugged. "Maybe. Is this your room?"

We arrived at the double doors. "Yes."

Lucius pushed inside. "Which bed is yours?"

"We haven't really picked, though I think Brianne took that one over to the left."

"So yours is next to Gavin's?" He stepped between the beds and pushed one all the way to the far wall. "That's better."

"That's juvenile." I crossed my arms over my chest.

"Maybe. But I don't want him touching you."

"Well, when you're living it up in your suite tonight and we're down here afraid, I doubt there's much you could do to stop us from touching."

He strode to me. "If he touches you, we're going to have a problem, Stella. A big one. We clear?"

"Sure. He won't touch me. Don't you worry." I put the least amount of conviction into my words as possible. I didn't know why I was trying to get a rise out of Lucius, but I was. Perhaps to repay him for his Dylan tirade.

He yanked me into his chest, the movement so sudden I gasped. "Do you ever shut up?" He kissed me.

I shoved him away. "Are you trying to cheat and get first dibs? Won't that piss off the sadistic buddies you're trying to impress?" I sneered. He'd shown me off for hours, parroting his talking points like he was running for office.

"Come here." He fisted his hands at his sides.

"No."

"Come. Here. I won't tell you again, Stella."

"Fuck you." I stepped up onto the bed and then down the other side and turned back to face him.

"You want to do this right now?" He grinned and pulled his sweater and t-shirt over his head. His skin was smooth, light brown hair at the center of his chest and disappearing into his slacks. The V tattoo swirled out of his heart, the thick brambles snaring him. He was leaner than Vinemont, but just as fast. And he was determined, given the look in his eye.

"I want you to leave right now." I was playing with fire. Something was so wrong about all of this. But I needed to feel something other than fear, other than horror.

"I don't think that's true." He let his gaze run down my body, lingering at my neck, breasts, and thighs before returning to my face. "Your pulse is racing, your nipples hard, and I can just bet your pussy is wet, Stella."

"Guess you'll never know." I backed away.

In one smooth movement, he leapt over the bed and tackled me onto the other bed against the wall. The air was squeezed out of my lungs as he wrestled my hands over my head. He stared down at me, his eyes alight with passion and need.

He claimed my mouth, his tongue sure as it swirled around mine, tasting and touching as he spread my knees apart with his. He was hard, his cock rubbing against me as his hips moved slowly. His kiss was hypnotic, the way he took me over, took my breath, and lit up every nerve ending. I wanted this, something to take my mind off the rest of it. Some small bit of fleeting pleasure before the devastating weight of reality crashed back down.

He moved to my neck, his lips worshipping my jugular as he switched my wrists to one hand. When he slid his hand under my top and squeezed my breast, I moaned. He ripped the cup of my bra down and twisted my nipple between his thumb and forefinger. My hips rose against him, his cock giving more delicious friction. I ignored the flash of deep sapphire eyes that crossed my vision.

Lucius hissed when I raised my hips again, working him through his pants.

"Lucius," I breathed, though another name was on my mind, hovering right along my lips. He sank lower, his mouth on my breast as his free hand yanked at the button and the zipper on my jeans.

He bit me hard, and I arched up to him as he slid his fingers into my panties. I was wet, and my skin was on fire wherever he grazed me with his mouth or his hands.

"Fuck." He reached farther, pulling wetness from my entrance and smoothing it around my clit.

I squirmed and moaned as he circled my hard, sensitive nub. He relinquished my nipple and kissed back up to my mouth, his bare chest pressing into my skin.

He sank a finger inside me and groaned. "I need you, Stella."

The words grated on me. Someone else had needed me, too. Vinemont—his eyes were there again in my vision. He was the ghost that lingered in every corner of my mind.

Lucius brought his fingers up to his mouth and licked them clean. He kissed me again, but his taste was wrong. Everything was wrong. I was a furnace that had burned out, the flame gone, the room cold.

I turned my head. "I don't want this."

"Yes you do." He bit my neck.

"No. I mean it."

The tone in my voice froze him, and he brought his face back to mine. "Are you fucking serious?"

"Yes. Please, just go."

He let go of my hands and sat back, his eyebrows knit together in confusion. "Why?"

I shook my head and yanked down my top. "Please, Lucius."

He stood and stared down at me. "It's Sin, isn't it?"

I looked away.

He didn't need any more confirmation. He turned and retreated, his movements jerky and full of anger, before swiping his sweater off the floor.

I jumped when he slammed the door behind him.

What am I doing? I bounced my head on the mattress, trying to sort through what the hell I was thinking.

Seducing Lucius was a necessary part of the plan and a welcome distraction. And I'd just blown it all up because Vinemont said he *needed* me. Because of a single sentence from a man who ran hot and cold faster than a tap.

I stood up and straightened my clothes before going to the bathroom. I splashed warm water in my face and stared at the mirror me. She was just as inscrutable as before, the reflection doing nothing more than reiterating how lost I was.

The bedroom door opened. I dried my face and walked out to find Gavin and Brianne. Gavin looked at the rumpled bed, then up at me, but I scooted past him with my head down.

Brianne went into the bathroom and took an inordinately long time getting ready for bed.

"So, um, the bed? Anything I need to know about?" he asked.

"No. I'm sad to say." I rubbed my eyes. "Nothing happened. Well, nothing substantial."

"Second base?"

I looked up and he was grinning at me. How he managed to smile so big on the eve of an Acquisition trial was beyond me. But his smile was contagious, because the corners of my mouth turned up despite my mood.

"Something like that. I'm not even sure what the bases are. But let's stick to second."

"I can do that." He kicked his shoes off as Brianne walked out of the bathroom.

She crashed on her bed, not even bothering to get under the covers.

While Gavin was in the bathroom, I took off my boots, feeling inside for the knife. The warm metal was comforting. Then I stripped my jeans and sweater off, but kept my undershirt on. Gavin came out, removed his shirt and pants, and slipped into his sheets. I did the same, pulling my covers up to my chin. We lay silently for a while, listening to Brianne's steady breathing.

"I'm too afraid to turn the light off," Gavin whispered.

"Same here." I flipped over to my side and looked at his profile as he stared at the ceiling.

"Do you think they'll do it in the morning or the afternoon?"

"I don't know, but I intend to be ready to go at sun up."

He turned his head toward me. "How can you be ready for something like this?"

"You can't, I guess. We just have to survive." My voice was small and I felt even smaller. One person in the huge crush of malevolent strangers scattered throughout this mountain retreat.

"Stella?"

"Hm?"

"Can I sleep with you?"

What? "You want to …"

"I mean, in your bed." He smiled. "I mean actually sleep. Not the other thing. I just thought maybe it would make it easier is all."

"Oh," my face reddened. "Sure."

He got out of bed and padded over behind me. The bed shifted and then his warmth was at my back. He pulled the blanket up and slung an arm over me. "Is this okay?"

"Yes." I barely knew him, but his arms were the safest place to be for miles and miles. I settled back into him.

"If it makes you feel any better, that kiss we shared last week was the first time I'd ever kissed a woman."

"Oh." So that's what Brianne had meant by "powder puff Gavin." *What a bitch.* "Well, I'm glad to be your first?"

He must have heard the smile in my voice because he laughed lightly. "Yeah, I was just trying to help. But it wasn't bad. Not really. Just different, I guess."

"Your hand sure went up my skirt fast." I reached behind me and pulled his arm under my neck so he could get more comfortable.

"Thanks. And I was just playing the role. Apparently, I need to work on it since Red still jumped on us."

"A for effort. Nicely done."

"I appreciate it."

We fell silent. His presence was a comfort in and of itself. I was afraid if I kept talking, I would focus on what would happen tomorrow. I didn't want to think about that pain until I had to, until I couldn't escape it.

Our breathing evened out, but neither of us slept. I worried away one hour, then another.

"It's okay, Stella. Sleep. I've got you." Gavin's voice was colored with exhaustion as he pulled me so I turned over to face him.

I let my head fall into the crook of his neck. He rubbed his hand up and down my back in a soothing motion until he drifted off.

"I've got your back," I whispered as sleep took me, too.

CHAPTER FOURTEEN
Stella

SOUND. SO MUCH of it that I instinctively covered my ears. My eyes flew open, my vision sharpening on a multitude of bodies crushing through the suite door. People swarmed into the room, black batons in their hands. They wore white masks, holes cut for their eyes and mouths, with the rest of their features obscured.

I jolted up right along with Gavin.

The men chanted some rhythmic song, unintelligible but somehow vicious. I clutched at Gavin's arm as he gripped my thigh through the blanket. We were both frozen, fear eating up any response we could have mustered.

The throng quieted suddenly, the loss of sound almost as terrifying as the noise. A woman, her long dark hair flowing from the back of her mask walked through the center of the crowd and threw down two white dresses and a white shirt and pants. She retreated back into the mass and Cal, maskless, stepped forward. His gaze flitted about between the three of us before landing on mine.

"Acquisitions, we have something very special in store for you." He pointed to the clothes on the floor. "But first, strip."

Neither Gavin, Brianne, nor I moved. Cal held his hand out behind him and someone put a black baton in it. He walked up and slammed it down on the footboard of my bed, the sound like an explosion through the now cramped space.

"I said strip." He spoke to all of us, but his malevolent gaze was fixed on me.

Gavin pushed me out of the bed and stood next to me.

"Just do it." His whisper was loud in the silent room.

The dozens of masked devils watched as Gavin and I took our clothes off. Brianne did the same, her eyes wide and no longer quite so glassy. The drugs must have worn off, because she came and stood at my other side, shivering and trying to cover herself.

I draped an arm across my bare breasts and used my other hand to cover between my legs. I didn't look at Gavin, who stood on my other side. I wouldn't add to the unwanted eyes already on him. All those masked faces—was Lucius there, watching?

Cal walked forward and put his index finger under my chin, pulling my face up until our eyes met. His pupils were huge, taking in every last bit of me.

A tremor ran through me at his touch, his look.

He let me go and backed up before pointing at the clothes the woman had dropped on the floor. "Dress."

I grabbed a dress and threw it on over my head, wincing at how bare I was before the material covered me. It was short and thin, and would offer no reprieve from the elements. My fear had been stunned right along with me at the sudden intrusion, but it roared back to life. I tried to fasten the top button of the dress at my throat, but my fingers were numb and clumsy.

Cal surveyed us and grinned, apparently pleased with our outfits. "Now, we're going to play a little game. Sound like fun, Acquisitions?"

Some of the masked figures smiled, their teeth showing

through the holes in their masks.

"This game is simple. It's about three a.m. right now. Perfect time for a little stroll in the woods. So, this is what we're going to do. We're going to take you outside and let you go. Let you enjoy the fresh, *cold* air. Stretch your legs."

Oh, god. I reached for Gavin's hand. His skin was like ice.

"Then at daybreak, we're coming for you."

A barrage of shouts went up, gleeful and bloodthirsty.

"Whoever catches you first, wins. That person will fuck you. That person will do whatever they want with your body, because your body was made for our enjoyment. When the winner is done, they may choose to pass you around or bring you back here for more of their own enjoyment. Anything goes. But the winner gets the first fuck and the final say. Simple, right?" Cal nodded and raised his eyebrows at us, as if wanting us to agree with him.

Brianne did. I just gripped Gavin's fingers tighter.

"Your time starts…" Cal glanced at his watch-less arm. "Now."

Another cheer, and the masked figures began filing out. Cal remained and approached, clearly reveling in the power he wielded over the three of us.

"Run, rabbit, run," he whispered. Then he turned and whistled as he followed the pack the rest of the way out of the room.

Only two stayed behind—one of the masked men and the woman with the long, dark hair.

"Come on. Outside." Her voice was harsh, but her nerves made the sound wobble.

I took a chance and darted to my bed and sat, pulling on my socks and boots before grabbing my jacket. The knife rubbed against my ankle, reminding me I still had some measure of defense.

"Gavin, clothes," I urged. "More clothes."

He yanked on his socks and shoes before throwing his

coat on over the white pajamas he was wearing.

The woman came toward us, her baton held above her head. "I said let's go."

"Brianne, shoes!"

She jolted at my words and finally moved, the white dress hanging loosely from her as she pulled on her sneakers.

"Hit her." The male hadn't moved from the door, but his hand ran up and down his baton.

The woman swung at me. I ducked back, but she nailed me on the forearm when I held my arm up to ward her off. Pain exploded down to my wrist and up to my shoulder. I screamed, and gripped the injury.

Gavin finished donning his coat and advanced on her, but the male guard moved forward.

"Enough bullshit," the guard barked. "Let's go."

Brianne had no coat, nothing to keep her safe from the chill wind in the darkness. My arm stung and ached, but I stood and snagged my sweater off the floor and tossed it to Brianne. She yanked it down over her head as we filed out the door under the watchful eyes of our guards.

They led us through the house and then down to the road. A curve of silver moon hung in the sky, and my breath shuddered out in white puffs. Icy patches dotted the road, and the air was keen and cold, faintly burning my lungs on each inhale. The sting took my attention away from the throb in my arm.

Laughter rang out above. A host of masked ghouls crowded the deck and peeked through the windows of the home. Cal stood at the top of the stairs and raised a pistol into the air.

"As an added incentive to our little rabbits, I am offering them a prize beyond value." I couldn't see his eyes from this distance, but my skin crawled enough for me to know he was watching me. "If no one has caught you by noon, you will remain unscathed. No one will touch you."

The crowd booed and hissed. Cal laughed, the sound

loud, fake, and booming. "Now, now calm down. We must have a carrot, after all. It can't always be the stick." He grabbed his crotch for emphasis, and the mob erupted in laughter.

May the best man, or woman, excuse me ladies—" a smattering of feminine laughter coursed through the crowd, "—win!" Cal pulled the trigger, and a hollow pop echoed across the ridges and back to my ears.

"Come on." Gavin tugged at my arm, and we both took off at a sprint away from the house.

I looked over my shoulder. Brianne remained still, staring at Cal and the masked assemblage above her.

"Brianne, come on!" I cried.

She turned and followed us at a jog.

"Which way should we go?" I asked.

"I don't know. Just away from here." Gavin took the lead, moving across the parking area, then through an open field, and finally to the tree line.

Brianne was several yards back, but still followed. I couldn't slow down. We had to make it, had to get far enough away somewhere and hide, or just run and run until the sun was high enough overhead that we knew we were safe.

The woods were shadowy, the crescent moon doing little to illuminate our path. We crashed through the underbrush, not caring what sort of trail we left as we jumped over logs and climbed the first hill. The house gleamed in the night, the windows brightly lit, and the sounds of laughter and music floating along the chilled air. They partied as we ran, enjoying themselves before sinking their claws into the three of us and ripping us apart.

We crested the hill and started down the other side, the house finally out of view. Knowing that they couldn't see me anymore gave me the slightest bit of comfort, but we had to keep moving and put as much distance between them and us as possible.

Gavin stopped and leaned against a tree as we waited

for Brianne to catch up.

"Do you think we can hide?" I asked and peered up into the trees.

Gavin shook his head. "Not in the trees. No cover without leaves. We'd be sitting ducks."

Brianne was breathing hard already, and her cheeks burned a bright pink from the frigid air. My cable-knit sweater wouldn't keep her warm for long, especially not when the wind soughed through the trees as it did. My legs were cold above my boots, and hers must have been freezing. She wore only tennis shoes. I dug in my jacket pockets, ignoring the pain in my forearm, and found my gloves and the knit hat I'd stuffed inside.

"Here." I handed Brianne the hat and the gloves.

Her eyes opened wide. "Th-thank you."

"We aren't competing, Brianne. I promise. Red lied to you."

She took the hat and pulled it down over her blonde locks, which shined almost white in the moonlight. "I know. I don't know why I said all that. All he does is lie to me and, and...other things." She looked away as she pulled on the gloves.

"It's okay. This isn't easy." I slipped my chilled fingers inside my boot and drew out my blade before stuffing it into my pocket. "But we've got to stick together and keep moving. Can you do that?"

"Yes. I think I can."

"Good."

"Take mine." Gavin drew some leather gloves from his coat pockets and handed them to me.

"No, I'm good. I can just stick my hands in my pockets when they get cold. You wear them."

He shook his head and peered down at me. "I can do the same. Go ahead and take them. At least I'm wearing pants. This will make us even."

He wasn't fooling me. The white linen pajama bottoms offered him no more protection from the piercing wind than my bare legs had, but I took the gloves to cut off any more argument. We needed to get moving.

"I'm ready. Let's go." I pulled the too-large gloves on and began picking my way down the slope. It was slow-going because the leaves were covered with a slick of frost, were wet underneath, and the terrain was uneven. It quickly became clear my boots were made more for looks than use, with each step turning into a balancing act.

Once we'd reached the bottom where a small stream ran, we paused.

"Up and over the next ridge, or should we break off to the right and follow the water?" I didn't want to keep moving in a straight line, but I also wanted to get as far from the party as possible.

"Let's follow the stream and then cut up the next hollow we come to." Gavin said.

Brianne nodded, her teeth chattering.

We stayed along the water's path, moving as quickly as we could with Brianne lagging behind. Large stone boulders dotted the landscape, and I wondered if we could hide against one of them. But it was still too out in the open. They would find us in no time. And they would expect us to hunker down, to try and wait them out. That's why we had to keep moving. We slogged through the dead leaves and cracking branches, grunting with the effort of climbing over trunks or boulders. The woods were silent except for our exertions and the inconsistent wind which whistled and pushed easily through the naked branches, chilling the sweat on our skin.

Gavin and I surged ahead, urging Brianne to step where we did to avoid any mishaps. We followed the stream for maybe a half mile before a long hollow opened up to our left. I was sweaty and cold, perspiration rolling down my back, though I didn't dare take my jacket off.

"Brianne, keep up," I called as we started to climb up the hollow.

A screech cut through the still woods, and I glanced

over my shoulder. Brianne floundered, one leg in the icy stream as she tried to climb back to her feet.

"Shit." I raced back down to her and gripped her forearm, dragging her from the shallow stream.

She shivered, her teeth chattering. "I-I slipped."

"Come on." I eyed her wet feet and legs.

"She okay?" Gavin made it back to us.

"I think so, but she got wet."

He shook his head, frustration creasing his brow.

"So cold." Her eyes squeezed shut, misery pouring out of them in delicate tears.

"I know." I had nothing else to say, no promises of help or warmth. We were hunted and freezing; hope was out of reach. "Let's go."

I took her arm and we resumed our trek, her one wet shoe squishing with each step. Our pace slowed even more as her breathing grew labored. The cold was seeping away her strength, her will. I felt it, too.

She paused to rest against a tree as Gavin and I kept going.

"Move, Brianne. Come on," Gavin barked.

Wiping her face with the back of her glove, she started trudging upward again. When we were halfway to the top of the ridge, I slipped on a wet pile of leaves and slid before Gavin caught my arm and hefted me up.

"Thanks."

"No problem."

We were both winded, but wouldn't stop. After more long minutes of climbing, we reached the top.

I bent over, gulping in air.

"Stand up straight and put your arms over your head," Gavin said through wheezes. "It helps."

I did as he'd instructed, though it was agony at first. I leaned my head back, gripping my wrists at the back of my neck. I inspected the sky. No longer an inky black, it was dotted with stars. The Milky Way split the center, its mass of blooming light like a road we could follow. A beautiful path, but cold and distant.

The burning in my lungs subsided as I scanned the bright dots marking the heavens. I dropped my gaze earthward as Brianne sank to the ground at our feet, soiling her dress as she gasped for air.

The moon was lower now, and I could still make out the gleam of lights from the cabin over the last ridge. We were too close. We needed to travel faster.

"Brianne, get up. We have to move."

"I can't." She wiped her runny nose with my glove. "I can't go any further."

"You have to."

"I don't. It doesn't matter. They're going to catch me. They'll catch all of us." She looked up, her eyes brimming with tears. "There's no way out."

I knelt. "Brianne, if you just sit here and don't move, you could die of hypothermia before they even find you."

She dropped her gaze to her knees. "Would that be so bad?"

"Yes." I pulled up my sleeve and showed her my scars. "Yes. It would. Trust me. Now get the fuck up and let's go."

Gavin offered his hand, and Brianne took it. We were on our way again, moving down into the next valley, skidding on leaves and climbing over fallen trees. Once at the bottom, we decided to cut even farther sideways instead of continuing straight up the next ridge.

The moon lowered, its disappearance heralding the coming dawn.

"What's that?" Gavin stopped ahead of me.

I came to stand beside him. "What?"

"You see that light?" He pointed ahead.

Something glimmered between the trees, maybe fifty yards ahead. "Yeah. What is it?"

"I don't know. Let's go. Maybe it's help." He took off faster, his steps becoming less careful at the promise of salvation.

"No, Gavin, wait." Foreboding took hold inside me, and I struggled to catch up with him. "Don't."

"Stella!" Brianne fell to her hands and knees behind me. "I can't feel my feet. I-I can't walk."

"Shit." I dashed back to her, my feet sliding over the leaves and stones. I gripped under her arms and pulled her upright.

"Gavin, don't!" The frigid air swallowed up my voice. I could barely see him through the trees now, but I spied the light. It infused me with dread.

I slung Brianne's arm over my shoulder and half-dragged her.

Gavin's scream sliced through the air, through my mind.

Brianne stiffened at my side. "What happened? What was that?"

He screamed again, agonized and frantic.

"I don't know. But you have to keep walking." I dropped her arm and scrambled over a boulder before taking off toward the light and Gavin's screams.

"Stella." Brianne's voice cracked behind me, but I couldn't stop. Gavin's cries compelled me forward. I tripped as my muscles burned and my lungs struggled to pull in enough air, but I kept moving.

The light grew brighter as I lurched from tree to tree, trying to get a look at what it was.

Gavin's screams subsided into a gasping "Stella" that he repeated until my heart was shredded.

I slowed and crept closer. The light appeared to be a gas lantern hung in a tree. Beneath it dangled a bulbous net bag of clothing—knit hats, jackets, gloves—all warm and welcoming. Gavin lay beneath the bag in a shallow, concealed pit, a narrow bamboo shoot piercing his calf.

"Oh, shit." I dropped to my knees at the edge of the hole and reached down for him.

He grimaced and raised up on his elbow. "I am so stupid. So fucking stupid."

"No, no." I bent over toward him. "Can you get up? Give me your hand."

"It hurts." He stared at his calf, his eyes wide with shock.

"I know. But we have to keep moving. They'll come here first. Please, Gavin." Desperation colored my voice.

He nodded and turned on his side, more bamboo shoots rolling beneath his large frame.

"Is it just your leg?" I asked as he took my hand.

"I think so. Isn't that enough?" He pulled hard enough on my arm that I thought it might come out of the socket, but he managed to perch himself on the edge of the pit next to me. "So fucking dumb. I saw it and thought… I don't know what I thought." He examined the injury. "I guess I wasn't thinking."

The bloodied shoot had been sharpened into a curving tip, penetrating Gavin's flesh cleanly.

"We have to pull it out and keep moving." I took his booted foot in my hands and placed it on his other knee so I could get a better look at the spear. Blood soaked into the white fabric around the wound.

Gavin shook his head, a dazed expression in his eyes. "I don't know—"

"Oh, god." Brianne caught up and retched into the leaves behind me.

"I'm going to pull it from this direction, okay?" I gripped the longer end of the spike. "Just hold still."

"Fuck! I don't think I can do this." Gavin clutched my hand.

I put my gloved palms on his cheeks and stared into his amber eyes, now awash with pain. "We can do this. I've got your back."

He nodded, sweat running down his face.

I bent over him and gripped the underside of the shoot again. "On three."

He took a deep breath.

"One, two—" I ripped it free in one smooth jerk.

Gavin's scream pierced my ears, leaving them ringing long after the air was gone from his lungs.

He lay back and pulled his knee to his chest, his hands clutching at the punctured leg. I fought back my tears and glanced to the lightening sky.

"Here." I ripped the thin edge of my dress, tearing off a long strip. Wrapping it around Gavin's wound, I pulled it tight to try and stem the flow of blood. He grunted as I tied it off.

"Brianne, help me get him up."

She sat on the stony ground, her chest heaving and her hands clapped over her ears.

"Brianne!" I took her forearms and shook her. "Snap the fuck out of it."

"I can't." She shook her head and her tone was reminiscent of a tired child.

The moon was gone, time running away from us just as we ran from our hunters. Bitterness welled in my stomach, then a seething hatred. I wasn't angry at Brianne, but I needed her to function. I grabbed her hair where it flowed from beneath her cap and ripped her to her feet. She screamed. I didn't care.

"Stella—" She protested.

I shook her again, this time by her hair, putting every ounce of nastiness into it that I could. "Shut the fuck up and help Gavin."

Her lip trembled, but when I released her, she didn't fall. Instead, she knelt next to Gavin. I took his other side and we lifted him.

"Can you walk?" I asked.

"It hurts, but I think everything still works." He grunted. After a few steps, he was able to walk on his own with a pronounced limp. Our pace slowed to a crawl, but we keep plodding through the never-ending trees.

My legs burned, the pain in my arm now a dull throbbing ache. My cheeks were wind-chapped and stinging. And, above all, I was cold. The sort of cold that nothing short of a soak in a hot bath or a long shower could alleviate. It was in my bones.

We trekked and trekked before coming to another shallow ravine crossing up the hill in the direction we were going.

Gavin and I turned and started heading up the slope when Brianne collapsed behind us.

We rushed back to her. Her chest heaved, big white plumes of her breath floating in the air.

"You okay?" I asked. I yanked a glove off and smoothed her hair from her face. Her skin was cold and clammy. Had I pushed her too hard?

"No. I can't. I can't go on."

"You can." I wrapped my arms around her chest and lifted. "Get up."

She remained limp, every last bit of fight expended. "No, I can't. I'm tired. I'm too tired. Leave me." Her voice was weak.

I glanced up to Gavin. "What are we going to do?" I didn't want to face the truth. "We have to take her with us."

He leaned against a tree. "I would carry her, but I can't. I just can't." He gestured to the crimson stain on his pant leg.

"Just go. Please. It's all right. I knew what would happen. I knew." She closed her eyes as I kept my palm on her cheek. Her words came in shuddering breaths. "You did all you could. It's okay. I was never going to make it."

The knowledge that I couldn't save her ate at me like acid. She put her hand over mine and leaned into my touch, her eyes closed.

"I'm sorry." I choked down my sob.

"You did all you could." Her voice stuck in her throat, but she shed no more tears. She peered at me, her light eyes unfocused. "Run."

I scanned the hollow for any sort of camouflage, something to at least give her a chance. A fallen branch caught my eye. Several limbs sprouted from it, and the crisp leaves were still attached in places.

"Gavin, if we can get her to that limb, maybe we can hide her under it and cover her with leaves to keep her warm."

He stared up the hill. "That'll take time. Sunrise is soon."

"I know. But we have to. We can't just leave her."

He wiped a hand down his sweaty face. "You're right. I'm sorry. You're right."

I pulled my glove back on and dragged her to her feet. We made it to the fallen limb, and she climbed under the branches. I gathered up armfuls of leaves from a little farther up the slope and piled them around where she lay curled up. Gavin helped as best he could, and after a while, she was completely hidden. I got on my hands and knees and spread the leaves out around where we'd taken them to hide the disturbance.

The sky was brightening, the sun threatening. The hunt would begin soon.

I clambered back up from my aching knees. "Okay, Brianne. Just stay there until the sun is high. It'll be okay."

"Thank you." Brianne whispered her absolution, though I would never forgive myself for leaving her behind.

"Let's go." Gavin started ahead of me, using saplings to help pull himself up the steep incline. He groaned with each heavy step on his injured leg, but he kept moving.

I turned and followed, using the same sapling technique.

When we got to the top of the ridge, my legs shook, fatigue settling into my deepest parts.

"What's that?" Gavin pointed down into the next valley. Smoke rose through the darkness, floating along the tops of the skeletal trees. It must have been a cabin of some sort.

"I don't know, but it's probably another trap."

"A warm trap." His gaze lingered on the plume of smoke.

The smell of wood burning floated in the air, and I had never smelled anything more wonderful. I forced myself to scan farther down the ridge, away from the toasty lure of a roof and a fire.

"Come on." I trudged away from the beckoning cabin, toward the west and the dark azure sky.

Gavin fell in behind me, his injured leg crashing heavily with each step. We stuck to the crest of the ridge until it started sloping down into a ravine with hollows running up either side.

The sun peaked over the farthest ridge I could see, and a gunshot cracked in the distance.

Gavin gripped my gloved hand and squeezed. "This is it."

"I know." I leaned into him and we just stood together for a moment.

"We'll be alive, Stella. On the other side of this, we'll still be alive." His voice shook.

"My heart will still beat. I'll still draw breath, but I don't know if I'll still feel alive." My words flattened in the air and sank to our feet as we began to pick our way down the embankment.

Once we reached the relatively flat bottom of the ravine, we were able to pick up more speed. Maybe it was our second wind, or maybe fear fired our nerves and muscles to push harder. We continued a slow trot. Gavin favored his bad leg, but powered through all the same. Several hollows fell away as we continued deeper into the gorge. My heartbeat thundered in my ears until a buzzing noise cut through the rapid thump.

Gavin hauled me sideways until we hid against one of the large rock outcrops that dotted the forest. A square drone flew by, its four helicopter blades whirring as it eased down the ravine. The machine passed us by, then hovered for a moment. I held my breath and closed my eyes. I was in Cuba beneath the pool's surface again, the vines snaking around my ankles and holding me under.

The noise of blades cutting through the air increased, and Gavin pressed my fingers until I lost sensation. Then the sound retreated and the drone kept going, the morning light reflecting off its metal surface as it purred away in the lessening gloom.

"Did it see us?" I whispered.

"I don't know. I don't think so."

We stayed put until we were sure the drone was gone, and then took off again, running faster even though we were drained. Gavin's limp grew worse. The terrain turned rocky again, the sides closing in as the slopes became more treacherous and the hollows petered out. Over stones and up steep hills, we climbed and descended, hopped streams and ducked under fallen trees.

Every muscle in my body was on fire, but I forced myself forward. I wouldn't sit and wait for them. They would have to come get me.

The ravine ended in a wide open grassy plot. A hunting blind stood at one end of it, and some deer were munching in the field. As soon as we burst from the trees, they scattered, silently disappearing back into the woods. The sun had risen higher than I'd thought. We'd spent at least an hour in the ravine. What time was it? Nine, ten?

For the first time since we started running, I entertained the hope that we could make it. That we could get far enough away to where they'd never catch us. The stale, dead grass grew waist high as we picked up speed on the open terrain. We jetted across, the faded trees at the edge of the grass becoming an oasis in the desert. If we could just make it through the field and into the woods on the other side, we could outwit Cal, outwit them all. It was like turning a page. Gavin must have felt it too, his feet thundering unevenly on the dirt as we pushed ourselves as fast as we could.

Then we heard the buzz, the familiar whir of flight.

The drone had come back.

"Down," Gavin hissed.

We both dropped, lying in the grass and hoping the drone hadn't seen us. I held my breath as the sound grew closer, the hiss of the helicopter blades like a hand at my throat, cutting off my air.

The drone passed overhead and I could breathe again. The whir lessened, and I was about to get up when the noise grew louder and louder until horror atrophied my senses. I turned my head to the side and it was hovering over us, sitting in place. They'd seen.

"Fuck. Run, Stella!" Gavin lunged from the ground and took off.

I pushed my aching muscles, the stiffness already setting in even though I'd only been still for a few moments. I dashed after him as the machine lazily followed.

We finally made the tree line.

Gavin crashed ahead. Limbs scratched my face like clawing fingers as I tried to keep up.

The machine whirred above us now, floating above the trees and keeping track. Gavin stopped so quickly in front of me that I slammed into his back.

"What?"

"We have to split up." He ran a hand through his sweat-drenched hair.

"No." I peered up through the branches. I could feel the drone staring back.

"We have to. It can't follow us both. It's our only chance."

"No. I can't. I've got your back, remember?"

His eyes softened, and he ran a cool hand across my cheek. "I know you do. We'll still be alive. Remember that, okay? I'll see you again."

"Here." I shucked his gloves off and handed them back to him. "My hands are warm. You need them."

He tried to refuse but I shoved them into his palms.

"Please."

"Fine." He pulled them on and hugged me tightly before glancing sideways at the woods around us. "Left or right?"

It didn't matter. "I'll go left."

"Okay." He kissed my forehead, his lips like ice. "Go."

He limped to the right, and I hopped the fallen tree trunk to my left, skittering across the leaves and rushing between the trees. I stood at the base of a gentle slope. Turning back, I caught a flash of Gavin's white pants before he was lost in the browns and grays of the woods. The rumble of engines cut over the sound of the drone, some sort of off-road vehicles moving far faster than I could ever hope to. I balled my hands into fists and forced myself to move, fear and rage mixing to give me one final jolt of energy.

I kept going, slower now, the pain in my body, the lack of food, and the constant exertion killing what little physical ability I had left. The sun still rose, the minutes ticking off the clock. The whir of the drone never stopped. It had chosen to follow me instead of Gavin. I couldn't do anything about it, just keep moving, keep striving.

When I reached the top of the slope, I stopped to catch my breath. I felt heavy, heavier than I'd ever felt in my life. My dress was drenched with sweat, and my legs were an ugly shade of red. The wind and cold had burned them. My face was tight, the skin stinging as my silent tears flowed down over them. The sun continued its climb, but I still had at least an hour before noon.

"Stella!" A man yelled out in a perfect mimic of Marlon Brando from "Streetcar," followed by howls of laughter from others. It was distant, but not distant enough. The yawning pit in my stomach opened even wider, dragging me down.

I pushed my legs into motion, ignoring the wave of nausea and aching hurt. My feet were blistered, and my socks dug into the swollen skin. Even so, I hobbled away from my pursuers. The drone flew toward my right, toward Gavin. It had abandoned me. Why? Was I as good as caught?

I tripped halfway down the slope and tumbled into the wet leaves and over a rock before skidding to a stop against a tree. My leg was bleeding. Still, I picked myself back up and kept going.

More yells, this time "Gavin" and "Brianne" added in. They must not have found her yet. I smiled, my chapped lip splitting as I did so. Maybe she would make it.

The sound of an engine grew louder and then died. Voices. They were close.

I stumbled and wrapped my arms around the nearest tree, catching myself before falling again. I retrieved the knife from my pocket, ripping the tape off as I lurched forward. No matter what happened, I would fight. The consequences be damned.

A desperate yell met my ears and then was quickly cut off. Gavin. They had him. I wiped the back of my hand across my face, erasing the tears as I put one foot in front of the other.

I was almost to the bottom of the hill when I glimpsed movement in the trees ahead of me. I stopped, but the multiple voices at the ridge to my back had me moving again. I prayed a deer was in front of me, running from the hunters just like me. I would have laughed at the absurdity of hope, but I didn't have the energy.

My steps lingered, my feet leaden and my limbs spent. I tripped over a root and caught myself, my hands on my knees as I raised my head and peered through the shadowy trees. More movement. A man strode right toward me. The hair on the back of my neck stood up and I rose, scurrying back the way I'd come. The man's steps didn't falter. He was large and not the least bit winded. He wore the same white mask as the others, the rest of him covered in camouflage.

Blood roared in my ears as I scrambled back up the

slope, back toward the grasp of the others. In the open woods, the sun filtering down in orange rays, I was caged. The crackle of leaves and heavy footsteps behind me spurred me faster. I didn't turn around, only pushed my legs harder. The steps picked up their pace, the thuds growing louder. A scream built in my throat. I turned to face him.

He was only yards away, his large arms swinging as he advanced, my destruction balled into the palms of his hands. I froze. There was nowhere to go, no one to save me. Caught. I held my knife at my side. I wouldn't go down without a fight.

He slowed when he was but steps away, then stopped and stared. His white mask obscured everything but his mouth and eyes. He took another step.

I held the blade out in front of me.

He smiled and shook his head calmly. "Stella."

I peered into his eyes. I knew them. "Dylan?"

"I told you I'd take care of you."

"Oh my god." My knees buckled, and he rushed to me, taking me in his arms before I sank to the ground. The knife tumbled from my hand and landed in the leaves at my feet. "It's you."

"It's me." He pulled me to his warm chest.

Hope exploded in my heart. "Oh my god." I wrapped my arms around his neck and buried my face in his shoulder. I had never felt so grateful in my life. I was blinded by it. "Thank you. Oh my god! It's you."

"It's me. Calm down. Shh." He moved his hands up and down my back as I clung to him.

"But how?"

"I may have gotten a head start." He smirked and cocked his ear toward the sound of male voices along the ridge at my back.

I glanced behind me, but they were still out of sight. "We have to go."

"Don't worry. I won't share you. It'll be nice to have an

audience, though."

I pulled my hands away from his neck as his words slithered around in my mind. "Audience?"

"For the big show." His hands ventured lower and gripped my ass.

"Dylan." I tried to back out of his grasp, but he squeezed me to him. "What—"

He crushed his mouth to mine, his tongue stabbing at my lips. Ice trickled down my spine.

I pushed as hard as I could. "Dylan, no!"

"Shut the fuck up." He pushed his fingers between my ass cheeks, only the thin dress separating us.

Panic rose in me, twisting like a tornado, until I was biting and scratching wherever I could find purchase.

He threw me back and ran his fingers along a deep scratch in his neck. "You fucking bitch."

I darted past him and took a few long strides down the slope. His thudding steps were at my back in moments.

"Gotcha!" Dylan tackled me to the ground. We slid through the rotting leaves and careened to the base of the hill.

We rolled a few more times until I landed on top of him and tried to scramble off, but he gripped my throat and slammed me onto the ground before climbing on top of me.

"No!" I fought, scratching at his wrists, his neck.

He batted my hands away and unzipped my jacket. Then his warm hands were on my thighs, hiking up my dress.

"Dylan, please stop. What are you doing?" I let go of his neck and pushed at his shoulders, as if that simple movement would snap him out of whatever dark daydream had taken hold in his breast.

"What I have to do." His light brown eyes, the same ones I'd trusted, shown through the mask.

"No. You don't." My mind tumbled, the thoughts not connecting. I squirmed and tried to get out from beneath him. "Stop."

"I do. This is what you need. What I need. Mom was right. I need to stop having a fucking schoolboy crush." He squeezed my throat and reached between us with his other hand.

"Dylan, no. You aren't one of them." I could barely push the words past his palm at my neck.

"No, Stella. You aren't one of *us*." I felt his hard tip pushing against my thigh.

He gripped my breast so roughly it hurt, and a strangled scream burst from my lungs. I thrashed, fighting with all I had left, but he was too big, too strong. I didn't have a chance even at full strength. He reared back and slapped me, dimming my vision. My body stilled for a moment at the force of the hit.

"That's better." He squeezed my throat as my eyes watered. "One fuck when we were kids?" He shook his head. "God, I was such a fucking pussy. I should have taken all of this a long time ago. Every time I stood over you as you slept. Every time your dad left the house and I jerked off as I watched you shower. I should have fucked you like you deserved. Like the little cunt you are. But I didn't, because I was trying to be something I'm not."

"Please don't, Dylan. Please." I cried, my tears flowing in a never-ending river as I hit and kicked at him to no avail.

He leaned closer, his eyes boring into mine. "But I'm going to make up for it now. I'm going to show you what a filthy whore you are. And I can't wait until I get you back to the house so everyone can see how I treat cunts like you, especially Lucius. I want him to watch while I fuck you until you pass out from the pain."

The rough stones dug into my back and the smell of peat and earth sank into my pores as he crushed me. "Please."

"I like you this way." He smirked down at me as his cock pressed closer to my entrance. My skin screamed as his palm tightened at my throat, his fingertips digging into the back of my neck. His hot mouth was at my collarbone, and I thought I might vomit.

"Stop!" I screamed.

And then his weight was gone.

Another masked man stood over him, a pistol in his hand, butt out. Dylan had gone completely limp next to me. I skittered back, kicking at the leaves as the man advanced, his steps sure and steady.

"Please, don't." My progress stopped as I backed into a tree trunk and I put out a shaking hand. "Please, I'm begging you. Please, I won't survive. I can't survive it."

"Stella. It's me." He gripped my hand and pulled me up.

"Sin?" I couldn't trust my senses anymore. I glanced at Dylan's prone form and then quickly back to the man. I couldn't trust anyone.

He lifted the mask. It was him.

I wanted his warmth, his strength. I couldn't move.

He yanked the mask back down over his face.

"Are you going to do it?" I stared into his eyes, the tempestuous blue so familiar, the man behind them so strange.

His eyes narrowed, as if I'd hurt him. He stepped toward me, but I had nowhere to go. My stomach twisted in a knot as he glared down at me. Then he bent over and threw me over his shoulder.

"Play along or we're both dead. Got it?"

I didn't say anything. I didn't even know what he meant. The blood rushed to my head and my vision swam.

He slapped my ass, the sting worse because of the cold. "Got it?"

"Yes."

I heard shouts at the top of the ridge. More men coming for me.

He kicked a break of leaves down on top of Dylan and lumbered up the slope, me swinging limply at his back. "I raped you. You hate me. I'm going to take you back to the house and rape you some more. Oh, and I'm Lucius. All that clear?"

"Yes."

"Good." He hefted me higher on his shoulder, my ribs pressed against his back. "The hate part should be easy enough."

"Wait, my knife!" I scanned around the area where Dylan had first found me. There was a slight glint in the leaves. "There it is!"

"What knife?"

"Please, I need it. It's right behind you."

"Dammit, Stella." He whirled and knelt before standing back up, lifting my weight easily. "I got it. Hang on. This is actually a stroke of luck." He made a fast movement and then his left hand was all over my ass.

"What—"

"It's done." He growled. "Now, shut up. Or cry. Either would work."

The voices got louder. "Fuck, someone already got her."

"Shit!" A younger man's voice. "Hey man, you sharing?"

"No, I already bottomed her out anyway. Now I'm going to take her back and rip the fuck out of her ass."

"Which one is that?"

"Stella."

"Goddammit. That one was my favorite."

As if I were a toy and he could collect them all. Rage rose in my worn-out body, but I stayed silent. I would do whatever it took to get out of here.

"Son, there's still one more. Come on. Let's keep hunting." An older man's voice, his antique drawl right out of the antebellum South. "But I am curious. Who is the lucky hunter?"

"Lucius," Vinemont called, his steps slow and steady up the hill.

The old man cawed out a laugh. "Well I'll be damned. The Vinemont boy caught his own goddamn Acquisition and took the cherry. Good work, my boy. Cal will definitely be impressed with that. Did she cry?"

"Of course she did. She's weak. Begged, pleaded, and screamed when I shoved it in. Fucking bitch didn't know when to shut up. I had to cover her mouth, and you know I hate that. I prefer it when they scream."

"As do I. As do I. Come on, Brent, let's get back to business. This little chat has my blood up. I'm going to tell Cal about your performance, Lucius."

Vinemont shifted, and I felt him shaking hands with the stranger. "You do that. Sovereign would look pretty damn good in front of my name."

Another laugh from the older man.

"You sure you're not sharing?" The other one—Brent—spoke, and a hand ran up my leg and gripped my ass.

"I'm sure. This cunt is just sweet enough for me. Go find your own, boys. Better luck next time. But if you catch Brianne, I might just trade up."

The man squeezed harder, and I cried out.

"Sounds good to me. We'll take you up on that when we find her." The hand released me.

"Good hunting."

"Congratulations again, Lucius. Keep up the good work." The older man said, his voice farther away now, and mixed with the sound of crunching leaves.

"Yes sir."

CHAPTER FIFTEEN
Sinclair

I WALKED PAST the dozens of congratulations and offers to fuck Stella. The house was abuzz with a Vinemont victory. I nodded and waved, smiled at them all as I still carried her slung over my shoulder like the spoils of war.

"Take the mask off. Let's see you." One of the older ladies crowed as I stomped up the stairs to Lucius' suite.

"No can do, ma'am. The mask makes her scream almost as much as the rest of me."

She laughed and smacked Stella on the ass. "Get her."

Once past the crone, I had one more set of stairs to ascend before she'd be safe.

"Caught your own girl?" Red leaned against the railing. From where he stood, he'd seen me from the moment I walked in with her over my shoulder.

I gave a curt nod. I wasn't sure if he'd recognize my voice. His gaze shifted to Stella, to the blood from my palm I'd smeared on her.

"Looks like you put it to her the way she deserves." He slid his hand up her leg and she tried to kick him. He dodged but backed up a step, still eyeing her. "I sure would like a little taste."

I shook my head. "Not sharing," I said as quickly as possible.

His eyes widened for a split second. Did he know who I was? I wasn't going to wait to find out. I walked past and felt Stella's hand pressing on my lower back. I glanced over my shoulder to see her pushing up from me so she could give Red the finger.

He gripped his crotch in response. "Next time, bitch."

I continued toward the suite, passing an open door on my right. I glanced in. Gavin was there, his hands tied behind his back and a gag in his mouth as Judge Montagnet rutted on him like a boar. *Fucking animals.* I glanced away from Gavin's mournful eyes. I had enough pain without sharing his. Stella swung hard against my back as I turned so she wouldn't glimpse her friend.

The rest of the way was smooth sailing to Lucius' room. I kicked the door, and he swung it open before shutting it tight behind us and propping a chair under the handle.

"Did you get to her first?"

"Mostly." I hurried through the main room and into the bedroom, setting her down on the bed and kneeling in front of her.

Her lip was split, her cheeks and forehead wind burned. There was a cut on her leg. She was dirty, with black dirt under her fingernails and smudges on her face. The urge to kill everyone who'd hurt her, chased her, tried to violate her rose up inside me and threatened to block out any rational thought.

She reached out with a trembling hand and stripped off my mask, tears welling in her eyes and spilling down her cheeks. "You came for me."

"I told you I always would."

"Jesus." Lucius kicked an accent table, breaking the leg off.

Usually, I would have scolded him for the outburst, but

for this the noise was necessary, desired even. Everyone needed to believe Lucius was rough fucking her while she cried. The more brutal, the better.

"Get the first aid stuff I brought."

Lucius unzipped a case and yanked out some of my clothes and other items, including a bag full of medical supplies. He handed it over to me. "If that's all you need, I'm going into the other room."

"Go ahead. Make plenty of noise."

"Not a fucking problem." He slammed the bedroom door, cranked up the sound system with some angry metal, and then there were a series of crashes.

"Stella, I'll need you to scream for me. Can you do that?"

She nodded as I moved the pads of my thumbs over her cheeks, wiping away the tears. A shallow cut ran along my palm. I'd used her knife on myself and smeared the blood on the bottom of her dress, made it even more believable as I'd carried her around like a trophy.

"Go ahead. Scream."

She let out a peel of shrieks, her body quaking from the effort.

"Okay, that's good for now."

She stopped and shivered, shaking uncontrollably, her teeth chattering. She needed heat.

A scream sounded from somewhere else in the building. They must have found Brianne.

"No." Stella's faced crumpled and she covered it with her hands. "No. I hid her. I hid her."

"It's not your fault." It was mine. I'd seen Brianne's hiding spot when I'd first set out for Stella. I'd radioed back to another party that something appeared odd at that break in the forest and intentionally used an open channel so everyone heard. The ensuing search for Brianne bought more time for me to find Stella first. But I'd still failed. I could only hope that Dylan would keep his mouth shut about what happened. He'd turned out to be more intelligent than I'd originally thought, and definitely more devious. I might have even liked him if he weren't trying to take what was mine.

I gently pulled her wrists away, the coldness of her skin shocking me into action. I rose and went to the bathroom, finding a whirlpool tub with a forest mosaic of tiles surrounding it. I turned on the water and adjusted it until it was just north of lukewarm. Once the bath was running at the right temperature, I went back to her. She sat unmoved, fear and sadness painting her face, turning her eyes into sad emerald pools.

"Come on." I helped her up, but she groaned as she stood and fell back. "What is it?"

"Everything, but mostly my feet." She bent over and tried to unzip her boots, but her fingers couldn't grasp the tabs. I eased her hands away and slid the zipper down on each one.

Her legs were burned like her face, and I was as careful as I could be. I pulled the first boot off. Her sock was bloody, and she cried out as I stripped it from her foot. Blisters had risen and burst all along her feet and ankles.

"Shit." The bath would sting like hell, but I need to clean all her wounds. "Just hang on to my shoulders, okay? You can hurt me all you want. I don't care. Just hold on to me."

She grabbed me as I pulled the second boot away, her nails digging into my thermal shirt and the skin underneath. When I peeled the sock off, she let out a strangled scream, and I heard something break on the other side of the suite door.

"I got it. I got you." I looked up at her. The pain in her eyes tore me apart. I wanted nothing more than to stop her hurt.

I eased my hands to her shoulders, keeping it slow as I pushed her jacket off. Underneath was nothing more than a paltry white shift, the bottom hem ripped away. I clenched my jaw at the thought of her out in the woods, frightened, and wearing nothing more than a thin nightgown. Cal was a sadistic piece of shit.

I gripped the muddied hem. "I have to take this off."

She shivered more and placed her hands over mine. "Don't."

"It's dirty, Stella. The bath is going to be nice and warm." I moved my hands up the slightest bit, lifting the skirt up her thighs. "It's okay. Here, just guide my hands."

I kept my grip on the nightie at her upper thigh until she pulled. I lifted it higher, almost to the apex of her thighs when she pushed against me and I stopped.

"I'm not going to prey on you, Stella. I just want to help." I knew my words sounded hollow to her after everything I'd done, but I held her gaze and tried to make her believe them.

She hesitated, then pulled more. I raised the shift higher and stood, drawing it from her arms and tossing it in the floor. An ugly bruise—purple edged with yellow and green—covered a large part of her forearm.

"What happened there?"

"A woman. She hit me." Stella blinked down at the injury. "Before we ran."

I made a mental note to find out who it was and punish the bitch accordingly. "I'm going to lift you and take you to the bath."

I bent over slowly, treating her like I would a skittish horse that was too afraid to be treated. I slid my hands under her knees and across her upper back.

She made a noise and bit her lip. "It hurts."

"I know." I carried her to the bath and lowered her into the tub.

Her face twisted in a mix of relief and pain as the water rushed up to meet her. Once she was in, I turned off the water and stripped off my wet shirt, tossing it out the door in the same heap with her dress.

She glanced up, taking in my chest and stomach before she closed her eyes and leaned her head back.

I sat on the edge of the tub, my gaze tracing the curves of her body beneath the water. I'd tried not to look when she was on the bed, but my cock was hard all the same. Because I was a bastard.

The water trembled as she shivered, the heat not seeping into her fast enough. Her hair floated around her shoulders, the red strands delicate against her pale skin and the white of the tub.

She shifted and groaned, but her teeth no longer chattered, and some color was returning to the parts of her skin that weren't chapped.

"You can't stay in here long. Hot water isn't the best for the blisters."

"Just let me sit for a little while longer." Her eyes didn't open, and her voice had a distant quality, relaxed and sleepy.

I went to the vanity and dug around in the cabinets, finding towels, shampoo, wash cloths, and soaps. I grabbed a bar, smelled it, tossed it, and then picked another. This one was more on point, sweet without being overpowering.

I sat on the edge of the tub again and dipped the cloth in the water before using the soap to lather it up. Stella's head lolled to the side as her breathing smoothed into a steady rhythm. Something warmed inside me at the thought that she felt safe enough to fall asleep in my presence. That, or she'd simply been pushed beyond exhausted.

I put my arm down in the tub and gingerly lifted her leg. The blisters were clean from the water, but still an angry red, with deflated skin around the wounds. They would hurt for a while. Good news was I had something in the first aid kit for it. Bad news was I didn't think Stella would willingly let me drug her. Not that it mattered. I would do it either way to help her through this mess.

I soaped up her foot and she woke, sucking in a pained breath.

"I'm done. I'm done." I moved up her calf and massaged as I cleaned.

She moaned.

"This okay?"

"Yes. Don't stop." Her throaty whisper had my cock straining against my pants, but I ignored it.

I continued working my fingers into her muscles, and her mouth opened. She was panting as I got to her thigh and massaged out the knots there. When I neared her pussy, I forced myself to stop and place her leg back on the bottom of the tub. Then I lifted the other one and did the same.

By the time I was done, she watched me with half lidded eyes. I had the impulse to jump in the tub with her and sink between her thighs. Instead, I dutifully soaped the washcloth again and worked up another good lather. I gently scrubbed her face, her delicate neck, graceful shoulders, and arms. The bruise seemed even uglier now that the rest of her was clean.

I soaped her chest and ran the washcloth along her pert breasts, the nipples hard and begging for attention. I swiped lower, cleaning her before putting a hand behind her back and leaning her forward. I rested her upper chest on my palm as I washed her back. She was like dough in my hands, soft and pliable. Vulnerable.

I leaned her back and poured water in her hair. I shampooed her scalp, the first time in my life I'd ever done such a thing. Her neck bore ugly bruises from Dylan's hands. Anger coiled in my stomach like a snake waiting to strike, but I shut it down and concentrated on Stella. Once I rinsed the suds from her hair and she was clean, I hit the drain.

"No." Her protest was weak.

I gripped under her arms and lifted her until she stood, the water sluicing down her body. She was more than I could take, so beautiful that it hurt. I wrapped a towel around her and scooped her up again before carrying her back to the bedroom. The king size bed with the black comforter swallowed her whole.

I inspected her feet. They were still in a bad way and needed antibacterial ointment and bandages. Her eyes were closed, her wet hair fanning out against the pillow. I would kill two birds with one stone. I got the first aid items and laid out alcohol, ointment, gauze, tape, and one final thing—a syringe.

"Stella? This is going to hurt."

She murmured something unintelligible. With the syringe in one hand, I dabbed alcohol onto a blister with the other. She awoke on a scream, the sound raising the hair on the back of my neck. It was perfect.

I gripped her arm hard and kept it still as I slid the needle into her vein and depressed the plunger. She looked at me, lightly shaking her head as one tear fell. Then she was out. Hitting a vein on a struggling woman was one of my specialties, thanks to my mother.

Another crash from the living quarters. This time it sounded like Lucius had ripped the flat screen off the wall.

I took my time with her, cleaning every blister, every scratch. An hour later, she was bandaged and sleeping comfortably. I undressed and took a quick shower, though I hated letting her out of my sight. Lucius would guard us, not that I expected any guests. I'd made clear that Stella was mine and that I wasn't sharing. Or, that Lucius wasn't sharing, as they thought.

I was still amazed that he'd called me last night. That he'd given up and wanted to transfer her back to me. It didn't work that way, of course. He never gave me a reason why, though I suspected the rules had something to do with it. And when he'd explained this particular trial to me, I knew I had to get to Stella first. To be the one who took her or saved her, as the case may be.

I hated myself for knowing that I would have done it if I'd had to. If someone had been watching, I would have committed the act. I had no choice. It was the only way to keep her safe from the others, and the only way to win the Acquisition. Would she have ever forgiven me? I shook my head, not wanting to consider that alternate outcome.

She rested peacefully, her chest rising and falling, and every so often a sweet sigh escaped her lips as if she were in a pleasant dream. The drugs wouldn't wear off for a few hours. I dug through my bag, pulled on some boxers, and picked out some panties and pajamas for her. I slipped the towel away from her body and my cock was rock hard in an instant. I slid a pair of panties up her legs, careful to avoid the bandages, followed by a pair of shorts. Once I pulled her top over her head and threaded her arms through it, I pulled the sheet down and lay down beside her.

I couldn't look away. She was the only thing I'd seen for months. Even when she wasn't in my presence, I saw her. More than that, I felt her. She'd taken up residence inside me. I shifted closer, her body so near mine that I could feel her heat. It was a comfort. I watched over her. I was here, with her, and she was safe.

CHAPTER SIXTEEN
Stella

I WOKE WITH one thought. *He saved me.* I was warm, with my head on his chest and his arm around my shoulders. He was everywhere—his scent, his body, him. I stretched against him and my muscles ached. My feet stung, and my arm felt as if it were broken. The morning came back in a rush, and I sat straight up despite the pain.

Vinemont sat up with me and scanned the room before turning his gaze back to me.

Dusk had fallen outside. How long had I been here?

"You drugged me." I felt along my arm where the needle had gone in.

"You needed it."

"Maybe, but you can't just drug me!"

"It won't happen again." He smirked, the signature twist of his lips familiar enough to be comforting. "It won't happen again unless you are in extreme pain and by drugging you, I am easing that pain."

"Is this the shit they taught you in law school? Because it doesn't work."

"It does work." The smirk grew. "Just not on you."

"The others?" Gavin's yell played in my mind, joined

by Brianne's scream. My heart sank.

"I haven't heard a peep for an hour or so. I think they've finally been given a reprieve."

His nonchalance was like a slap in the face. I tried to scoot toward the end of the bed and stand, but the movement made my body scream. My left thigh cramped, and I rolled onto my side, gripping it. The tightness ramped up, like my muscle was being twisted around a corkscrew, and I gritted my teeth through the ache. Vinemont got on his knees, his strong hands rubbing the muscle hard until the pain subsided.

"I'm okay. It's gone now." I flipped to my back, and he fell next to me on his elbow. I met his eyes. "Just don't talk about them like that. They're people. It could have been me." I remembered Dylan, what he'd tried to do, and I put a hand to my throat. "It almost was me."

"Don't think about it." He slid his arm under my neck and pulled me into him. "I'm sorry. Just don't think about it."

"Did you just say sorry?"

He let out a low laugh, his Adam's apple bobbing. "Maybe."

"You did. I'm not falling for this again." I moved my head back so I could see into his eyes, and perhaps even deeper. "I know you're going to turn back into Mr. Hyde tomorrow."

"Likely." He clutched me to him, his fingers splayed across my back.

"Why can't you be like this all the time?"

"Because I can't."

"But why?" I wouldn't let him get away, not this time. I pushed back from him again so I could see his eyes, and I rested my palm on his cheek. "What changes?"

His eyes softened the slightest bit as he considered me, and he was here. The man I knew he could be. Not the vile monster he so often was. My heart burned to know why. But just as soon as the softness came, it was gone again.

"I remember my obligations." He rolled away and sat up before running both hands through his hair. "I won't discuss it further."

I lay back, shut out again like I had been so many times before. What wouldn't he tell me? What was the game within the game? Something more was happening. Something just beyond the periphery that I couldn't see.

"I need you to do something for me." He looked back over his shoulder.

"What?"

"I need you to tell Cal that you want to transfer your ownership back to me."

"Why?"

"I'll explain later. But you need to do it today. Will you?"

"Shouldn't we talk to Lucius?"

"No. It's already been decided between the two of us. Now it's up to you." He turned to face me, the late afternoon sun shining over his shoulder. "Will you be mine again?"

It was a twisted proposal, one that should have come with a ring and love. Instead, it came with a lock and key.

"It doesn't really matter who owns me, does it? It just matters that I'm owned." I sighed. "Fine. I'll tell him."

"Good. Now that that's settled, let's get the fuck out of here as soon as possible." He rose, the chiseled planes of his body on full display. Desire rushed through me like a wildfire. I intentionally pressed my foot into the bed for the sting of pain to cut off my need for him. It didn't work. The sting only heightened my arousal, the pressure between my thighs growing.

He contemplated me, his eyes locked on mine. I didn't have to look down to know he was hard, to know he wanted me.

I wanted him, too. But could I deal with the consequences? When he threatened me and hurt me again the next day, would I hate myself? I knew the answer and turned away, breaking the moment, severing the tie.

Vinemont helped me down the stairs with Lucius following a few steps behind. It seemed more believable since Lucius was my supposed rapist.

Cal was glad-handing guests as they left.

"That was one hell of a party." Judge Montagnet was ahead of us, grinning and patting Cal on the shoulder. "That boy Gavin, whew!"

"Glad you enjoyed him. I enjoyed watching, I can tell you that."

"Can't wait to see what spring holds."

Spring. My stomach churned at the thought of what happened to Gavin and the trials that remained.

"You're going to love it." Cal smiled as the judge made his way out into the falling night.

Cal's smile fell away as I hobbled up on Vinemont's arm. "I heard we had an unannounced guest."

"My apologies, Sovereign." Vinemont hefted me closer into his side, and I kept my eyes downcast.

"Lucius, my man." Cal beamed and patted the younger Vinemont on the back. "I heard quite a story from Senator Calgary about how you bagged Stella here."

"All true." Lucius shook Cal's hand, but I still didn't raise my eyes.

"Maybe you finally broke this little filly. Stella, look at me, darling. Let me see those gorgeous green eyes."

I shook my head.

"Do it." Cal's voice was instantly cold.

I raised my head slowly. He peered at me, his watchful eyes studying every inch of me.

"Oh, I don't know. I think I see some spirit left." He

grinned. "All the more fun for the next trial."

Vinemont cleared his throat. "About that, Cal. Stella has something she wants to say."

"And what's that, little Stella?"

I looked to Vinemont who gave me a small nod. "I want to go back to Sinclair."

Cal chuckled and glanced to the juncture of my thighs. "Was Lucius too rough on you?"

I dropped my gaze again.

"Do you even want her back, now that she's all used up, Sinclair?" Cal crossed his arms over his chest.

"Not particularly, but if Lucius has to spend all his time in Cuba fighting off threats from other families, sacrifices must be made."

"The Eagletons trying to cozy up to the regime again?" Cal asked, his tone conspiratorial.

"Not sure just yet," Lucius said.

"Well, the Acquisition does get to choose between first and second born." Cal tapped his chin. "I don't think we've ever had one change hands twice, though. This will set an interesting precedent. But I'll allow it. Of course, Lucius' performance at this trial won't carry much weight in my final determination, but if this is what you want, Sinclair, then it's fine with me. Just keep it this way, is all I ask. More paperwork for me, you see?" Cal clapped his hands, signaling an end to the conversation.

Vinemont helped me hobble away.

Cal's voice called out behind us. "You better perform the best at the next two, Sinclair, or you may be in for some trouble."

Vinemont stiffened but kept moving. "Got it, Cal."

The open air enveloped us, and I was finally able to breathe. Vinemont gave up trying to help me along and swung me up in his arms as he took the stairs down.

Luke held the back passenger door open and Vinemont placed me inside before joining me.

Lucius leaned over in the window. "I've got a ride with,

um, Amanda over there. I'll catch you two later."

The woman we'd met on the way in the day before stood next to a sports car, watching Lucius like a lion eyeing a gazelle. And I sincerely doubted her name was Amanda.

Lucius didn't look at me, just gave a sarcastic salute to Vinemont before straightening.

"Don't stay gone too long," Vinemont said. "We've got business."

'Fuck off." Lucius strode away toward 'his ride'.

"Dick." Vinemont shook his head with a slight smile. "Luke, take us home."

"Yes sir." Luke pulled around the circular drive and followed the line of cars down the lane.

I yawned, fatigue still so deep in my bones that I wondered if I would ever feel at full energy again. I rested my head against the window, the coolness giving my chapped skin the slightest relief before the glass warmed. The trees hurried by, along with the now too familiar hollows and boulders. I hoped I'd never see these woods again.

I sat up and leaned my head back, not wanting to see anymore. The dark material of the car's roof was a much more palatable view. I closed my eyes, but opened them again immediately. Brianne's frightened face, streaked with dirt and scratched by branches, had appeared. I couldn't think about her, about Gavin. Not yet.

Vinemont shifted. I let my head loll sideways toward him. He'd stripped off his long wool overcoat. "Come here." Before I could move, he'd put one hand at my back, the other at my knees, and pulled me into him, laying me down so my head rested in his lap.

"What are you doing?"

He gazed down at me, his dark hair shading his forehead. It was longer than I'd ever seen it. And I knew it was soft, perhaps even softer than mine. He seemed older now. Or maybe I was the one who'd aged in the months since we'd met. He draped his coat over me, and I slid my feet toward the door. I wasn't going to fight it. I didn't have the strength.

One of his hands rested lightly on my waist, and the other trailed through my hair. "Sleep. I've got you. I know you're drained."

"I'm scared." I hated myself the moment I said it. Admitting things like that to him was like laying my neck bare and handing him a blade.

"I know." His fingers started at my scalp and smoothed another long lock of hair. He glanced up as we finally left the drive and entered the main road, his soft v-neck sweater falling right below his collarbones. His strong chin and jaw, along with the darker shadow on his cheeks, threw him in sharp relief. He was so beautiful. I moved my arm from under his coat and reached up, tracing my fingertips down his jaw and neck, feeling every little bit of stubble, every piece of sinew, every strong pulse of his blood.

He looked back down as I dropped my hand.

"Close your eyes."

I shook my head against him. Gavin and Brianne would be there, their bodies ruined, their hearts ripped apart.

"You're safe. I promise. And I always keep my word." He moved his hand from my waist and put his warm palm on my cheek. "Close them."

He ran his thumb over my lips lightly, the feeling more soothing than sexual.

Safe in his arms, I closed my eyes.

I didn't remember how I got to my bed, but I woke the next day to torrential rain. I glanced at the clock. It was already past noon. I lay still for a long time, letting my body slowly wake up, each sting of pain a reminder that I was alive, just like Gavin said I would be.

Gavin. I rolled to my side, the effort making the muscles in my legs try to seize. The hurt subdued me, and I focused on breathing through it. A tray was at my bedside with a sandwich, an apple, some chips, and a glass of tea. It looked like it hadn't been there long.

"Renee?" My voice was hoarse, but plenty loud enough.

I heard the creak of a floorboard and then heavy footfalls. Not Renee's. My door opened and Vinemont came into view. He flipped on the light. I closed my eyes against the sudden glare. The light flicked off again, and he strode to my window where he pulled back the curtains and let in the soft glow of sun through rain.

"Better?" His deep baritone washed over me.

"Yes, thank you."

He stood over me, inspecting my face before moving to the foot of the bed checking the bandages on my feet. Seemingly appeased, he returned to my side.

"You need to eat." He put his hands under my arms and pulled me into a sitting position before placing a pillow behind my back and resting me against it.

I ached all over, groaning even though he was gentle with me. Once I was settled, he drew the blanket back up and set the tray in my lap.

"Where's Renee?"

"Just eat. I'll have the doctor come in when you're done and fix you up proper." He opened the little bag of chips and placed it back in front of me.

"Will you just tell me if she's all right?" I placed my hand on his arm and wondered if the rest of him was as warm.

"Take a bite and I'll tell you if she's buried out back, okay?"

My eyes grew large, the loss too much for me to bear, but then I saw his mischievous look, the corners of his mouth turned up.

"Are you *teasing* me about killing Renee?"

"Maybe. Now take a big bite since you didn't do it when I asked the first time."

I did as he said. The sandwich was actually delicious, made just the way I liked with fresh tomatoes and turkey.

"She's fine." He slid his arm down, and I thought he was going to pull away, but instead our fingers met and he entwined them. "She's here. She's just occupied elsewhere."

I swallowed, relief flooding me, before taking another bite. I was suddenly ravenous. Vinemont smiled and handed me a napkin. I took the hint and wiped my mouth, Dijon mustard coming away on the cloth.

"Elsewhere?" I asked between bites. "Do you mean upstairs?"

His fingers tightened on mine. "You know, then?"

"I know your mother's alive. Not much else. Feel free to fill me in." The chips were salty and perfect, and I downed the sweet tea to finish it all off.

"There's nothing to tell. She's been up there for years." He stared out the window at the sheets of rain, milky white in the gloom. He slipped his fingers from mine and took the tray before standing. "I'm going to send in Dr. Yarbrough and Laura. Keep resting."

When he got to the door, my emotions got the better of me. "When are you coming back?" I knew I was a fool for wanting him, for my weakness. I couldn't stop it any more than I could stop what happened to Gavin and Brianne.

"Soon." He walked away, and not long after I heard more footsteps—the doctor and Laura as promised.

Laura stripped my gauze and helped me bathe, then she ushered me back to the bed so Dr. Yarbrough could clean my injuries and re-bandage them. He laid out some pills on the bedside table and made sure I took one.

"For the pain." He didn't have much of a bedside

manner. Perhaps he'd seen too much. With his age, I suspected he may have doctored Renee during her Acquisition year. He must have seen it all, become numb to it. Competent and distant—maybe it was the smartest way to be around these people.

"I'll be back around tomorrow." He picked up his black leather bag and left while Laura puttered around my room, a certain nervousness in her quick movements.

"What is it?" I asked as the faint rumble of thunder rolled over the house.

"Nothing." She straightened my blanket, even though I would just kick it off once I was asleep.

"Something." I tilted my head at her and patted the bed. "Sit. What is it?"

She paused and then slowly walked over to me and sat, her small frame barely making an indention in the bed. The thunder grew louder, the rain pouring over the higher eaves, making a small waterfall outside my window.

"It's Renee."

I sat up. "What about her?"

"It's just," she glanced to the closed door and back to me, "I'm not supposed to talk about..." She looked up.

I took her meaning. "About Vinemont's mother?"

She nodded and dropped her voice to a whisper. "But I've heard things when I've been in Teddy's room." Her cheeks pinked. "Cleaning in Teddy's room," she corrected herself.

"Like what?"

"Bangs and yells and crying. All sorts of things that never happened before. I've never been allowed up there, and I know neither of us are supposed to go and see. But I know that's where Renee is. I prepare meals for two now instead of one, and send them up with Mr. Farns."

I gripped her arm. "Do you think Mrs. Vinemont is hurting Renee?"

"I think so." She shrugged, her narrow shoulders carrying more weight than seemed possible. "It's worse up there now. And it's worse down here, too. Teddy hears it and he sort of, I don't know. He just gets so sad, and it doesn't matter what I do or say; I can't help him." She wiped at her eyes with the hem of her white apron.

Something upstairs had changed. The silent partner in this Acquisition mess was making plenty of noise all the sudden. I moved my feet under the blanket. I winced as a stinging pain erupted along my injured skin. I didn't have a chance of getting upstairs anytime soon, especially not stealthily. Maybe a week or so. Then I could investigate.

"Why tell me?"

She sniffed and brought her gaze to mine. "You're the only one I've ever seen get to them. I mean, Teddy talks about you like a sister." She laughed. "I was even jealous at first when you came." Her giggle died on her tongue. "But then that morning in the dining room, when Mr. Sinclair made you stand and m-made Teddy watch. I didn't envy you. I still don't fully know what the Acquisition is—"

"Join the club."

"But I know it's ripping them all apart. I don't want Teddy hurt. I lo—" She stopped herself.

"It's okay to love him, Laura. He's a good boy. Man, I guess. He's a good man."

The two of them wouldn't have an easy road, but the love they shared was obvious. I hoped that one day they could leave the Vinemont legacy behind entirely and strike out on their own.

Tears rolled down her round cheeks. "I know. I'm worried about him. I'm worried about Renee." She picked at the hem of her apron. "I just don't know what to do. I would march right up to the third floor, but then I'd lose my job and my chance to see Teddy."

I patted her arm. "I'm already in hell. Going down another circle won't hurt me too much. I'll check it out as soon as I'm able." I waved at my legs and feet.

She turned her body toward me, staring at me head on. "How are you so brave? How do you do it?"

Brave? That's not a word I'd ever associated with myself. "I'm just surviving."

"You *are* brave." Tears still shone in her bright eyes. "I know what they did to your back. I heard a rumor about where you went the last couple of days, what they were going to do to you." She dropped her gaze. "I would have given up if I were you."

"No, you wouldn't." I leaned my head back, the pill starting to do its work. "You would do what you had to do. You would go through hell. But you would be alive on the other side. You'd be different. I'm different. But I'm alive."

"Brave," she said again, and rose. The thunder boomed right overhead, the sound vibrating in my lungs, my mind.

I turned my head and stared out the window, the streaking rain becoming nothing but a gray blur as she left and clicked the door shut.

The next few days were spent in bed, Laura visiting more and more frequently. I sketched and sketched. Most of my drawings were of the wisteria in bloom from the house in New Orleans, or skeletal trees spiking in a desolate landscape.

I didn't see Vinemont or Lucius, though Laura told me they were out of the country on business. I wondered if that meant Cuba. Teddy came by to visit, though he avoided any questions about how I came to be laid up like I was.

By the third day, the weather had turned frigid, and Laura said we had a chance at some snow that night or the next day. It was Christmas Eve. I'd been up and around a few times, the pain in my feet subsiding and my bruises maturing into light yellow hues.

I sketched some more, this time a man's face. I roughed in the first few harsh lines and kept going. More strokes, and lines, and shading, until a familiar, square jaw emerged, and then full lips, and the sharp line of a nose. His eyes were difficult. They could be so emotive at times, so impassive at others. In the end, his look was something warm. The way he'd looked at me after the lightning strike, or when he cradled me in his lap on the way back from the woods. He'd worn the look enough for me to picture it, to capture it in charcoal.

The day grew late, the sun setting through a bevy of high, billowing clouds. Music began drifting through the halls. I halted my drawing and listened. At first it was just the rumble of drums, the whine of a guitar, and the tinkling of piano keys—all of it a discordant mosh. Then, a song took shape, the drums setting the rhythm and the guitar playing the melody while the piano filled out the sound. Was there a party?

I set the drawing aside and swung my legs out of bed. The muscle soreness had thankfully diminished, but my feet were still tender. I snugged them into the fluffy slippers Laura had brought me and stood. I could stand the twinges of pain, so I slowly maneuvered around the room, slinging on a bath robe to cover my pajamas before creeping into the hallway.

The sound came from downstairs. The music room off the foyer. It took me a while, and the song seemed to be almost finished by the time I reached the bottom step, but I relished the feel of finally moving. By the time I turned the corner, the song was over and a new drum beat began. Lucius sat at the drums and counted off before Teddy began riffing on the guitar. Vinemont sat at the piano, his back straight, and his fingers at the ready.

I smiled. It was a genuine grin that I couldn't contain. It grew even bigger as the piano joined in, Vinemont picking up and playing to Teddy's notes. I eased into a high-backed chair and Vinemont looked up, his fingers still working the keys. He didn't miss a note, and his answering smile made my chest warm. Shots were lined up across the top of the piano, three sets of five glasses, though one of each had already been drained.

Teddy's nimble fingers ran back and forth on the frets and strings like he was in an eighties hairband. They played well together, following the squeals and improvisation of the guitar, but staying within the parameters of Lucius' beat. We all laughed when Teddy went even more over the top, started a run toward me, hit his knees and slid up to my chair, still wailing on the guitar.

"Big finish!" He hopped to his feet from his knees and bopped his head along to the beat before letting his fingers fly so fast over so many notes that Vinemont threw his hands up and leaned back, grinning at his brother.

With the piano out, Lucius kept the beat going until Teddy ended on a screechingly high pitch that made me want to cover my ears. Then he tossed his pick at me. I was more surprised than anyone when I actually caught it.

I applauded and heard more clapping; Laura and Farns stood in the doorway at my back.

"Another," I demanded.

"What would the lady like to hear?" Teddy swiped his hair off his forehead.

I glanced over my shoulder at Laura. "Requests?"

"Well, seeing how it's Christmas Eve, can we do a carol or something Christmasy?"

"Sin? You feeling it this year?" Teddy asked.

Vinemont looked at me, then quickly back down at the piano. "No, not that one."

Teddy grinned even bigger. "'Last Christmas' it is."

"Shots!" Lucius leaned over to pluck one from the piano.

Vinemont and Teddy grabbed their respective glasses, clinked with each other, and then drained them.

Teddy's face twisted up and he rubbed the back of his sleeve across his mouth. "Damn." He walked back over to me. "Um, I'm going to need that pick back."

I laughed and handed it to him. He shed the electric guitar and picked up an acoustic, slinging the strap over his shoulder.

He winked at Laura. "You'll love it. It's my fave." He backed up. "All right, Lucius. Hit it."

Lucius tapped the cymbal and then started a beat on the snare punctuated with the bass on the downbeats.

Vinemont smirked as he began playing lightly in the background. I knew the song. It was an eighties staple from some long-defunct boy band that played on the radio every year at the holidays.

Teddy's voice rang out, smooth and clear. I was shocked at how exquisitely and freely he sang. He made the notes sound easy as he played along, rocking slightly as he kept Lucius' beat. All three of them worked together beautifully.

This was how they were supposed to be. A team, a unit that functioned best when they were all in accord. Even Lucius was smiling, his happiness making him seem younger and far more carefree than I knew he was.

Teddy held Laura's eye for quite some time as he belted out the lyrics—heartfelt and cheesy at the same time. But he pulled it off, and the smile never faltered from my face, though I watched Vinemont watching me more than anything else. He swayed to the music, not at all like a concert pianist; more like someone who felt the beat but wasn't ruled by it.

My stomach fluttered as if I had joined in on the last round of shots. He wore a simple black t-shirt, the ever-present vines wrapping around his biceps and to his forearms. I studied each movement, each sway, each time he moved to the lower notes or the higher.

Teddy reached the end of the song, singing soulfully about giving his heart to someone special.

I leaned back and whispered to Laura. "Are you going to throw him your panties?"

She giggled and slapped at my shoulder.

The song wound down, and Teddy held the last note for longer than I could hold my breath. Everyone laughed, Farns gripping his stomach and looking positively gleeful. The only one missing was Renee, and I intended to make my inquiries as soon as possible. This little trip downstairs was proof I was ready to roam a little farther.

"What next?" Teddy asked.

"'It's Cold Outside'?" Laura suggested.

"Can we handle that, boys?" Teddy asked.

Lucius did a drum roll in response, and Vinemont matched it with a flourish.

Teddy grinned. "That's a duet, Laura. Come on up."

"Oh no. No." She backed away. "I couldn't carry a note in a bucket."

"We have to have the woman's part." Teddy strummed, searching for the right key.

"Stella?" Vinemont asked, raising an eyebrow at me.

I could sing. But I wasn't sure if I could sing in front of him. I shook my head, color heating my cheeks.

"Aww, she can sing. Look at that face." Teddy laughed and put his guitar on the floor. He hurried forward and scooped me up.

"Hey!" I cried. "Why does everyone manhandle me around here?"

He set me on the piano. "You okay?"

My legs hung over the edge and blood rushed to my feet, though the slight tingle of sensation didn't hurt. Despite my irritation, I couldn't help but smile at Teddy. "Yes."

"Good." He grabbed two glasses from his line of shots and handed me one.

Lucius and Vinemont seized theirs, and we toasted before throwing them back. The liquid stung my tongue, my nostrils, and burned all the way down. I sputtered and slapped the glass back on the gleaming dark wood of the piano.

"You're harmony." I pointed to Teddy and tried to clear the pure alcohol from my lungs with a cough.

"Not a problem." Teddy leaned against the piano next to me. "These pipes are lined with gold."

I peeked over my shoulder at Vinemont as he began the accompaniment. He nodded to me, urging me to start the song. I waited a few more bars and closed my eyes before singing, "I really can't stay." My voice wobbled, but hit the right notes. Teddy jumped right in, telling me it was cold outside and adding, "It really is."

Laura linked her arm in Farns' and they swayed back and forth as Teddy and I sang the tune about responsibility and desire, the two dancing around each other.

Teddy's perfect harmony made my voice sound even better, though alone it was middling at best. My nerves seeped away as Teddy got into it, putting his arm around me though I knew he was singing right to Laura's heart. It was working, her gaze glued to him.

We reached the end, our voices melding and joining in unison as Lucius tapped the cymbal and the piano softened and quieted.

Applause from Farns and Laura rang out. I peeked over my shoulder at Vinemont and the look was there—the one from my drawing. Kindness, and something else that was undefinable. Something even warmer, even deeper. The same feeling had a stranglehold on my heart, my soul. Even in the barren ground of the Acquisition, love still grew.

"Beautiful voice. Like a bell." Farns beamed. "I think—"

His words were cut off when a tall woman with flowing white hair barreled past him, ripped the front door open, and ran out into the freezing night.

CHAPTER SEVENTEEN
SINCLAIR

I'D BARELY SEEN her ghostly form flit past when the front door slammed. *Fuck*.

"Teddy, take Stella to your room and lock the door." I didn't think my mother would be violent, but I couldn't tell anymore.

Stella opened her mouth, no doubt in protest, as Teddy scooped her up and headed for the stairs.

"Laura, you and Farns stay in the kitchen," I said. "Run out the door to the garage if anything happens."

Laura helped Farns from the floor as Lucius and I rushed past, no time to don shoes or coats, and took off after her. A blast of arctic air rushed into the foyer and stung my exposed skin as we darted into the night.

She fled across the moonlit lawn, her hair glowing silver in the luminous rays, and her white nightgown floating around her ankles. Ethereal and determined, she was making decent time. All the same, Lucius and I gained on her. My feet burned from the frost on the freezing ground, but we pounded after her, ignoring the pain.

She was slowing, fatigue already making her lag. We caught up, both darting around to corral her. She stopped and shrieked, her eyes wild and glancing from Lucius and back to me. I barely recognized her. The woman who'd raised me, tormented me, was now a screaming banshee on the same front lawn she used to rule.

"Mom!" Lucius tried to shout her down, holding his hands out in front of him as he crept nearer.

"Don't you touch her! Don't you touch her, you bastards!" She snarled, spit flying from her pale lips.

"Mom, it's me." I stepped closer and stared into her eyes, the ones I knew were the same shade as mine.

"Stop hurting her." She put a hand to her mouth, gasping as if someone had knocked the wind from her lungs. "Please stop."

"Mom! It's me, Sin." But she wasn't seeing me. She was seeing Renee's trials. They played over and over again in her mind as if she were sitting alone in a movie theater, strapped to a chair with her eyes pinned open.

"Stop!" she screamed and raked her nails down her face. "Take me instead. Please, take me."

I moved slowly, the individual blades of icy grass crunching under the soles of my feet with each step. She grimaced and tore at her hair, ripping at the silver strands as her wild gaze turned skyward. Lucius and I both darted in, grabbing her around the waist. Then the screams began in earnest as she clawed and fought.

"Mom, calm down." Her nails were on my neck, gouging deep lines as she bit at Lucius. She was feral, the mother I'd known long since gone.

A brutal wind whipped past, carrying her screams out into the night. She was barefoot. If my feet were any indication, we were all in danger of frostbite the longer we stayed out here.

"Get her legs," I yelled.

I gripped her upper body, pinning her arms to her sides, as Lucius grabbed her around the knees. Together, we lifted her and hurried back toward the house. Once we reached the steps, she stopped struggling and her screams ceased. Defeated and limp, she fell silent. I took her full weight, cradling her in my arms.

"Lucius, go on up and see about Renee."

"Oh, shit. I didn't even think about her. Mom, what did you do?"

She was unresponsive as Lucius took the steps two at a time.

"Can I help?" Farns came down the hall, wringing his hands as Laura gripped his arm.

"Everything's fine." A lie. "Just one of her episodes." I hurried up the stairs to the third floor.

The door to her room was open, and I carried her in before laying her on the bed. Renee sat on the floor by the fireplace, hand pressed to the side of her head. Blood trickled down her face.

Lucius knelt down beside her, pulling her hand away to check the wound.

"You okay?" I asked over my shoulder.

"I-I think so," Renee said.

Mom lay on the bed and stared at the light green ceiling. Her mouth moved, half-formed words passing through her lips that held meaning only to her.

She'd made this large suite her sanctuary, the place she'd retreated to when Lucius and I were old enough to take care of the estate and the sugar business. I'd thought it was a blessing to be rid of her at the time, but I didn't know how much darker her thoughts would grow while she stayed alone up here.

"What happened?" Lucius pulled Renee's hand away to inspect the damage. The wound seemed to be somewhere in her dark hair, and was bleeding profusely.

"I don't know," Renee said. "She was lucid. We were talking about you boys when you were little. She was telling me a story about how Teddy used to ride his tricycle into the house and how it drove her batty. We were laughing, actually laughing. Then she swung something at me. I don't know what. I don't remember anything until you two came in."

I knelt beside her and pulled her hair away. It was a small gash that wouldn't need stitches, but the lump around it was troubling. I looked back at Mom, but she was still in her daze. Would she regret this when she came back to life? I doubted it.

"Give me the key to the medicine cabinet." I held my hand out. Renee dug in her black skirt and produced a key ring, but couldn't seem to focus on which key it was.

"It's fine. I got it." I went to the armoire, unlocked it, and swung it open. Two syringes were loaded and ready to go, but Mom was calm now, so I didn't bother. I grabbed up some alcohol and bandages. I handed some to Lucius and then took the rest over to Mom.

I worked on her feet, dabbing the alcohol on each small cut. It had to sting, but she didn't react at all, remaining perfectly still. I'd done this only days before on a different woman, one I hoped wouldn't end up as damaged as the woman who lay before me. Once I'd bandaged her, I checked Lucius' work on Renee. He'd done well, the wound clean and Renee comfortable. I sat next to him and we wiped the blood from our feet.

"This is fucked up." Lucius glanced to Mom. "Keeping her up here like this."

"If there was a better way, I'd do it."

"I just wish we could get her some sort of care."

"There's no care for what's wrong with her." Renee had looked like hell even before Mom clocked her. But she wouldn't leave Mom's side, no matter how many times I asked her to get some rest, to go downstairs, to visit Stella. Tired eyes, gaunt cheeks, and sallow skin were her reward.

When Mom was like this, the only person she could tolerate was Renee. And now she'd attacked her.

"She's fine now," Renee said. "I'll stay with her. She wore herself out with that little episode." She tried to gain her feet, but wobbled before Lucius caught her and helped her stand.

"No. You need to go and get some rest."

"But Mr. Sincl—"

"Go!" I pointed to the door. "I'll stay with her for a while. Lucius, take Renee to her room and have Laura sit with her tonight."

He paused like he was going to challenge me, but seemed to think better of it. Taking Renee's arm, he said, "Come on. Sin's right. You're beat. In every way." He gave her a smile that she didn't return before walking her out.

At the door she turned. "Rebecca, I'll be back to see you tomorrow. I'm okay. Don't worry about what happened. You didn't hurt me." Her pleading voice broke on the last few words, as if she were injured more by having to lie to her lover than by the bloody wound along her scalp.

Mom made no move, just kept staring at the ceiling, her mouth slightly open. Lucius closed the door and I scrubbed my hand down my jaw. This was her worst episode yet. It was as if her memories grew stronger every day, the fear gripping her more tightly and turning each of her thoughts dark.

I moved her slender body up the bed so her head rested on a pillow. After pulling the sheet and blanket over her, I sat on the edge of her bed. I took her cold hand, the back pale, each vein a blue ridge leading to her bony wrist. The small crisscross of raised scars was still there, a matching set on my right hand.

I sandwiched her hand between both of mine, trying to instill some warmth in her. I knew I couldn't. She'd never given me enough to start with, so I had none to give back.

"Mom. Come back." How many times had I made the same request? Countless. More so when I'd been a child. But the words were empty. The Mom I'd known before her Acquisition had long been gone. Only Renee still encountered her from time to time. Never me, or Lucius, or Teddy. To us, she remained the strict matriarch, ensuring we maintained our dominance over the other families by coercion, deceit, or force.

Her breathing was even, but her eyes remained open and unseeing. A knock sounded at the door, and Farns shuffled in.

"How is she?" He'd known my mother longer than anyone. His eyes swam with sadness as he contemplated her expressionless face.

"She's coming down. I'm going to give her something to help her sleep." I stood and returned to the armoire, pulling out a syringe before locking it up and pocketing the key.

Farns walked over and took my spot on the bed, patting her hand. "Everything's going to be all right. The boys are fine. Everyone's fine. We just have to get you well again."

She would never be well again. There was no cure for the regret that had blackened her heart and eaten away at her mind. There was only management. Farns held her wrist as I pushed the needle into a vein on the back of her hand and depressed the plunger. After a few moments, her eyes finally closed.

She was peaceful. I should have felt relief. Instead, I felt what I always did. Despair.

CHAPTER EIGHTEEN
Stella

I SAT ON Teddy's bed as he paced the room. When we heard the commotion on the stairs that eventually settled on the third floor, we knew it was over.

"Does that happen a lot?" I hugged my knees and watched as he came apart with each fitful step.

"No. She's done…things before. But she's never done this." He sank next to me and cradled his head in his hands.

I leaned over against his back and listened to the rapid beat of his heart. "I'm sorry." It wasn't enough, but it was all I could say.

"She'll be okay, I think. They caught her quick, right?"

"Speaking from experience, I've made that same dash across the lawn and didn't make it far at all."

"I remember. That was a fucking weird day."

"You're preaching to the choir." The memory of Vinemont, the sun high and blinding as he glowered over me, was something I would never forget.

"I know." He sighed. "It's because of Christmas, you know? Why she's like this."

I put my hand on his shoulder. I'd guessed that the

time of year had something to do with it, especially after Renee told me how hard her Christmas trial had been on both women.

"I understand." I didn't know if I meant that I understood Teddy or his mother. Maybe a little of both. My mother was dead by her own hand, and Teddy's seemed to have killed herself in much the same manner. Winning the Acquisition was a self-inflicted, fatal wound.

"She wouldn't hurt us." His eyes met mine, as if begging for agreement.

"I'm sure she wouldn't." I had no idea, but I would say anything to wipe the pain from his kind heart. "I think Vinemont just wanted us out of the way so he could tend to her."

"Yeah."

Footsteps sounded in the hallway. Two sets. Teddy unlocked the door and peeked out. Lucius walked by, Renee's arm slung over his shoulder as he helped her to her room.

"Is she okay?" Teddy asked.

"They both are. Sin is staying with Mom. I'm putting Renee to bed. She's exhausted. You can take Stella back to her room."

I wanted to run to Renee, but by the time I'd made it to the door on my sore feet, they'd turned the corner, and the house was quiet again.

Teddy offered his arm. "Come on. I'll take you over to your place."

I peeked down the hall. "I really want to see Renee, if that's all right? I promise I'll go straight to my room after."

He raised an eyebrow. "I don't think Sin would—"

"Teddy!" Laura rushed down the hallway and into his arms. "Is she okay?"

"Yeah, I think so."

I took my chance and began hobbling away as some wet noises erupted at my back.

Teddy broke their kiss for long enough to call over his

shoulder. "If you don't get back to your room, Sin is going to kill me."

"Okay, okay. I'll go just as soon as I see Renee."

"You better." The kissing noises resumed as I turned the corner.

This was the same hall where Lucius' and Vinemont's rooms were. They stayed along the side of the house, and Renee's small suite was at the very back. I passed Lucius' door, a lamp burning on his desk and some rock music playing low. I kept going and came to Vinemont's door, but it was closed.

I leaned against his doorframe to give my feet a momentary reprieve. I stared at the closed door, and curiosity got the better of me. I turned the glass knob and swung it open just a bit.

A beam of moonlight lit the curves and lines of a piece of my soul—the painting I'd made after the first Acquisition trial. He'd hung it in his room, the stark image made even harsher in the low light. I pushed the door the rest of the way open and flipped the light switch. My breath left me.

Every painting I'd ever exhibited, save one—*The North Star*—covered his walls. I was everywhere, my heart, my thoughts, my emotions covering every bare inch of space in his room. I walked in and spun in a circle, disbelieving my own eyes. But it was real. All of me was here, in this room, with Vinemont.

"I bought them a little while back." Vinemont leaned on the doorframe and crossed his arms over his chest. His face and neck were scratched, but the marks appeared to have been cleaned. He no longer bore even a shred of the merriment from the music room. His mother had stripped it all away, leaving him cold and raw.

"Why?"

His eyes pierced me but he gave no answer.

My heart began to thump in my ears as we held eye contact. I wanted to turn away. I tried. I couldn't. His gaze dropped to my lips. Instead of cold, his eyes were suddenly alive with heat. He filled the door, his wide shoulders the perfect barrier.

I felt the urge to run. It was instinctive. My breath caught in my throat.

"Stella, if you keep looking at me like that…" His strained words trailed off as he walked in and shut the door, clicking the lock in a smooth movement behind him.

I took a step back, but there was nowhere to go. One more step and I'd be against his bed.

He covered the short distance between us, his aggression hitting me like the wave of a turbulent sea. I placed my hands to his chest and found his heart beating just as fast as mine, if not faster. He put one hand in my hair and another at my throat.

I tilted my head back, wanting to see every bit of his emotion, his need. My own surged inside me and created a blaze in my core.

"You're still hurt." He squeezed my throat and used his thumb to turn my head to the side. His lips ran along my jaw as he ghosted his mouth to my ear. "And I won't be gentle."

The blast of heat that shot through me at his darkly whispered words was beyond reason, beyond anything I could comprehend. I didn't want gentle. I wanted everything he had. And I wanted it just as real, just as raw as he was.

"Then don't be."

"You don't know what you're saying." He moved his hand down my body and gripped my wrist, rubbing the palm of my hand against his hard cock. "I can't control myself with you, Stella. Especially not now. I want to make it hurt, make you scream."

Something in his words clicked inside my mind. He *wanted* to hurt me. My thoughts flickered back to the first trial—each time he'd hurt me, it was as if he was hurting, too. And he'd never wanted to bring me pain. The second trial proved that beyond doubt. But, here and now, we were two people who didn't have to be master and slave. Here and now, when I could choose, I wanted him to hurt me.

"I want you to." I rubbed my hand up and down his cock as it strained against his jeans. My pussy was already wet, and my heartbeat pulsed in my clit.

"You're making a mistake." He groaned and yanked my wrist away, twisting it up behind my back. The slight pain sent a buzz straight between my legs.

He grabbed a fistful of my hair right at my scalp and pulled so I was completely at his mercy, my body arching into him. His lips were at mine, his gaze bearing down on me. "If we do this, there is no safe word, Stella. There is no tapping out. I will hurt you. Do you understand? You're mine."

"Sin, please." I wanted every dark thought he'd ever had. I wanted to cede him control freely, not have it taken from me.

He closed his eyes when I used his name. "Say it. Say you're mine, and I'll show you how much I can make it hurt."

My knees grew weak and fear kicked in my breast like a snared rabbit. But fear didn't rule me. Not here in his arms.

"I'm yours," I breathed.

He released his hold on me and gripped my robe before yanking it down. His hands were all over me, his eyes locked on mine as he fisted my tank top and pulled it, the seams coming apart with a popping sound. My body jerked forward but he put a hand at my chest. Then, he gripped my shorts and panties with his left hand and yanked twice before ripping them off.

He stepped back, breathing hard, and raked his gaze down my naked body. Goose bumps rose along my flesh, and when he stopped at my pussy, the tightness inside me increased. I felt like I might come just from the pressure of his stare.

"Lay on the bed on your back, head toward me."

I backed away as he watched, his body completely still. When my knees hit the bed, I sat and then spun so I was on my back and looking at him upside down. His hands went to his belt, his strong fingers nimbly unbuckling it and pulling it slowly loose. He tossed it on the bed next to me. The faint smell of leather filled my nose. He unzipped and pushed his jeans and boxers down while drawing out his rigid cock. I swallowed hard.

His jeans at his hips, he walked to me and gripped my shoulders, pulling me so my head hung off the bed. Blood rushed to my brain, pooling there as the lust pooled between my thighs.

Oh my god. When he rubbed his wet tip across my lips, my nipples stiffened and I scissored my legs, my clit desperate for attention. I darted my tongue across his head and savored the salty taste.

He groaned. "Open."

I opened my mouth as wide as I could and he shoved into me, his head hitting my tongue and then moving to the back of my throat. I gagged, but he only pulled back and pushed in again. I closed my eyes and fastened my lips tightly around him, sucking and playing my tongue along the top of his shaft.

He leaned over and squeezed my breasts to the point of pain as he fucked my mouth in hard strokes.

"Spread your legs. I want to see what's mine." His voice was an animal growl.

I obeyed, parting my legs as I squeezed his thighs. He continued shoving in and out of my mouth.

"Wider!"

I pushed my heels as far apart as they could go, cool air against my hot, wet pussy.

"Fuck." He pushed in farther and my eyes watered, but I didn't stop sucking him, his cock filling my mouth and making my jaw ache. I wanted every last bit of him, though

I couldn't possibly have taken him all in my mouth.

He pinched my nipples, making me squirm and moan around him. He backed away, and I gasped for breath. His cock stood at attention, out of reach and tantalizing.

"That's going to make me come, and we aren't anywhere near done yet."

He stripped his shirt over his head and pushed his jeans and boxers the rest of the way off. "Get on your stomach. Head on my pillow."

I rolled over and did as he said, burying my face in his clean, masculine scent as he prowled up to the bed. The jingle of his belt got my attention and I turned to stare at him. His eyes were wild, every muscle on his body tense.

"On your hands and knees."

I slid my legs under me and pushed up as he ran a hand down the line of my spine from my neck to my ass. I shivered under his touch.

"Spread your legs more." I shifted my knees apart and he teased a finger down my pussy and to my clit.

I moaned and pushed back into his hand. He withdrew his fingers. "Not yet."

He gripped the belt in his right hand and for a moment I was back at the first trial, chained to a tree. I hung my head, taking in a gulp of air, and tried to stay in the moment.

"Stella." He gripped the back of my neck. "Look at me."

I turned my head and caught his gaze. His body was drawn tight, tension infusing every muscle, but his eyes were steady, reassuring. "I've got you. I'm right here. Just you and me. I've got you."

I was doing this because I wanted to. Not because I was chained against my will. I nodded, and he placed his hand on my cheek, gentle for a moment before he reached behind my head and gripped my hair tight.

"When you scream, make sure it's my name."

"Yes."

"Yes what?"

"Yes, Sin." Hearing the words spill from my mouth made my pussy tighten even more, my arousal reaching new heights each time I gave in to his demands.

"Good." He let go and stood with his knees against the bed, his cock pointing at me straight and stiff.

He reared back, and a sting erupted along my ass, a sharp crack echoing around the room. I grunted and fisted the blanket.

"My name, Stella." He hit me again, harder this time.

"Sin!" I cried in unison with the sound of the leather on my skin.

He fisted his cock and hit me again, this time the leather grazing against my pussy lips and making me shudder.

The impact went straight to my clit. I gave him his name again and again and again. My ass stung, but I leaned back into every strike, begging for more. I wanted the pain. It was mine. I owned it. I'd chosen it.

One more stroke and I buried my face in his pillow, screaming his name and breathing hard. The belt jingled to the floor and the bed shifted. His hands were on my ass, spreading me apart and pushing me forward, and then his tongue was on the hot flesh between my legs. I jerked as he licked from my clit to my entrance.

He groaned and stabbed his tongue inside me, fucking me in and out with it. I rocked my hips back to him, and he moved to my clit, sucking it between his teeth as I pushed back into his face. He sucked until my moans grew louder, my pussy tensing. I was at the edge, so close, his tongue swirling and flicking me into a frenzy.

When he stopped, I yelled my frustration into the pillow and tried to flip over. He gripped my hips hard and kept me right where I was.

"Don't you fucking move." His voice was gravelly, filled with unrestrained lust. "Not until you have my permission, Stella."

He slapped my ass hard and I screamed at the sudden pain.

He hit me again on the other side even harder, and his name flew from my lips. I remained still, his cock pressing against my pussy as his hot palms marked my ass again and again. I jerked with each hit, his head teasing my clit until I was desperate for him to fill me.

"Sin, please," I said as he rubbed my ass, soothing the sting.

"Begging me, Stella?"

"Yes!" I pushed against him again, my hot clit seeking his cock for the slick friction.

"What do you want?" He slipped a finger between my cheeks and rubbed the wrinkled skin around my asshole. I made a keening sound and twisted so I could look at him.

"I want you to fuck me."

He gripped my hip so hard it hurt and shoved forward, my clit singing at the increased contact of his cock. Then he flipped me over with one rough movement and crashed down on top of me, crushing the air from my lungs. He pinned my wrists over my head with one hand, covered my mouth with the other, and thrust inside. I screamed into his palm as he sank to the hilt.

Pain and pleasure exploded within me as he started a hard, rough pace. I was still yelling into his hand as he dropped his mouth to my ear.

"Is this what you wanted, Stella?" He released my mouth and rose up on an elbow.

Yes.

He jarred my body with each impact and looked down to my bouncing breasts. He captured a nipple in his mouth and bit down. I moaned and writhed, his thrusts getting stronger as he reached down and gripped one thigh under the knee and yanked it up, spreading me wide for him. He groaned as he surged and surged, his cock so thick inside me and every crash hitting my clit. The slapping sounds of our skin reverberated off the paintings and mixed with my moans.

"Sin, I'm getting close."

"No, you aren't." He switched to my other nipple, sucking and taking me higher.

My pussy was screaming for release.

"Please, I'm going to come," I cried.

He released my nipple and wrapped his hand around my throat. "Not until I say."

He maintained the same pace, a hard fuck that kept me perched at the edge, ready to tumble over at any second.

I was there. "Please!"

He withdrew and I wanted to cry. I growled with rage, but he just smirked and flipped me to my stomach again and pushed my legs together. He straddled me and raised my ass and spread my cheeks before shoving his cock into me again.

"Fuck, you're tight." He groaned and leaned over me.

I moaned at the sensation of being filled again as he fucked me in steady pumps. He grasped my hair and wrenched my head to the side before fastening his lips to the back of my neck, his tongue tracing the tangle of vines that lived there. My pussy clenched him tighter as he possessed every bit of me. I jerked against him, but he kept his other hand at my hip, yanking me into his cock with each thrust.

He kissed my shoulder, running his tongue along my skin, and I gripped the pillows. I was desperate to touch my clit. As if reading my mind, he snaked his hand beneath me and rubbed the swollen nub with two fingers. I arched my back, pushing my ass farther up into him so he could get even deeper.

"Sin." It was all I had. The only word on my tongue.

He grunted with the effort, the rough fuck taking everything out of him as I gave him all I was. He strummed my clit harder as his cock grew inside me. I teetered on the edge again, my pussy gripping him tightly, desperate for release.

"Please, Sin, please." It was a strangled cry.

He kissed to my ear and kept working me. I shook with the pleasure and fought against coming. I would wait for his permission. I had to.

"Sin!"

"Come on my cock." His voice was in my ear and I couldn't stop.

I cried out his name as he bit down on my shoulder. I shuddered as wave after wave of bliss blew through me, my pussy spasming as he kept pounding.

He grunted and bit harder. I felt his cock kick inside me, but I was too lost in my own high to do anything other than sink beneath him and take everything he gave me. He pulsed a few more times and kissed my shoulder where his bite had stung. Then he rolled off to my side and let out a whoosh of breath.

I was still floating, my mind and body in two separate locales. He reached over and moved my hair off my sweaty neck. I turned toward him and it was there again. The look that I'd drawn. It was mine. I'd never seen it any other time than when he looked at me.

My heart swelled, and so many emotions I thought I'd given up on rose to the surface, not the least of which was hope. Hope that this would change things. Hope that he would value me more than just a means of winning the Acquisition.

The warmth that bloomed in my heart was almost too much to bear, and I wanted to hide it, nurture it—let it grow under the harsh sun of the Acquisition. I slid over to him and rested my head on his chest, listening to his heartbeat slow and even out. He ran his hand up and down my back and my side.

I was awash in him, soaking up his heat, his sweat, his emotions. He sighed deeply and his hand stopped, resting at my waist. I held my breath, never wanting the spell to break.

"Sin?" Teddy's voice from the other side of the door

made me jump.

Sin covered me with the blanket before tugging on his boxers and going to the door.

He clicked the lock and opened it a crack.

"What?" Sin's voice was rough.

"I know she's in there," Teddy said. "I just wanted to ask about Mom. Is she going to be okay?" The worry in his voice was enough to make me turn toward the door, more concerned than embarrassed.

"I gave her something so she can sleep. You know how she gets this time of year."

"Yeah, but it's never been like that."

Sin ran a hand through his hair, his back muscles flexing with the movement. "I know."

"Can I go up and see her?"

"Yeah, she's out. Farns is sitting with her."

"Okay. I'll check on her. Bye, Stella."

"Bye, Teddy," I called.

Sin turned and lowered his eyebrows at me before closing the door and locking it again.

"You two think you're clever, don't you?" He smiled, warmth and hunger mixing in his eyes.

Yes. I shrugged. He stalked to the bed, ripped the blanket off and settled on top of me, pushing between my legs and wrapping his arms around me, pinning my elbows to my sides.

He kissed my collarbone, light caresses that made the butterflies in my stomach swirl and dip. His lips were warm and soft as he moved to my neck, sucking my skin between his teeth. I squirmed as my body awoke from its momentary reprieve, but I was trapped in his arms with nowhere to go.

He nibbled at my jaw and surged against me, his cock hard again and seeking entrance. The only thing to stop him was the material of his boxers. I moaned as he bit my ear, and I was hyper aware of every sensation—his mouth, my hard nipples pressing into his chest, the exquisite ache between my thighs.

When he took my mouth, I moaned. He swallowed the sound and sank his tongue into me, demanding and hot. I gasped when he slanted over me, his body hard against me as the softness of our mouths melded. I was on fire again, needing even more of him. He slid a hand down to my ass and I was free to run my fingers through his silky soft hair. When I gripped it hard, he thrust against me, his head pushing at my veiled entrance.

He rose onto his knees and shucked his shorts before falling on top of me again. I moaned as he sank inside without warning, my pussy clenching at the sudden intrusion. I dug my heels into his ass, ignoring the sting of pain. He thrust smoothly and bent his head to my breast, teasing around the nipple. I buried both hands in his hair.

He sucked me into his mouth as he surged deep and stayed, grinding against my clit with small movements of his hips. I was already panting, my body on a hair trigger from his touch.

"I want to see you." His deep voice was an aphrodisiac of its own.

Gripping my back, he flipped us over so I was on top. I sank down completely on him, his cock stretching into my deepest core as I threw my head back. His hands were at my hips as I rose and fell on him, working him in and out. I spread my knees even wider, and he thrust up into me, pulling a deep moan from my lungs.

I leaned forward, planting one hand on his chest and the other at the pillow next to his head.

"Fuck, yes, Stella. Look at me. Make yourself come on my cock." He palmed a breast with one hand while his other stayed at my hip, pulling me down tight as I ground my pussy against him.

I held his gaze as I worked him. His grunts and thrusts made my pleasure spiral higher and higher. And when he pinched my nipple hard I cried his name.

"I'm so close," I whispered, and put my forehead to his.

His cock hardened at my words, and my clit pulsed as I was filled so completely.

"It's mine. Every orgasm is mine, Stella. Tell me."

"Yes. Yours. All of me, Sin. I'm yours."

His jaw tightened even more. "Then give me what's mine."

My hips bore down even harder, the sweet friction on my core too much as I came.

"Sin—"

He kissed me, taking his name from my lips as I froze and shuddered. He thrusted hard once more and tensed as he shot inside me. My orgasm was still rolling, burning me with skittering sparks of pleasure as I convulsed and moaned my bliss into his mouth. I was gone, my mind shattered as I broke our kiss and took in a gulp of air before dropping my head onto the pillow next to him.

He encircled his strong arms around my back and crushed me to him. I was limp, utterly spent. I didn't move, just lay on top of him and allowed myself to remain in pieces.

"Stella, look at me."

I lifted my head and stared into his eyes, the shutters to his soul open and giving me a view of something more beautiful than I could have ever imagined. The real him, the one he kept hidden, the one I knew existed deep beneath the cold exterior.

He kissed my lips softly and ran his hand over my cheek. The wonder in his gaze made so much inside me open and warm. Then a shadow flitted across his eyes, some dark thought or memory that clouded our connection. He gave me one more lingering kiss before pressing me to his chest and covering us with the blanket.

I began to drift to sleep as his fingertips stroked my back, my hair. Love was in every touch. I'd never felt so safe, so content. A comfortable darkness began to fall over me, but my last thought was about the shadow.

CHAPTER NINETEEN
Stella

I STARED AT his face in the early morning light for far too long. Sleep wiped the cares away from his brow, making him seem young, almost reminiscent of Teddy. I wanted nothing more than to stay in his arms, in his bed, in the sanctuary that he'd covered with my art, but I needed to check on Renee.

The house was quiet, my steps the only sound as I crept down the hall. Her door was open when I got there, and she was gone, her bed made like usual. I stared at the ceiling, wondering if she was upstairs again.

I felt a deep ache in my body as I snuck downstairs to my room. Sin was still with me, his scent on me, his body still making mine feel everything we'd done the night before. My ginger steps told the tale of a night spent with him.

I showered and slid naked into my sheets, staring out the window as the cloudy, cold Christmas day began. I couldn't go back to sleep, the memories of Sin's mouth, his hands, and his eyes making me tingle.

I was toying with sneaking back to his room when there was a forceful knock at my door. *Renee?*

"Who is it?"

"Merry Christmas, *Krasivaya*."

My mouth dropped open. Dmitri, my manly masseuse I'd met before the Acquisition ball.

The door swung open and Alex, his hair a bright shade of indigo, rushed in and jumped on my bed. "It's a Christmas miracle, beautiful!"

Dmitri scowled at Alex as he lumbered inside.

I put my hand to my mouth, joy rushing through me. "You're here!"

"Juliet's downstairs getting set up. Sadly, Yong couldn't make it. She's busy waxing an entire clan of reality stars in Hollywood. Serbians. Super hairy."

"But why?" I reached out and touched Alex to make sure he was real.

"Few days ago, the honorable counsellor Sinclair Vinemont requested our presence as a Christmas treat for you and offered some choice coin." Alex winked and lay back, threading his fingers beneath his faux hawk. "This ain't so bad." He surveyed the quilts. "Nice room. I didn't know you sewed."

"I don't." I finally accepted they were really here and wrapped my arms around Alex's neck.

"Eww, naked woman." He patted my back awkwardly.

I pulled back and yanked the sheet up, having totally forgotten I hadn't dressed yet.

Dmitri smiled, his large frame ridiculous against the backdrop of a particularly dainty white and pink quilt, and started cracking his knuckles.

"Come on down to the spa when you are dressed. A day of leisure awaits." Alex hopped up and fired an imaginary pistol at me before leading Dmitri into the hallway and back down the stairs.

Did Sin give me friends for Christmas? The thought made me laugh, mostly because it was true. I rose and dressed simply, knowing full well I wouldn't be wearing clothes for long.

I skipped the empty breakfast room and hurried straight to the spa. The cloudy sky imposed on the glass panes above and cast a gray gloom on the usually sunny room.

A small table was laid out with croissant, fruit, and juice. Alex had already powered through some strawberries, and Juliet was mid-chew on a chocolate croissant when she saw me and squealed. After an intense hug, she allowed me to take a seat. It felt natural—all of us eating, drinking, and laughing.

"Did you win the beauty pageant thing we did you up for last time, or what?" Alex downed his coffee and poured more.

I shifted in my seat. "Umm, the results aren't in yet. I'll let you know, though."

"Well, if you didn't, then I'd like a word with the judges because you were amazing." His eyes lit. "Do you still have the dress?"

I dropped my eyes. I hadn't seen it since the ball. "No, I think the designer took it back for a show or something."

"Well, shit." He leaned back and murdered another strawberry.

"You win, *Krasivaya*. I know this." Dmitri had some new ink along his neck, something in Russian.

"What's that say?" I pointed to it.

"Oh," he laughed, the sound almost nervous. "Nothing."

Juliet raised an eyebrow, met my eye, and sipped her juice.

"Embarrassed?" I asked, teasing in my tone.

"No." He straightened in his chair, the joints creaking under his weight. "It is not meant for ladies such as you to hear."

"Oh my god, Dmitri! Are you blushing?" I asked.

Alex crowed with laughter and I couldn't help but

join in. The big Russian rubbed a hand over his shaved head and grinned.

"Dmitri went and got something inapropes tatted on his neck and won't share." Alex giggled some more.

"It say." Dmitri shook his head. "It say my *chlen* proud."

"Your what?" Juliet asked through her smile.

"My—" He gave an obvious look down to his crotch and then back up. "It is proud."

"What is your dick proud of, exactly?" Alex snickered.

Dmitri waved his meaty palm at Alex and let out a string of Russian.

Alex nodded. "Right, right. Very proud. I'm not denying it. So is it cut, or are you sporting foreskin?"

Juliet spit a mouthful of orange juice back into her glass, and I examined my feet.

"Let's get you buffed up, shall we?" Juliet rose and, thankfully, saved me from any further discussion about Dmitri's 'chlen'.

An hour later, I sat comfortably as Juliet buffed my legs, the sensation refreshing but also intense.

"Damn, Russian. If your hands feel this good, I can't imagine how your chlen must feel." Alex lay on the massage table, having talked Dmitri into warming up by massaging him first. Alex grinned at me and then grunted as Dmitri used his elbow on his lower back.

"Turn it on over," Juliet instructed.

I flipped on the table, staying under the towel as best I could, but I lost my grip and it fell to the floor. I winced, knowing what was coming. I'd already made an excuse about running in the wrong shoes about my feet. Now I had to explain the rest.

"What happened to your back?" Juliet ran her fingers over one of the scars. "Is this why Renee asked me for the scar serum?"

Dmitri loomed up next to me. "Who has done this,

Krasivaya? The *suka* who came before?"

"Lucius? No. It doesn't hurt. Not anymore. Please don't worry about it. It doesn't bother me." I looked over my shoulder, my eyes pleading with Dmitri to leave it alone.

"It bother *me*." Dmitri smoothed his wide palm down my back and frowned.

"I don't want to talk about it." I rested my forehead on my hand.

"Come on, big guy. You heard her. Take it out on me," Alex said.

I breathed a sigh of relief as Dmitri's shadow receded, and Alex's deep grunt of pain filled the room.

"From the looks of them, the serum helped. But this should make them even less noticeable." Juliet patted my shoulder and started doing her thing. Coarse crystals rubbed against my skin, then finer and finer until it felt like she was floating thin sheets of silk across my body.

Once it was Dmitri's turn, I was in heaven. What little muscle soreness I had left was worked away by his strong hands. Alex snored on the table next to me, his hand on his stomach and his silver nipple rings rising and falling with each breath. I could relate. Dmitri worked magic.

When he was done, he draped my towel up over me and I remained in my haze of relaxation.

"Juliet. Your turn." Dmitri waved her over and smacked Alex on the arm. "Up!"

"Hey!" Alex sat up and rubbed his eyes.

Juliet shook her head and backed away. "I'm not doing that."

"You shy, baby girl?" Alex asked.

"No." Juliet dropped her gaze to the river-rock floor, her blonde bob hiding her face.

"It okay." Dmitri frowned. "I understand."

"I'm sorry. I'm just not…" She gestured toward my body.

"What? You're beautiful." I looked in her eyes.

"Inside and out."

"Yes, beautiful," Dmitri said, and stared at Juliet as if this were an obvious fact.

"Me three." Alex stood and smacked me on the ass. "Get up, woman. Let's go in my room and play with hair stuff. Leave these two alone to negotiate."

"What?" Juliet's big blue eyes widened.

Dmitri smiled. "Yes. You go, Alex. I handle."

I tucked my towel around me and rose before pointing my finger at Dmitri. "Go easy on her, Russian."

"Of course." Dmitri smiled down at me as he motioned an unmoving Juliet to come to him.

I wanted to stay and watch, see if the large Russian could coax the skittish Juliet, but Alex pulled me into his booth and shut the door.

He clapped. "This is going to be good. You think they'll fuck?"

I cocked my head at him in the mirror. "Of course not. She'll probably run screaming before he even gets a finger on her." The words came out and whistled around my consciousness, a flash of barren tree limbs darting across my mind and the scent of earth and rotting leaves in my nose.

"Hey, you okay?" Alex patted my shoulder.

I forced a smile. "Fine."

"Let's give you a cut. Spruce up these ends. And, just for you, I'll tell you all about my newest boyfriend while I do it." He whipped out a black cape and tied it around me. "Have you ever seen a pierced dick?"

I spent the next forty-five minutes laughing and telling Alex just how bad he was after he regaled me with tales of his conquests, the most recent being a TV star on some show about zombies.

When he was done, I felt lighter, and my hair was cut, shampooed, and styled to fall in waves.

I ran my fingers through the strands. "Thanks, Alex. I'm a new girl."

He bent over, caught my eye in the mirror, and kissed my cheek. "No. You're the same one I fell in love with a couple months ago."

I smiled. This was by far the best Christmas present I'd ever received.

"Let's see if the coast is clear or full of Russian dick." Alex silently opened the door and crack, then swung it all the way. "What the—"

I peeked over his shoulder. Dmitri and Juliet had disappeared.

A smell wafted to my nose, something rich and delicious. My stomach growled.

"I think lunch is ready." Alex walked into the room and grabbed my clothes from the nearest rack before tossing them to me. "Get dressed. I'm starving. And please tell me I'm invited."

I dropped my towel and pulled on my underwear, jeans, and t-shirt. "Of course. But we need to find Juliet and Dmitri first."

Someone cleared their throat. I stared around. The sound came from a closet along the front of the room. The door opened and Dmitri stepped out, his eyes everywhere but on Alex and me.

"Where's Juliet?" Alex asked.

The door opened again and she hurried out, though Dmitri slapped her ass as she went by.

"I'm not discussing this." Her face was on fire.

I grinned, happy that the simple enjoyment of another person, no dark motives at play, was possible under this roof. "Fine. Come on. I bet you two worked up an appetite."

Juliet tucked her hair behind her ear before thinking better of it and plucking it back out. I led the procession, up the main hallway, past Sin's study, past the breakfast room, and to the large dining room where I'd signed the contract that fateful day. It seemed so long ago now. So much had changed.

Laura puttered around adjusting plates, but the table was perfect. A large roast sat in the middle, flanked by sides of green beans, mashed potatoes, corn, sweet potatoes, and any number of foods placed around like decorations.

"Wow," I said. "This is beautiful. I almost hate to eat it."

Laura smiled and motioned to the chairs. "Everyone sit. I already told the boys it's ready."

We took our seats, leaving the three spots around the end for Sin, Lucius, and Teddy. There were three more places set, and I wondered if Renee would join us. I missed my friend something terrible, the loss a nagging ache.

Deep male laughter bounced into the room for the foyer, Teddy and Lucius appearing in the doorway.

Lucius' eyes opened wide as he surveyed the room. He clearly had no idea there was company.

Dmitri growled.

"Keep it civil." I laid my napkin in my lap as Laura poured the wine.

Lucius leered at Dmitri before sitting in his usual chair. "Yeah, keep it civil, *comrade*."

"Very nice to see you again, Lucius is it? I'm Alex." Interest lit his face, the charm switch flipped.

I smothered my laugh as Lucius simply eyed the eager stylist.

Teddy bumped my elbow and grinned at me. "Have a good night?"

Lucius shifted in his seat and scowled at Teddy.

More steps in the hallway saved me from having to respond. Sin walked in, his black button down open at the throat with the sleeves rolled up. He wore a pair of perfectly fitting jeans with a familiar belt. Was the room suddenly warmer? My heart skipped a note as he strode to the head of the table.

"I'm not much for ceremony…" He paused when I raised my eyebrows at his words, but then continued, "But seeing as how we have this lovely meal—thank you Laura—and seeing as we have some of Stella's friends over, we may as well indulge in a little tradition." He sat and motioned for us to dig in.

Alex wasted no time grabbing some rolls and scooping mashed potatoes. Laura helped everyone fill their plate.

"Laura, please sit," Sin said. "Where's Farns?"

"Here, sir. Sorry for my tardiness. My knees, you know." Farns walked in slowly and took his seat. Laura fixed his plate and then sat next to him. Only one place remained empty.

"Renee?" I asked.

Sin cut his eyes to the ceiling and then back to me. "She may come in later."

I stared at the empty place setting for a moment before the clatter of silverware and the rhythm of small talk filled the room. I didn't know why Renee had stayed away, though it obviously had to do with Rebecca. I decided it was long past time for me to find out.

I spent the afternoon with Dmitri, Alex, and Juliet, just talking and laughing. It was as if we'd known each other for years, not just the small space of months. Dmitri and Alex competed on their storytelling abilities.

Dmitri kicked it off by explaining how he became the most skilled rabbit skinner in his town when he was five years old. Then he shared how he was a well known prize fighter in Russia, replete with lots of muscle flexing for emphasis.

Juliet and I, bundled up on the couch in the library, giggled as Dmitri puffed out his chest with pride, and told yet another tale about how he was the first boy to ever talk the town prostitute into giving him a free ride. When he was twelve.

"Was it the pride down below that got her?" Alex snorted.

"Yes." Dmitri grinned.

Juliet sank back into the cushion next to me and I wrapped my arm around her. "No shame in your game," I whispered in her ear.

She nodded and snuggled into me. Alex started into a story about the time he went skiing, ran into a tree, and wound up in an infirmary with a ski patrol dick in each hand. We laughed until the sun fell, though the clouds made it impossible to tell whether the gloom was true night.

On Juliet's turn, she shared her most embarrassing moment—the time she went to a red carpet event with her skirt tucked into her panties. When I was laughing so hard my ribs hurt, Sin walked in.

His stern face softened as he watched me. "I hate to do this, but our guests have to be on their way. The snow is supposed to start in an hour, and they need to be on a plane by then."

I knew they'd have to leave today—they had other family and friends to visit over the holidays—but I was beyond grateful that I got to see them, even if for such a short time. I forced myself not to cry as I hugged them goodbye and reluctantly let them go. Luke was already waiting outside with their things packed in the limo.

After saying our farewells on the front porch, Dimitri's face darkened as he approached Sin. Sin met his eyes, not even the slightest hint of fear in his demeanor. I supposed there wouldn't be, not after what he'd done in Cuba. Sin was capable of horrible acts if something important to him was threatened. The thought sent a shiver through me as sure as the chill wind that promised snow.

"If you hurt her, comrade, I come back here for you."

"You do that." Sin gave him a shit-eating grin.

Dmitri glowered, but backed away before squeezing me into a bear hug one last time and stomping down the stairs to the car. He ducked inside and closed the door. I fought back more tears as the car pulled away. Sin walked over and placed his arm around my shoulders as the first flakes of snow fell, the weather arriving earlier than expected.

"Thank you." I leaned into him.

"You're welcome." He kissed the top of my head and led me back inside.

CHAPTER TWENTY
Stella

The fun daydream over, I stared up into Sinclair's eyes as he pushed my hair behind my ear. He leaned down to my lips and hovered just out of reach.

"Sin?"

He closed his eyes, as if just hearing me say his name was pleasurable.

"I want you to tell me about the last two trials."

His eyes opened and he straightened, the link between us broken with a string of simple words.

"We have time enough to worry about that, Stella." His voice was cold.

"Please, just tell me."

He rested his palm against my throat. "What did I tell you at the ball, Stella? Anticipation just makes it worse. You have three months before the trial. Don't spend them worrying."

"But I worry more when I don't know." I gripped his wrist and slid my hand down his forearm. "Please."

He opened his mouth to speak and then closed it. His grip tightened at my neck. "No. I'm not discussing this. Don't ask again."

Stung at his harsh tone, I backed away. He let his hand drop, but he followed my steps until I was backed against the front door.

"Sin, pl—"

"I'm doing the best I can." He pushed me into the door, his gaze singeing me with its intensity. "I can't explain it to you, but I'm doing everything I can to keep you safe. But nothing has changed." His hand was back at my throat, the touch rough as he pressed me against the wood panel. "I still have to win. You aren't going to stop that. Understand?"

"No. I don't." I tried to shove him off but he didn't let me go, just came right back and pressed me harder, his chest crushing into mine, taking my breath away. I dug my nails into his hand.

Tears welled and ran down my cheeks. "Why is winning more important than me?"

"Because nothing is more important to me than winning the Acquisition, Stella. Nothing."

"Not me?"

"No." He said the word with a sharp edge that sliced me so fast I didn't feel it at first, but then the blood ran from my heart. "Do you think some fucking makes you more important to me than my name, than my own blood?"

I couldn't catch my breath. He scowled at me—the man who'd just given me the happiest Christmas I could remember, who'd given me more pleasure in one night than a lifetime of nights. Nothing but disgust was written on his face.

"Why can't you love me?" My voice was choked with tears, but I asked the only question I had left. The only one that needed to be answered.

"It's not that I *can't*, Stella. It's that I *don't*."

I pressed forward into his hand, forcing him to hold me tighter to keep me in place. I wanted to see his eyes. "You're lying."

"You don't know me, Stella. You've only ever seen what I wanted you to. What I needed to show you to keep you in line. Don't think for a fucking second I give two shits about what happens to you."

My tears turned to laughter, and I didn't care if it sounded insane. "You're *lying*, but not to me."

His body vibrated with rage, a frenzy of emotions churning from him. "Shut the fuck up."

I kept laughing. There was nothing else. He cared about me. I'd seen it. I knew it, and he couldn't take it away from me no matter what he said or did to me. He loved me.

"I don't love you, Stella." But he backed away, only his palm still making contact.

"You're a fucking liar. Don't touch me." I dug my nails in and wrenched his hand away.

I shot past him, darting up the stairs as I felt his eyes on my back. I ran to my room and sank onto my bed. I felt as if I were in shock. There were no more tears, only an empty expanse where my hurt should be. I felt nothing. Had he ripped it all out? Was I broken now? Is this what being broken meant? I lay that way for a long time, seeing nothing, hearing nothing.

Something, some sound—maybe the grandfather clock chiming—woke me from my reverie. I sat up, the night dark and a light layer of snow on the lawn. No moon, just black nothingness above. I let my eyes wander the window sash and then back to my own ceiling. *Upstairs. Answers.*

I opened my door slowly and peeked into the hall. It was clear, so I crept down the runner and hesitated as I eyed the rest of the way up to the third floor. My spine tingled, but I took the first step. Then another, then more until I was at the top.

The doors were closed up here, and the air was stale with disuse. The lights overhead were dim, but gave enough of a glow that I could creep along and listen at each door. Nothing. I kept moving until I heard a humming sound coming from the end of the hall. I moved closer, a cold sweat breaking out along my forehead.

I forced myself onward, looking for Renee, looking for some sort of answers.

The last door on the left hung open. I peeked inside. Renee sat in a rocking chair and hummed as she did needlework. The white-haired woman, Mrs. Vinemont, slept peacefully.

Renee must have sensed me, because the humming stopped and her eyes opened wide.

"Stella!" Her voice was a harsh whisper.

She dropped her needlework and hurried over to me. She wrapped her arms around me, but I didn't return the embrace, my arms numb.

"Why haven't you come to see me?" I asked.

"I couldn't bear to leave her. You shouldn't be here." She tried to guide me back into the hallway and pull the door closed behind her, but I pushed past her and into the room. Photos lined the walls. So many of Sin, Lucius, and Teddy—beautiful boys who grew into young men as the images continued from one corner to another. Another, larger photo was framed and hung above the fireplace. It was a young woman, her hair almost the same shade as mine, but her eyes the same light blue as Lucius'.

"Cara?" A scratchy, unfamiliar voice.

I turned to find Mrs. Vinemont staring right at me, her mouth gaping.

"Cara, is it you?"

Renee went to her side and gripped her hand. "No, your sister's gone. Remember, darling?"

"But she..." Mrs. Vinemont pointed a wizened hand at me.

"No, that's Stella." Renee's voice was gentle, as if speaking to a child. "Stella. Remember?"

"Stella." Rebecca's eyes cleared the slightest bit, then narrowed. "The peasant?"

"Rebecca, come on now."

"No, it's fine." I crossed my arms over my chest and stared down at Rebecca. "Her attitude helps."

"My *attitude*?" The older woman sat up in her bed, her familiar eyes perusing me from head to toe. "No wonder my son is having such trouble with you."

Her voice was brittle, like a dry, crumpled leaf being crushed under a boot.

"No trouble. I just want answers."

"Well, Stella, let me get up and pour you some tea and serve you some scones while I'm at it." She cackled.

Renee stroked her hand, but Rebecca ripped it away. "Get out of my room. Both of you are a curse. One after another. A curse!" She repeated "a curse" until the sound trailed off and she glared at me.

"I'll leave," I said. "I won't bother you again. But I have some questions first."

Renee put her hand up, as if warding off an attacking foe. "Please, Stella. Don't. Just go. I'm begging you. She can't handle any talk about it."

"About the Acquisition?"

Rebecca flinched at my words. "Let her ask her questions. We'll see if she likes my answers." She smiled, and I realized what a beautiful woman she must have been. But now, she was nothing more than a ruined, haunted wreck.

"What is the next trial?" I asked.

She hummed some bars of a song I didn't recognize and said, "Spring is the time for family."

"What does that mean?"

"I answered your question. Isn't my fault if you aren't smart enough to follow it. Next." She held her hand out, as if scooting me along, and I observed the same smattering of scars on the back of her hand that I'd seen on Sinclair's.

"What are those scars?" I pointed.

"These?" She held her hand out like she was showing me an engagement ring and batted her dark lashes. "These are from one wonderful night in Brazil. Shall I tell you about it?"

Renee blanched, the color draining from her face in an instant as she shook her head. "Please don't do this, Rebecca. Please."

"Have you ever been cut by a sugar cane leaf?" Rebecca's eyes drew me in, and I found myself walking closer until I stood at the foot of her bed.

"No."

"It's a very particular sting, you see?" She ran her fingernail across the lines, retracing whatever pain had put them there. "I took my eldest, Sinclair, to Brazil for a short vacation one time." She grinned. "He watched me kill a man. I had never killed anyone before. But I killed Mr. Rose. Shot him dead. Do you know why?" She didn't let me answer. "Because he was trying to tarnish my name, to take what was mine." Her voice hardened. "No one takes from us. Not again. Not ever. We are the ones who take things."

She leaned back, her face wistful, though she still watched me. "My son didn't understand. He kept crying." She threw her hands up. "The gunshots, the blood, the killing, the bodies—he couldn't handle any of it. He was weak. He was afraid. He clung to me like I was some sort of safety in the storm." She laughed, the sound harsh and jarring.

I put a hand to my throat, my hackles rising and my palms going cold. I could see the boy in the photos around the room, the one she spoke of. He'd been so happy, but something had changed, something was different in his older photos. Now I knew what.

She shook her head. "But I *was* the storm. So, after I'd gotten the Roses straightened out, I sat him down and took a sugar cane leaf. I retold the horrible things I'd done, the things he'd witnessed. Every time one of his tears fell, I cut him, and then I cut myself." She slid her nail sharply across her hand. "I cut and cut until I could make him relive it without a single tear, until he could recite it all himself without blinking an eye—how Mr. Rose had begged, how I'd shot him in the face, how the workers had run and screamed as my men hacked them to death. And then he was strong. Like he is now." She beamed, pride in her eyes.

My gorge rose, and I grabbed the footboard to steady myself. A bead of cold sweat ran between my shoulder blades.

"Ask your next question." She folded her hands in her lap, clearly pleased with herself.

Renee cried softly into her palms.

I didn't know if I could stand another answer. Could I bear more truth from the malice-filled creature before me?

"What are the rules of the Acquisition?"

Another song erupted from her lips, but this one with words, *"Seven rules to see you through. Seven rules to live by. Seven rules to make it hurt. Seven rules to kill by."*

I shuddered and my knees buckled, but I didn't fall, despite the heavy weight of dread crushing down on me.

She grinned, her teeth like tombstones in moonlight. "Let's start with the first, and most important rule of the Acquisition. If you lose, you must kill the last-born child of your line. Weeds out the weak, you see."

The floor moved under my feet, and I gripped the footboard with both hands. "If he loses the Acquisition, Sin has to kill Teddy?" My voice was far away.

She nodded, her grin growing wider and filling her face like a garish caricature. "Teddy dies."

Acknowledgements

Writing a book is a solitary endeavor. Sitting around, grumbling to yourself, glaring at a blank page, or staring at words that make you irrationally angry because they aren't exactly *right* and fail to convey your thought *concisely* – all lonely things. Thankfully, everything else to do with a book's creation is a much more social proposition. Brainstorming, editing, laughing at typos, laughing even more at phrases that turn out sexual that weren't intended that way at all – all collaborative things.

First, I am grateful to my family. A huge thank you goes to my publicist/accountant/plot-hole-finder/cheerleader/stress reliever Mr. Aaron. He is my first, biggest, and handsomest fan (Google it if you don't believe me). Also to my two evil little girls, especially the mini-me who likes to grab my red mark-up pen and draw on the wall. Devil.

To Sloane Howell, for reading and re-reading and making rude [hilarious] comments in my margins about dicks. He has made this book better, especially that **one** time he correctly called me on telling instead of showing. Great friend, great writer – check out his books, especially The Matriarch, my fave of his.

To my readers, especially those who give me insightful comments about content. I love hearing different perspectives, and I appreciate input – even if it's criticism – more than I can say. (Though I may prefer adulation, natch.)

I've always said that if you want to know what another person is thinking, read a book. That is not to say my consciousness is a twisted, arcane game of supremacy amongst rich assholes, but rather that I like sexy, troubled anti-heroes and smart heroines. I hope you like those things, too; otherwise, you've just wasted a couple of hours of your life that you will never, ever get back.

Above all, thank you for reading.

See you in Sovereign. Darker deeds are yet to come, but the faint glimmer of hope gives enough light to read by.

THE ACQUISITION SERIES

Coming April 2016

SOVEREIGN, Acquisition Series Book 3

THE ACQUISITION HAS ruled my life, ruled my every waking moment since Sinclair Vinemont first showed up at my house offering an infernal bargain to save my father's life. Now I know the stakes. The charade is at an end, and Sinclair has far more to lose than I ever did. But this knowledge hasn't strengthened me. Instead, each revelation breaks me down until nothing is left but my fight and my rage. As I struggle to survive, only one question remains. How far will I go to save those I love and burn the Acquisition to the ground?

Sign up at AaronErotica.com for news on SOVEREIGN's release date and an ARC giveaway.

EROTICA TITLES BY CELIA AARON

Forced by the Kingpin
Forced Series, Book 1

I've been on the trail of the local mob kingpin for months. I know his haunts, habits, and vices. The only thing I didn't know was how obsessed he was with me. Now, caught in his trap, I'm about to find out how far he and his local cop-on-the-take will go to keep me silent.

Forced by the Professor
Forced Series, Book 2

I've been in Professor Stevens' class for a semester. He's brilliant, severe, and hot as hell. I haven't been particularly attentive, prepared, or timely, but he hasn't said anything to me about it. I figure he must not mind and intends to let me slide. At least I thought that was the case until he told me to stay after class today. Maybe he'll let me off with a warning?

Forced by the Hitmen
Forced Series, Book 3

I stayed out of my father's business. His dirty money never mattered to me, so long as my trust fund was full of it. But now I've been kidnapped by his enemies and stuffed in a bag. The rough men who took me have promised to hurt me if I make a sound or try to run. I know, deep down, they are going to hurt me no matter what I do. Now I'm cuffed to their bed. Will I ever see the light of day again?

Forced by the Stepbrother
Forced Series, Book 4

Dancing for strange men was the biggest turn on I'd ever known. Until I met him. He was able to control me, make me hot, make me need him, with nothing more than a look. But he was a fantasy. Just another client who worked me up and paid my bills. Until he found me, the real me. Now, he's backed me into a corner. His threats and promises, darkly whispered in tones of sex and violence, have bound me surer than the cruelest ropes. At first I was unsure, but now I know – him being my stepbrother is the least of my worries.

Forced by the Quarterback
Forced Series, Book 5

For three years, I'd lusted after Jericho, my brother's best friend and quarterback of our college football team. He's never paid me any attention, considering me nothing more than a little sister he never had. Now, I'm starting freshman year and I'm sharing a suite with my brother. Jericho is over all the time, but he'll never see me as anything other than the shy girl he met three years ago. But that's not who I am. Not really. To get over Jericho – and to finally get off – I've arranged a meeting with HardcoreDom. If I can't have Jericho, I'll give myself to a man who will master me, force me, and dominate me the way I desperately need.

***

A Stepbrother for Christmas
The Hard and Dirty Holidays

Annalise dreads seeing her stepbrother at her family's

Christmas get-together. Niles had always been so nasty, tormenting her in high school after their parents had gotten married. British and snobby, Niles did everything he could to hurt Annalise when they were younger. Now, Annalise hasn't seen Niles in three years; he's been away at school in England and Annalise has started her pre-med program in Dallas. When they reconnect, dark memories threaten, sparks fly, and they give true meaning to the "hard and dirty holidays."

Bad Boy Valentine
The Hard and Dirty Holidays

Jess has always been shy. Keeping her head down and staying out of sight have served her well, especially when a sexy photographer moves in across the hall from her. Michael has a budding career, a dark past, and enough ink and piercings to make Jess' mouth water. She is well equipped to watched him through her peephole and stalk him on social media. But what happens when the bad boy next door comes knocking?

F*ck of the Irish
The Hard and Dirty Holidays

Eamon is my crush, the one guy I can't stop thinking about. His Irish accent, toned body, and sparkling eyes captivated me the second I saw him. But since he slept with my roommate, who claims she still loves him, he's been off limits. Despite my prohibition on dating him, he has other ideas. Resisting him is the key to keeping my roommate happy, but giving in may bring me more pleasure than I ever imagined.

***

Zeus
Taken by Olympus, Book 1

One minute I'm looking after an injured gelding, the next I'm tied to a luxurious bed. I never believed in fairy tales, never gave a second thought to myths. Now that I've been kidnapped by a man with golden eyes and a body that makes my mouth water, I'm not sure what I believe anymore... But I know what I want.

MAGNATE

About the Author

Celia Aaron is the self-publishing pseudonym of a published romance and erotica author. She loves to write stories with hot heroes and heroines that are twisty and often dark. Thanks for reading.